I0451060

Damaged
Desire

Qiana Rae
Princess of Erotica Books

Princess of Erotica Books
Copyright © 2018 Qiana Rae
All rights reserved.

Cover Design: SelfPubBookCovers.com/Tigerlily

No part of this publication may be reproduced, stored in a retrieval system, or transmitted, in any form or by any means, electronic, mechanical, photocopying, recording, or otherwise, without the written prior permission of the author.
This book is a book of fiction. Names, characters, places, and incidents are products of the author's imagination or are used fictitiously. Any resemblance to actual events locales, or persons, living or dead, is entirely coincidental.

ISBN: 978-0-9916187-8-1

Dedication

I dedicate this novel to everyone who has supported and believed in me thus far. You are, and forever will be appreciated.

Love,
Qiana Rae

Table of Contents

Acknowledgments

I acknowledge my Lord and Savior Jesus Christ because HE only truly knows what I went through to get this book done. My mind went through struggles only He can understand, but I was able to push through with his help. He gave me motivation by making me always remember that he had something special for me ahead and I had to keep on moving, so that I could move on to my next journey in life. I thank HIM for not ever allowing me to quit on what I believe in, and if no one believes in me, to always believe in myself.

I also thank all my fans that kept asking me when the new book was coming, which helped me to realize I had to keep moving because you all were waiting. I know you won't be disappointed and I pray it was worth the wait. I have to say this is book number five, and with my obligations to my family, I am now officially retired as an author. Thank you to everyone who stuck with me on this journey. You are all appreciated.

Love,
Qiana Rae

Chapter One

As my family and I headed home from Bone's, one of the most exquisite restaurants in Downtown Atlanta, I sat in the backseat wearing my earbuds, listening to my girl Rihanna, as I watched my mom caress the back of my dad's hand, which was comfortably placed on her thigh as he drove. She would look up at him from time to time and just smile. He would feel her staring, and look back at her. Like a shy schoolgirl, she would quickly look away as if she wasn't looking, but no matter how hard she tried, she was unable to remove the silly grin from her face. Eventually, she could no longer control it, and burst into laughter. From her beautiful profile, I could see half of her huge smile, and the one and only dimple she possessed on her left cheek. Her golden brown skin glistened from the sun that shone brightly through the moonroof in mid April. My dad laughed right along with her, as he squeezed her thigh. I pretended as though I wasn't paying any attention to them. It wasn't cool for a sixteen, soon to be seventeen, year old girl to admit to finding her parents interesting, but to be honest, I did. I loved the way that they loved each other, and I wanted to be loved like that one day. Not too many of my friends lived with both of their parents, but I had been lucky. My parents both had so much respect for one another. They would have disagreements, mainly due to the fact that my mom was very strong-willed. She was like many women in the aspect that she wanted what she wanted, how she wanted it, and when she wanted it. She and my dad had been together for so long that he was used to it, and of course, she would always end up getting her way. My dad was very easy going. As long as I met the expectations that he had for me, which were to help around the house, stay involved in at least one extra-curricular activity, and keep my grades up, he was satisfied. I didn't have a favorite parent, like some do, so you couldn't call me a momma's girl or a daddy's girl. Every now and then, I would favor my dad over my mom, only because my mom was so strict. As soon as I became a teenager and got my first period, she wanted to lock me up in my room, and the only time I was allowed to go anywhere was when I was with either her or my dad. Only sometimes would she allow me to go places with other adult relatives without her trailing along. Whenever I asked my dad to go somewhere, his answer to me was always "yes". That was because he always trusted me to do the right thing.I could see my dad looking at me through the rear-view mirror, and my mom turn around in her seat to look at me, which meant they were probably trying to include me in their conversation, but I couldn't hear them over trying to decipher what Rihanna was saying in her song, "Work". I took my earbuds out and asked, "Were you saying something?"

"Your dad was talking to you," my mom said, as she faced the front again.

I waited for my dad to repeat what he'd said.

"Can you hear me now? You got all of that ratchetness out of your ears now?" he said, jokingly.

"No, wait a minute. There's only a couple more verses left," I replied, as I began putting my earbuds back up to my ears.

My mom quickly turned towards me with the look she gave me when I was getting on her last nerve, and said, "Desiree'!!!"

which meant she was serious. Whenever she called me by my full name, I knew she wasn't playing. Any other time, she would call me by my nickname, Dezzi, which was what everyone else called me.

"I'm just playin'! Dang!" I said as I laughed.

"Little girl!!!" my mom said, as she rolled her eyes and turned back around in her seat.

"Yes, Daddy, I can hear you now," I said with a smirk on my face.

"I was just saying how good dinner was. We should go there more often."

"Yeah, we should. I think that was the best lobster tail I've ever had."

"It was pretty good, but I wouldn't say all that," my dad replied.

"Yeah, me neither," my mom cosigned.

"Well, the steak was nice and tender. You can't say that wasn't the best steak you've had," I said, trying again to get them to agree.

My mom and dad both looked at each other and simultaneously said, "Nah!" as they laughed.

"Forget ya'll then!" I said.

"We're just messing with you," my mom said. "It was definitely one of the best I've had."

As we continued our discussion about dinner, and debated about what was and wasn't the best, I secretly began a text conversation with my boyfriend, Adonis, who my parents knew of, but didn't know much about. We had only been talking for a few months, and they had never seen him. They had only overheard me talk about him to my friends that would come over to the house, which made them start asking a few questions about him, here and there. What they knew from what I'd told them was that we went to school together and shared some of the same classes. Yes, "Donnie", which everyone called him for short, except for me, had gone to my school, but he had already graduated. As a matter of fact, he had graduated three years prior. He was twenty-one years old.

In the middle of my ongoing conversation with my parents, on the side of the highway, we saw a woman standing outside of her car with the hood up. My dad, being the caring man that he was, pulled over a few feet in front of the stalled vehicle.

"What are you doing, Brandon?" my mom asked, sounding irritated.

Before opening his car door to get out, he looked at my mom, and in a way that made it sound like common sense, he said, "That woman needs help, so I'm gonna go see what I can do to help. Is that ok with you, sweetheart?"

My mom inhaled, then exhaled as she folded her arms and shook her head. "Ok, whatever," she said, making it very apparent she wasn't in agreement.

"Woman, you know you're a trip, but I still love you!" my dad said, smiling at my mom as he was getting out of the car.

He startled me when he knocked on my window before he went to assist the woman. I rolled down the window, and raised my eyebrows, wondering what he wanted.

"You good back here?" he asked, looking down at the brightly lit screen of my phone, seeming as if he was trying to get a quick glance of what I was doing.

I tried to unnoticeable flip my phone over as I said, "Yeah, I'm good."

"All right. I'll be right back," he said, and winked at me, before I rolled the window back up, trying to keep the cool air inside.

My mom and I both turned around to look out the back window as we watched my dad head over to the woman. He was six-foot four, and very muscular, which helped him look the part of the "Superman" that he always proclaimed to be. The woman stood there with her cell-phone up to her ear, probably trying to call for help. She obviously wasn't having any luck, because as soon as she looked up and saw my dad heading her way, she took the phone down from her ear, and lifted her dark sunglasses.

"Your daddy really believes he's Superman," my mom said, shaking her head once again as she watched my dad do what he did best.

The woman looked relieved as she talked to my dad. While she was obviously trying to explain the situation to him, she kept shrugging her shoulders, which led me to believe she had no idea what was wrong. As she talked, my dad began wiping sweat from his forehead with the back of his hand, and his warm beige skin began to become tinged with pink from the scorching sun. The woman finally got into the car and my dad proceeded to look underneath the hood. At that point, I was just ready to get home, so I could lock myself in my room and have a real conversation with Adonis. I faced back forward, while my mom continued to keep her attention focused directly on my dad. I kept looking up from my phone, feeling like she was watching me as I attempted to text Adonis in private.

Trying my best not to show how uncomfortable I really was, so that I could avoid an uncomfortable conversation with my mom about what I was doing in my phone, I glanced back once again to check the status of what was going on behind us. The hood of the car was still up, but it looked like the car was running. My dad was at the woman's driver's side window, having a conversation. I was relieved to know that he had finished his good deed for the day and we would soon be headed home. I turned back around and quickly texted Adonis before my mom noticed, telling him I'd call him as soon as I got home.

Not even twenty seconds after I took my eyes off of my dad, my mom screamed, "Brandon!"

She struggled as she tried to quickly unlock her door and jump out of the car, but by the time she did, it was too late. A semi-truck had come speeding down the highway and sideswiped the woman's car at the very spot my dad was standing. I jumped out the car with my mom as soon as I realized what was going on, and all I could see was my dad being dragged down the highway from the front, right side of the semi, and my mom running after the love of her life, as fast as she could, screaming my dad's name.

I couldn't watch. I was in a state of shock. I turned in the opposite direction with tears running down my face. I saw the woman that my dad was helping, still inside of her car, looking like she was in horrible pain, but I was too numb to even walk over to help her. I soon heard a loud explosion. I was afraid of what I would see when I looked back, but I had no choice. When I turned around, I saw flames everywhere, and the sky was filled with a giant cloud of black smoke. I couldn't see my mom anywhere. I suddenly heard a trembling voice behind me.

"Oh my God. I'm so sorry! I called the police. They should be here very soon."

I slowly turned around to face the woman who my dad had felt the need to help. She was holding her arm, and one of her legs looked as if it was broken. I could tell she had been crying, but I couldn't have much sympathy for her. I left her standing there, without saying a word. I began walking towards the smoke and flames, and soon begun to hear sirens coming from every direction. As I got closer and closer, the smoke became thicker and thicker. As I walked through the smoke, almost choking, there was an awful smell, which I later realized was the smell of burning flesh . . . My dad's burning flesh.

It was a horrible sight, and I knew that it would be one that I would never be able to forget. I became numb again as I stared at the burning semi, and SUV that it had crashed into the back of. My dad's lifeless, burning body was crushed between the two, burning relentlessly. There were people trying to help pull the people out who were trapped inside of the compacted SUV, and spectators standing around with worry and disbelief upon their faces. I still hadn't seen my mom. I was so lost in the millions of thoughts and emotions going through my mind, I hadn't even realized when the fire trucks had arrived and began blasting their hose, attempting to put out the fire from the explosion. Police cars had barricaded the road, so traffic was at a complete standstill.

"Young lady. Are you ok?" I suddenly heard a man's voice say. It was raspy and had a very deep, southern accent.

I didn't say anything. I wanted to, but nothing would come out. He began gently shaking me, and waving his hand in my face to see if I would respond.

"I need medics over here," the man yelled.

Finally able to speak, I looked at the tall, white officer and softly said, "My mom."

"Where's your mom, sweetie?" he asked, sounding deeply concerned.

I shrugged my shoulders. At that moment, the medics came running over with blankets and a stretcher. I began aggressively pulling away, trying to loosen myself from the officer's grip.

"No! I have to find my mom!" I shouted.

"We're going to find your mom. Just let us help you," the officer said in a reassuring voice.

After calming down as much as I could, I said, "I don't need the medics. I just need to find my mom right now."

"Ok. Let's go walk so we can find her, and you can tell me what happened here."

As we walked along the grassy area of the side of the highway, which was where I had seen my mom last, with tears continuously streaming down my face, I attempted to tell the officer what happened. Officers, firemen, and paramedics were running wild, trying to tend to everyone and everything affected, including the truck driver who had apparently fallen asleep behind the wheel. Not one of the people who were being treated was my mom.

"What's your mom's name, dear?" the officer asked.

"Calisa Kimbrough."

"Can you give me a description of her? Approximate height, weight, what she was wearing? I'm Officer Walton. I'm just trying to help."

As I opened my mouth to begin describing my mom, I squinted my eyes, and in the distance I could see her. I immediately began running towards her. I could hear the officer yelling for me to come back. I never looked back. I ran as fast as I could to get to my mom. When I finally got there, she was staring up at the sky. I didn't even think she noticed I was there. Her once straightened hair was now frizzy from the extreme heat and humidity, and wild from the wind blowing through her tresses as she chased after the semi that wouldn't release my dad. Her make-up was no longer perfect. She had black streaks running down her face from her mascara and eyeliner, and her eyes were puffy from crying.

"Ma?" I said, hoping I would get a response.

She lowered her head from the sky, and looked at me as if she didn't know who I was. The police officer finally arrived, out of breath.

"Is this your mom?" he asked.

I nodded my head.

The officer attempted to talk to my mom.

"Ma'am, I'm Officer Walton. Are you ok?"

Without taking one look at the officer, my mom began slowly walking across the bare road.

"Mrs. Kimbrough," the officer yelled after her, but she continued to walk.

"You stay right here," the officer said to me as he began following my mom.

Once my mom arrived at the median of the highway, she turned to look at me, with sadness in her eyes. She then turned back around as she saw the officer getting closer, and began walking faster. She quickly climbed over the silver, metal median of the divided highway and walked towards the road where the thick traffic was rapidly coming her way. The officer and I both realized what my mom was doing. The officer began running to try and stop her.

"Ma! No!" I yelled as I began running from the other side of the highway, disregarding Officer Walton's orders.

As I ran, I watched as my mom walked in front of oncoming traffic, and Officer Walton grabbed her in just enough time to push her back into an area of safety. As I reached them both, I fell to my knees, crying and breathing heavily at the same time. I felt like I was going to vomit. My mom laid on her back, next to the median, in the patch of pebbles and gravel, crying uncontrollably.

"I can't go on! I have nothing! My world is gone! Why couldn't God Just forgive him!!!" she shouted.

I crawled over to her, and laid on top of her, hugging her.

"You have me, Ma. We have each other. We'll make it through this."

The officer watched as I soothed my mom. I wondered what she meant by God not forgiving my daddy. The officer then called in on his radio for an ambulance to pick us up. My mom and I weren't physically hurt, but we had been severely wounded mentally. I knew for a fact that neither of us would ever be able to forget the horrible sight we had been subjected to. I also knew that life would never be the same for us. That was approximately one year ago, and even after therapy sessions once a week for the past year, I had been absolutely right. Nothing was the same.

Chapter Two

"Ma, wrap your arms around my neck and hold on," I said, as I carried my mom all the way up our spiral staircase.

I found myself having to do that more and more lately. Anytime something triggered any type of memory of my dad, and it was too much for my mom to handle, she had begun using alcohol as a temporary suppressant for her depression. It didn't seem as though therapy was working much at all for her. I could say the same for myself, but at least it was helping me to be able to better control my emotions when I felt like I was going to lose it. I missed my dad, but what made it worse than him not being here was the way he was taken from us, and the fact that we had actually witnessed it. No one deserved to go out like that. Especially my dad. He was a good man, and experienced one of the most horrific deaths I had ever known.

"We're almost there, Ma. Keep holding on," I said as we managed to make it up the last couple of stairs.

As we got to the top of the staircase, I helped her down the long hallway to her bedroom. After my dad died, neither one of us could bear the thought of staying in the house where we had become a family. There were just too many memories there, so we left the only home that I had ever known, in Smyrna, Georgia, and moved to Buckhead, which was one of the most upscale districts in Atlanta. We were able to afford almost anything we wanted after receiving the life insurance money from the huge policy my dad had taken out on himself after he and my mom got married, however, my mom refused to touch it. She put it in a bank account under her name, and added me as a signer just in case something ever happened to her. She used part of the money that she got from selling our house as a down payment on our new home, and got a job, which was something my dad would've never wanted her to do.

The only time my mom had worked was before they got married, and while my dad was in architect school, and I was too young to even remember that. I had only heard them talk about it, and from those conversations, I knew how much my dad loved to be able to take care of his family without sending his wife out into the workforce. My dad was young, but he had an old school mentality when it came to that kind of thing. After my dad finished architect school and got on his feet, my mom went to school and became degreed and licensed as a Registered Nurse, however, she had never gone out and worked in the field until now.

I knew that the huge life insurance policy that my dad had been paying for every month was so that he could be sure that if anything happened to him, my mom would still be able to live off of him without having to work. That was the last thing my mom wanted, though. I had questioned why she just didn't live off of the money my dad had made sure she would have, and she said that she didn't want to live off of the death of her husband because if she could, she would exchange all of that money for just five more minutes with my dad. In addition to the life insurance money, my dad owned sixty percent of Kimbrough-Scott, which was the architect firm he and his good friend, Ricky Scott, had decided to open years before. My mom sold the sixty percent that went to her after my dad died, to Ricky, and put that money into a separate account which we would live off of until it was gone. After that one time I questioned my mom's reasoning for not touching the money, I never did again because it hurt so badly for me to hear it. I did, however, ask her what she meant that day by "God not forgiving my daddy," but the only answer she gave me was to just make sure I always did God's will. From that, I assumed that my dad had done something really bad in the past for her to think that God would punish him in that way. I even know that God forgave us for our sins, but my dad's accident had convinced my mom that God punishes us, and does not forgive us. I just left it alone.

The short time that we stayed at our beloved home before moving was extremely painful. All of my dad's personal items, including, clothes, shoes, the cologne that made my mom walk by and sniff him all day long, and his tools he used anytime he needed to fix something around the house, mainly because of me, because I was always breaking something, all remained untouched until moving day. Even the drawings that he had recently finished for one of his clients, laid on his desk, rolled up, ready to be presented. Rick tried coming by to get them, but during that time, my mom wouldn't allow anyone over to the house. We sat in misery together. Neither of us could bring ourselves to move any of the things that tortured us on a daily basis, but when it was time to move, we had no choice. It was a very sad day as we threw all of his belongings in trash bags and boxes, which would remain in the garage of our new home until we could both be at peace with getting rid of it all.

When we finally got to my mom's bedroom, I walked her to the bed. She plopped straight down onto the plush mattress, and immediately began to snore. I stood over her, shaking my head, and then proceeded to take off her five inch heels. Before leaving her to sleep off the tequila that was seeping through her pores, I threw a blanket on top of her, which she probably didn't need because alcohol always made her hot. I then kissed her on the cheek, and even though I knew she couldn't hear me, I told her I loved her. This was a ritual that occurred at least four times a week, and I had become quite accustomed to it.

After shutting off all of the lights in my mom's bedroom, I closed the door, and lightly jogged to the other end of the house to my bedroom. I pushed open my door that was already cracked, and went inside, shutting and locking it behind me.

"Oh my God! I don't know how much more of this I can take!" I said to Adonis, as I took my robe off exposing my naked body. We had just finished making love minutes before we heard my mom stumbling at the front door. I laid in my bed, and cuddled up right next to his warm, naked body.

Whenever my mom wasn't around, Adonis would come over to the house and keep me company. He actually did more than that. He gave me the love that I felt like I was missing. He filled the void that I felt when I was all alone. I knew my mom would've never approved of him being at home alone with me, but I sometimes felt like he was all I had. After all the time that had passed, I still hadn't introduced Adonis to my mom, and didn't plan to until after I turned eighteen, for obvious reasons. He had come to my dad's funeral, but so many others did, too, so there was nothing strange about him being there amongst all the other mourners.

After laying next to Adonis, he wrapped his arms tightly around me and said, "It's only a matter of time and you won't have to be a mother to your own mother anymore, and won't have to listen to her when she finds it convenient to actually be a mom to you. You'll be eighteen before you know it and you'll be able to leave and come with me. Can you believe you finish high school tomorrow? What are you going to do with your mornings until your new chapter begins?"

I quickly sat up and said, "And where will I be going, Adonis? To live with you and your mom?"

"I'm gonna get a place! You just have to give your man some time. Since you decided to stay here and go to a community college, you know I have to make sure I take care of you the rest of the way. I appreciate you not going away so that you can stay close to me."

Adonis kept hounding me about going off to college and leaving him, and I started becoming confused every time he would bring it up. I knew I didn't want to leave him, but I also knew my parents always wanted me to go to one of the best schools, and take advantage of every opportunity available to me. I had worked extremely hard when it came to my academics to make sure that I would receive a full ride to the college of my choice. That choice was Texas A&M. Adonis was not aware that I had already been accepted to and awarded a full four year scholarship to Texas A&M. I just felt like community college was beneath me, especially when my ultimate goal was to become an anesthesiologist. I hadn't broken the news to Adonis yet, but I still had approximately three months to do so. I was just hoping by then, Adonis would have a little bit more motivation and more flexibility when it came to his willingness to leave Atlanta. I would've loved if he agreed to come to Texas with me.

Adonis was somewhat of a momma's boy, but he denied it. Let him tell it, he was just "protective" over his mom. I understood what protective meant, and when my mom wasn't drunk, she was "protective" of me, meaning she wanted to be sure to keep me out of harm's way. I was sure Adonis felt the same way about his mom, but the way he talked, sometimes it sounded like he never wanted to move out of his mom's house. It wasn't like he was actually being productive in Atlanta. He had dreams of becoming the next Meek Mill or Drake, so he spent a lot of time in the studio that one of his boy's owned Downtown. He had a few tracks on SoundCloud that he got paid a little bit of something for, and he had some mixtapes that he would sell, but other than that, he had nothing going on.

Don't get me wrong. Adonis wasn't broke, but the majority of the money he did have wasn't coming from his music. He was out in those streets, and he thought I didn't know, but he failed to realize just how much the streets talked. I had gotten up enough nerve one day to ask him if he was selling, and he made it very clear that I had offended him, and he became very defensive. That made things between us uncomfortable for a while, so I never mentioned it again. He always told me how he had big plans to take care of me, and of course, his mother. I just never wanted to feel like pressure was coming from my way because I knew that would've just pushed him out in the streets even further. That was the last thing that I wanted him to do. I definitely didn't want him to end up dead or in jail. I had already lost my dad, and I guess you could say, I had lost part of my mom, too. I most definitely couldn't lose Adonis.

Adonis looked at me with concern and said, "You are still staying here, right?"

"Of course, baby," I said, grabbing his chin and giving him a kiss on the lips.

"Ok. Just making sure you haven't changed your mind on me."

"Now you know I can't be without you. You've been my rock lately."

I wasn't lying. I couldn't see myself without Adonis, especially during this rough time in my life, and he had definitely been there for me in ways no one else could have.

"Don't worry. We'll be together. I'm not letting you go that easily," I laughed.

I meant it when I said we'd be together. Whatever it took, I was determined to somehow get Adonis to move to Texas.

What seemed like minutes later, I heard my mom's heels clicking against the hardwood floors, and her yelling my name.

"Dezzi!" she yelled, as the clicking sound got closer.

Remembering that I had fallen asleep next to Adonis after our conversation, I jumped out of bed and began shaking him.

"What's up?" he asked, not realizing what was happening.

"You gotta go! She's coming!" I said, as I hurriedly hopped into a pair of shorts and a tank.

Adonis was dazed for a moment, but once it dawned on him what I was talking about, he said, "Oh, shit!"

He jumped up and began scrambling for his clothes, but by that time it was too late. As my mom began turning the knob from the other side of the door, and banging like the police at the same time, I pushed Adonis into my walk-in closet.

"Dezzi! What are you doing? Open the door. School's not over yet!"

I then noticed Adonis' clothes on the floor at the foot of my bed, and I quickly threw them in the closet with him. My heart beating a trillion times a minute, I opened the door, rubbing my eyes as if I had just awakened.

"Girl, I was about to take this door off the hinges!" my mom said, as she tried to secretly scan the premises.

"I was still asleep. I guess I was tired," I said, raising my arms and stretching in order to trigger a big yawn that I so needed at that moment to convince my mom I was telling the truth.

"Mmhmm," she said, still looking around with doubt upon her face. After her dark, slanted eyes had completed their full 360 degree inspection of my room, they focused in on me, and she said, "I guess I was tired, too. I don't even remember getting in bed."

Sarcastically, I said, "Because I had to help you get there . . . again."

Politely dismissing my comment as she always did after reminding her of how sloppy drunk she was, she said, "I'm running late for work, so you need to hurry up so I can drop you off at school."

"You can go ahead. I'll have Ess pick me up," I replied.

Ess, which was short for Essence, had become my closest friend since moving to Buckhead. She was the only person outside of Adonis who I felt like I could confide in, and the only person my mom really trusted me to be with outside of school. I would sometimes spend weekends at her house just so that I could feel like I had a functional family again. Her mom and dad were so perfect, just as my parents had been before the accident. I didn't really plan on calling Ess to take me to school. I was just going to have Adonis take me, as he did most mornings when my mom was running late. I didn't really care for riding with her because she left out so early that I would be one of only around five other students there. Even though Adonis would have to drive all the way across town from Smyrna to pick me up, he didn't mind. He had become very familiar with my side of town. A little too familiar, and I had learned from friends I was currently in school with, who would see me getting dropped off in Adonis' gold Seventy-three Cadillac Eldorado, that he had a pretty big clientele within the area. I didn't want rumors to start spreading about me dating a drug-dealer, so when people started talking, I would cover for Adonis and tell them he wasn't about that life, and they must have him confused with someone else. That would shut their gossiping asses up for a while, but I would still see them watching. I figured Adonis probably felt like he could make some fast easy money in the Buckhead area. Even faster than he had been making it in other parts because of the higher income levels. What I didn't think he realized was that the police didn't play any games out here, and the last thing I needed was for him to get locked up. That's why I knew I had to get him away from that life asap.

"You know I don't like you riding with your classmates," my mom said, still trying to feel me out to see if I was up to no good.

"I still have to take my shower, and you know Ess is not just a classmate! She's like a sister to me."

My mom loved Essence, and most of the time, as long as I was going to be with her, she was cool about it because she knew Ess was a good girl and didn't get into any trouble.

She finally gave in and said, "All right, but make sure you let me know you made it."

"Yes, mommy dearest," I said, before wrapping both arms around her neck, and standing on my tiptoes to give her a kiss on the cheek, as she stood five-foot eight without heels, to my five-foot five frame.

"I'm serious, Dezzi. Don't play with me."

"Ok!"

"Excuse me?" she replied, questioning my tone.

"I'm just saying … I do what you tell me to do. I'm seventeen years old and you don't let me go hardly anywhere. Can I just ride with my friend to school without being harassed? It's our last chance to ride to high school together. I'm sure there's some type of sentimental rule to that. There has to be."

My mom looked at me with rage in her eyes as if she had a mouth full for me, but she knew she didn't have time to let me have it.

"Just do what I said," she said rolling her eyes as she quickly walked out, wearing her turquoise, pink and black scrubs.

As soon as I heard the chime, which alerted me that my mom had left out of the front door, I quickly made my way to the closet to tell Adonis it was ok to come out. When I opened the door, he stood there, shaking his head, wearing only his pants, and sweating like a pig. His caramel skin glistened from the moisture, causing his abs to be even more prominent than they already were. I bit my bottom lip in awe of what I was looking at.

As Adonis began walking towards me, he said, "See, that's what I mean. You're too old to have to go through that every time you want to do something as simple as hitch a ride to school with a friend."

Adonis was hot and frustrated, which I understood, but I also knew that combination would make a fabulous session of love-making. I stood in front of him and gazed into his eyes. I wrapped my arms around his neck and pulled myself up, wrapping my legs around his waist.

"Dezzi, you know we don't have time for this. I gotta get you to school, and I need to hit up this studio," Adonis said, disappointing me and spoiling the mood.

"Yeah, I just bet you do," I said under my breath as I went into my bathroom and slammed the door.

I knew I could be a baby sometimes, especially when I didn't get my way. That was one trait I had gotten honestly from my mother. I knew Adonis' real reason for trying to hurry up and get me to school. He was really trying to get out and make some money. While in the shower, I lathered up my mocha skin with my mango body wash that Adonis loved so much, while hoping he'd bust through the door any minute, taking me up on my offer. That never happened. While I fantasized as I washed my slender, but almost perfect body, I could hear Adonis at the door telling me to hurry up.

"Here I come! Damn!" I yelled, as I pushed down the lever to turn off the steaming hot water that had fogged up the entire bathroom. I stepped out of the shower and threw on my bathrobe. As soon as I opened the door and walked out of the bathroom, Adonis jumped out of nowhere, scaring the shit out of me.

"Who the hell you think you're talking to?" he said, as he picked me up and slammed me down on my freshly made up bed that he had obviously worked so hard on while I was in the shower. He held me down by my shoulders, and waited on a response without one trace of amusement on his face.

"Now you know you turn me on when you try to punish me," I said as I laughed and pulled his face so close to mine that I was able to smell his morning breath, that I didn't care about, and gave him a delicate kiss on the lips.

He tenderly kissed me back, and as we got caught up in the moment, my cell phone rang.

Adonis got up, grabbed it from my nightstand and said, "Guess who," as he handed it to me.

"Hey, Ma," I said, immediately after answering.

"Are you on your way yet?"

"No. Ess just called. She'll be pulling up any minute," I replied, with the lie I had quickly come up with.

"Ok. Don't forget to call me," she reminded me once more.

"I won't."

Adonis stood there watching me, shaking his head with his arms folded. More and more, I was beginning to see things the way he did. At first, I didn't think my mom was all that bad, but it seemed like she was getting worse and worse. The older I got, the tighter her grip became and I couldn't wait 'til the day I'd be released from prison.

By the time I hung up the phone from with my "probation officer", Adonis had put on his shirt and shoes, and had his keys in his hand.

"So, you're not gonna wash up or nothing, huh? You just gon' go out in the world funky today?" I asked.

"I'm going home to freshen up before I hit the studio, smartass."

"Just checking," I said, as I put my clothes on, and quickly threw my once straightened hair, that was now wavy from the steamy shower, up in a high messy bun.

Once I finished getting dressed, Adonis stared me up and down.

"Is there a problem, Sir?" I asked curiously.

"So, you just gon' wear that?"

I stood in front of my full-length mirror, threw my arms up and said, "What's wrong with it?"

"What's right with it?" he asked, and I could tell he was dead serious. "You givin' those little boys way too much to look at." Adonis came close, squeezed my ass that was perfectly defined in my extra-snug, "like-skin" jeans, and continued by saying, "All of this is supposed to be just for me."

"You know ain't nobody else getting none of this, so be cool. I look good, don't I?"

Adonis grinned and said, "Oh, yeah. You definitely look good, with yo sexy self! You know I was just messin' with you."

For some reason, I didn't believe Adonis had only been joking. He had never said anything before about what I was wearing. Maybe this was his way of just testing the waters to see how I'd react. Maybe he did have a problem with it, but didn't know how to say it. He knew damn well that I didn't play that "beating around the bush" shit. Man up and say what you mean!

When we finally pulled up in front of my school, Ess was standing out front waiting for me.

"I love you," I said after giving Adonis a kiss. I always had a sadness come over me when he'd drop me off. I finally had realized it was because I knew what he was out there doing, which was probably the main reason he kept it from me. He knew I'd worry, which I did. I worried that something bad would happen and that would be my last time seeing Adonis alive. I tried not to think that way, but I had learned the hard way that someone could be here one minute, and the next minute they could be gone.

"Hey, Donnie!" Ess said as she waved to Adonis after I got out the car and closed the door.

Adonis waved back and sped off into the distance.

I exhaled as I walked with Ess towards the entrance of the school.

"What's wrong, Dez?" Ess asked, sounding concerned.

"I just worry about him being out there, Redbone."

Redbone was my nickname for Ess because she was so light, and had long golden-brown hair that she wore wild, and naturally curly. Her mom even called us salt and pepper.

"Well, you already know how I feel about the situation, but you and I both know, you're gonna do what you want to do."

I knew exactly how Ess felt about it, because she was the type that when she felt a certain way about something, she made sure that everyone knew about it! She liked Adonis, but she didn't like the situation. The fact that he was twenty-one and I was seventeen didn't sit right with her. She also wasn't fond of the fact that he had no other goals outside of a rap career, but what took the cake was when she found out he was out there in the streets. She would always tell me how dangerous it was even being around Adonis, and I needed to be careful. She even attempted to set me up with a few guys from school who liked me, but in my mind, no one could compare to my Adonis, and I felt like no one ever would.

While in my own thoughts, my cell phone rang.

"Oh shit!" I said.

"What?" Ess said, sounding worried.

Without answering her, I shook my head as I answered the phone.

"Hey, Ma. I'm so sorry. I made it safely," I said without giving my mom a chance to say a word.

"Ok. I was getting worried."

"I'm fine, Ma. Ess got me here in one piece," I said rolling my eyes and glancing over at Ess.

Ess folded her arms and shook her head, which let me know she was not happy, and next I would have to listen to her bullshit.

"Good. Well, have a good day, Sweetie. Love you! If I'm not home before you leave for the graduation today, I'll see you there, and I'm so proud of you!" my mom replied.

"Love you, too," I said, before hanging up the phone.

"Really, Dez? You're still using me as your scapegoat? Now what if something were to ever happen to you, praying that it never does, and you've told everyone you were going to be with me? Then everyone is gonna be looking at me sideways."

Ess was the responsible one in our friendship. She would thoroughly think every decision through and was always logical in her thinking, which was very different from most kids our age. Most of us, like me, would do things without thinking twice about it, and deal with the consequences later. I was extremely impulsive, especially knowing how my mom was. I felt like I might as well had done what I wanted, hoping I wouldn't get caught, or be prepared to deal with whatever I had coming if I did get caught. I could admit, Ess was a good balance for me, although I didn't listen to her most of the time anyway. It was still always good to have that one angel on my side.

"I know, and I'm sorry, Ess, but how else would I ever be able to see Adonis? You're like the only friend my mom trusts me with. It's almost over anyway! Today is the last day of our high school career. We might as well end it with a bang. If we get caught up now, who really cares?"

"I just don't want to get caught in the middle when your lies come crashing down on you."

"Don't worry. My birthday is only a couple of weeks away, and then you won't have to worry about me using your name ever again, except, of course if I ever get arrested and have to use my fake I.D. with your name on it."

"What?" Ess said, as she immediately stopped in her tracks.

I laughed hysterically and said, "Girl, you know I'm just messing with you! Stop being so serious!"

As Ess slowly again began to walk down the hall, she said, "You know, I can never be too sure about you."

"I would never do something like that to my bestie," I smiled, assuring Ess that I was, in fact, just joking.

Ess could be so serious sometimes. I'd always joked around a lot, particularly with my dad. I had begun to joke even more since his death because sometimes I had to laugh to keep from crying.

"I trust you," Ess replied, right before letting me know just how much faith she didn't have in me. "You sure do have a lot of confidence that things are going to change with your situation with your mom and Adonis once you turn eighteen."

"It has to. Once I turn eighteen, I'll be an adult, and she's gonna have to loosen her grip. You would think she would since today is our last day of school and graduation is tonight. She just may shock us both."

"Ok," Ess doubtfully said, before we parted ways, heading to our homerooms.

Chapter Three

The day had finally arrived that I was now considered an adult. I still couldn't legally have a drink, but my mother would no longer have total control over my life, and that's what was most important to me at the time. I laid in the bed, as the bright sunlight came gleaming through my window. I became excited just thinking about what the future would hold for me. As a teen, I had always dreamt of this day being the beginning of my life. I had been sheltered for too long, and it was now my time to shine, and make some of my own decisions. This would also be the day that I introduced Adonis as my man, to my mother and all the other guests who didn't know about him. I knew my mom wouldn't be happy, but she would just have to accept the fact that there was nothing she would be able to do to stop me from seeing the man that I loved. I felt like this would be the perfect opportunity to introduce Adonis since my mom had planned a big bash for my eighteenth birthday. She thought it would be nice to have something I would always remember before going off to college. The only thing I remembered about my seventeenth birthday was that it was the first of many without my dad. That birthday had come only one month after the accident, so neither of us had been in the mood to celebrate.

It was a quarter to ten, and I had told Ess to be at my house by ten so she could help with the decorations for my big bash. I knew she was the perfect person to get to help out because she was a pro at decorating for any and every occasion. She loved it so much, she would spend the end of every summer break helping random teachers from our school decorate their classrooms for the upcoming school year. Ess always kept herself busy and involved in anything productive. I figured that was how she kept herself out of trouble, and from being dragged into any kind of reckless behavior.

Knowing Ess was always either early or on time for everything, I jumped out of bed and ran in the bathroom to wash my face and brush my teeth. I then threw on a pair of sweats and a t-shirt. After decorating, I would have the rest of the day to get cute, so I wasn't worried about that at all. It was time to create the perfect ambiance that I had in mind.

As soon as I walked out of my bedroom, I could smell the aroma of buttermilk pancakes and bacon rising up from the kitchen below. Before I could become lost in heaven from the delicious smell, the doorbell rang. As I walked along the catwalk, heading towards the stairs, I could see my mom below, walking briskly towards the front door.

"Hey, Ess! I didn't know you were coming by."

As I walked down the stairs I said, "Yeah. She came to help out with the decorations."

"Hey, Redbone!" I said, as I gave Ess a hug."

"Essence, please tell Dezzi to stop calling you that," my mom said. She hated when I called Ess "Redbone", but Ess didn't care. She thought it was cute.

"It's fine, Ms. Kimbrough. She knows if she gets out of line, I'll put her in her place," Ess said as she laughed."

"You don't have to tell me! I already know, and I'm glad she has you around!" my mom said with a wink, and beautiful smile that rarely ever revealed itself anymore.

Essence knew exactly how to get my mom to relax and stop being so uptight. It seemed like she knew my mom better than I did. Sometimes, it even seemed like my mom liked Essence more than she liked me.

"Well, I was going to help with the decorations, but I guess you girls can handle it. I have to go pick up some things for the party anyway."

"Yeah, we got this," Ms. Kimbrough."

"I know you do. I cooked some breakfast. Let's eat before we get started making the day perfect for Miss Desireé Arie Kimbrough!

"Yasssss, honey!" I said, causing us all to get a little laugh in.

My mom walked towards the kitchen, as Ess and I followed.

I was about to fix a plate for Ess and myself, as I always did when she was over, but my mom grabbed the plates from me.

"I got this! It's your birthday. You only turn eighteen once, so enjoy!"

I looked strangely at my mom, and walked slowly to the table, not quite knowing what to think. She was being so nice, and seemed happier than usual. I was starting to think maybe she was looking forward to this day as much as I was. Maybe she was tired of keeping tabs on me, and had secretly planned on putting me out. I sat down across from Ess, and when I looked at her, she had the same confused expression on her face as I did. She raised her perfect, naturally shaped, golden-blonde eyebrows, and shrugged her shoulders. Ess knew just as well as I did how much of a nutcase my mom could be. She had been on the phone with me on several occasions when my mom had completely lost it, and I had to calm her down. Something had definitely put her in the best mood I'd seen her in in a long time, but I was going to savor every moment of it.

My mom placed our plates in front of us, then sat down at the head of the table with her plate. She had a big smile on her face as she cut up her pancakes. Something wasn't right, and I couldn't resist the urge of asking some questions to find out exactly what was going on.

"Ma, you ok?" I asked before biting a piece of bacon.

"Yes, I'm feeling so good today! I was gonna wait 'til later to tell you, but I just can't wait!"

Becoming just as excited as she seemed, I said, "What is it?"

Ess looked up from her plate, curious to hear what all the excitement was about.

"Well," she hesitated. She took a deep breath and put her fork down as she began. "I saw Brandon last night."

I began coughing, choking on the piece of bacon I had just chewed up and swallowed. Ess jumped up and began patting me on the back until my throat was clear.

"Thanks. I'm ok," I said, gesturing for Ess to sit back down.

"Ma, what do you mean? You mean you saw him in your dreams, right?"

"No, he was in my room, sitting on the edge of my bed. He told me he loves us, and misses us both very much."

Essence looked at me, then down at her plate and began quickly inhaling everything that was left.

"The best part of it was when he apologized for missing your seventeenth birthday, but promised to be here today for your eighteenth. He even said that we'd be back together soon."

"Ma, you had a dream, and of course he's going to be here, in spirit."

My mom looked at me with disgust and said sternly, "It was not a dream, and of course I know he'll be here in spirit! I know people can't come back from the dead! I'm not crazy!" she said as she slammed her fork down on the glass and got up from the table.

"I thought you would be happy to hear your dad gave me confirmation that he's still with us, but I guess not! You two enjoy your breakfast."

As upset as my mom seemed, she calmly walked out of the kitchen and up the stairs.

"Oh my God, Ess! It's getting worse instead of better."

Ess continued to look down at her empty plate, not saying a word. This was one of those times, she wanted to say something, but she didn't want to say the wrong thing.

"What is it, Ess?"

"Huh?" Essence said, looking up and pretending as if she hadn't heard me.

"I know you want to say something, so what is it?"

"I just think you could've been a little more supportive of your mom. It's not like she was saying something had happened that was completely impossible. She had a vision of your dad, and it gave her some comfort. She was looking for comfort from you. It has only been a little over a year. She's not going to get over it that fast. He was the love of her life, and no matter how much you think you're over it, you're not, and that's completely normal. He was your dad."

This was exactly why I called Ess my voice of reason. She always made me see things in the way I should've seen it in the first place. She was right. I pretended like it didn't bother me anymore, but in that one moment, it hurt like hell to hear my mom talk about seeing my dad. It made me a little envious because I wondered why he had never visited me. Not even in my dreams. I used to intentionally think about him while I laid in bed before going to sleep just so I could dream about him, but I never could. I gave up on it, and even after an entire year, the last image of my dad was one that I tried my best to avoid recalling.

After Ess made me realize how I'd acted towards my mom, I left her sitting at the table and went to find my mom. I ran up the stairs and down the hall to her bedroom. Her door was closed, so I knocked softly.

"Ma, it's me. Can I come in?"

There was no response and I became nervous. I knocked again. This time louder.

"Ma!"

After she didn't answer the second time, I turned the knob and slowly opened the door, afraid of what I might find on the other side. Thankfully, my mom was sitting at the end of her bed, staring at the wall.

She spoke softly. "He was sitting right here." She looked at me and said, "Dezzi, I just miss him so much. Why did God have to take him? He told me he was sorry, and he corrected his mistakes."

I sat next to my mom and wrapped my arms around her. "I'm sorry. I miss him, too, and I don't know why God took him."

Truth was, I questioned God all the time. What did my dad ever do to deserve such a thing? It seemed like my mom knew something, but she wouldn't open up about it. In my eyes, he deserved a long healthy life of growing old with his wife and daughter. I cried for the first time in a long time, because at some point after my dad's death, it seemed as though I had run out of tears. I felt pressure being released from my entire body as my mom and I cried together, and mourned the death of our loved one all over again. After we'd both calmed down and cleaned ourselves up, Ess knocked on the door that was already cracked.

She peeked her head in and said, "You guys ok?"

My mom nodded, and in a slight whisper, I said, "Yeah, we're fine. Thank you so much."

She winked, and said, "No problem. That's what friends are for."

My mom took the tissue she had just wiped her eyes with, and blew her nose. She then stood up and said, "Ok, pity party over. Now let's get ready to party!"

She headed out to get the cake and a few other last minute things, while Ess and I decorated the entire lower level, and outside entertainment area with purple and silver birthday décor, which included balloons, gorgeous hand-made centerpieces, streamers, banners, and an arch at the bottom of the staircase where I would make my grand entrance. When I said I wanted my eighteenth birthday to be big, I actually meant I wanted it to be huge! So far, everything was panning out as planned, besides our early morning episode, but I wasn't allowing that to ruin my day. My mom returned home as soon as we finished decorating, and the three of us looked around in complete amazement at how absolutely beautiful everything was. Even my cake turned out picture perfect. I gave my best friend a hug, thanking her for all of her help before she left to go home and get ready for the party. We had a set start time of five o' clock sharp, meaning, I only had three hours to become a princess.

Chapter Four

I t was getting close to time, and Ess had returned to my house all dolled up. I had requested for my guests to match the décor, wearing purple, white, and silver, and Ess looked beautiful. Since she was my best friend, I wanted her to wear the same dress as me, but in a different color, which she did. My thigh-length dress was violet, with a sheer violet panel train that hung right below my ankles. Ess' dress was in silver, minus the train, with a violet, beaded sash around the waist. She wore her hair pinned to one side, but her ends still curly, wild, and free. She had placed a beautiful violet flower in it to add just enough color.

As Ess was putting the finishing touches on the master beat down she was putting on my face, I kept hearing the doorbell as the caterers, d-jay, and photographer arrived. My mom had definitely put a lot into making this day special for me, and I appreciated her for it. It was good for her, too, because it kept her mind occupied with other things, which meant there had been fewer nights of me hearing her in her bedroom crying uncontrollably.

When Ess handed me the mirror, I almost cried. Ess had accomplished the task of making me look absolutely flawless. She made my eyes pop with the soft hint of purple eyeshadow, and shimmering glitter mascara.

"Thank you so much, Ess. I love you, girl," I said, as I stood up and gave my best friend, who was more like a sister, a big hug."

"I love you, too, girl," she reciprocated.

Walking down the spiral staircase to Stevie Wonder's "Happy Birthday to You", I felt so loved as I looked down at everyone's smiling faces. I could feel all the love flooding the room. It just felt so good to know that so many people loved and cared about me. Everyone clapped as I got to the end of the staircase, and lined up to give me plenty of hugs, kisses, and beautiful birthday wishes. My beautiful mom was first in line. She looked genuinely happy, and at that moment I wished that every day could be just like this one. It was magical and I appreciated my mom for feeling like I deserved all of this on my special day.

While hugging my mom, and telling her how much I appreciated all that she'd done, behind her, in the distance, I caught a glimpse of someone standing in the doorway of the foyer. The sun was gleaming so brightly through the glass storm door, that I couldn't tell who it was. I released my mom and squinted my eyes, trying to decipher who the unintroduced entity was. My mom looked in the direction I was looking, looking as if she was trying to solve the mystery. I began walking, trying to get a little closer so that I could get a better view. As I got closer and closer, it became very evident of who I was looking at. As I stood right in front my dad, he looked down at me, nodded, and gave me one of his endearing smiles, letting me know everything was ok. He told me he was sorry, and then disappeared into thin air. When I came to, there were some guests standing on the other side of the door, waiting to be welcomed inside.

I couldn't believe what had just happened, but what I did know was that my dad had kept his promise to my mom, as he always had. I finally unlocked the door to let in the guests who were now looking at me as though I was crazy.

"You all right?" my mom asked, as she walked up behind me, putting her hand on my shoulder.

"Yes, are you all right? We thought you were going to just stare at us all day and never let us in!" one of my classmates, Latoya, said, laughing, as she and the rest of the group of people who were waiting outside walked in.

I turned to my mom, and said, "Yes, I'm great!" I said, smiling as I walked off.

My mom continued to look out the door, knowing that I had seen something, and something had just happened.

As I walked around, entertaining my friends, I began to look around every few minutes, looking for Adonis. My party was an hour in and he still hadn't arrived, or even called letting me know where he was. I was becoming more and more furious because he should've been one of the first to arrive. He wasn't the only one that was MIA. My mom had completely disappeared. The last I had seen of her was when she told me she was going to step outside for some fresh air. There were so many people inside that it had become extremely muggy.

While standing in the kitchen, talking to Ess and a few others, I looked through the patio door and saw Adonis standing on the deck amongst a crowd of people. When he saw that he'd caught my attention, he motioned for me to come outside.

"He's finally here," I whispered to Ess, rolling my eyes.

"Well, about damn time!" Ess replied sarcastically.

"I'll be right back," I said before sliding the glass door and heading outside to meet with Adonis. He just didn't know how much of a mouthful I had for him.

As soon as I stepped onto the deck, he reached out for my hand. I folded my arms and frowned.

"I know you're mad. Just come with me for a second," he said, with this amazing smile on his face. I just couldn't resist.

"Ok, but there better be a damn good explanation and apology coming," I said, pouting, as I reached out my hand for him to grab.

Adonis led me off of the deck, and we walked towards the pond in the back of my home, where the ducks were swimming, enjoying the beautiful weather. Adonis didn't say anything along the way, and neither did I, only because I knew I needed to choose my words wisely. I was pissed, and anytime I got to that point, I could sometimes say some things that I would regret, but couldn't take back.

Once we got to the pond, Adonis stopped, and let go of my hand. He turned his white and purple New York baseball cap, which matched his attire perfectly, to the back, and wiped the sweat off of his forehead with the towel he had in his back pocket. As he was doing everything except for apologizing to me, I folded my arms, then inhaled, and loudly exhaled.

"What's wrong?" Adonis asked, as if he hadn't done anything wrong.

If he was trying to get me to the point of no return, he was definitely pressing all the right buttons.

I squinted my eyes and said, "What's wrong? Are you serious? You were not only late to my party, but have yet to apologize, and now making me miss my party!"

Adonis smiled and said, "Well, you look very beautiful."

I tried not to smile and show that I was blushing, so I rolled my eyes and turned away from him to look towards the ducks that were paying us no mind.

"Ok, ok. I'm so sorry for being late. I know how special this day is for you . . . well, for the both of us. I had to do something before coming here that just couldn't wait. It took longer than expected."

I couldn't believe Adonis had basically just told me that he had put his street bullshit that I wasn't supposed to know about before me and my feelings. I had no other words for him at that moment.

"That's it, Adonis! I can't do this. I'm done!" I said as I turned my back on him and began to walk away. I needed to walk away from the situation before it got real ugly.

"Dezzi!" he yelled after me.

I stopped walking, and took a deep breath before turning around. When I finally did turn around, Adonis was still in the same spot that I left him standing, but instead of standing, he was down on one knee. I covered my mouth with both hands as my legs began to tremble and feel weak up underneath me.

Adonis smiled, and motioned for me to come closer. I slowly walked towards him. As I stood directly in front of him, I could then clearly see that he was holding a small black box. I tried to hold the tears back as my heart began beating uncontrollably.

I unsuccessfully tried to control my rapid breathing that was caused by my sudden elevated heartbeat as I said, "Adonis, what are you doing?"

"Dezzi, I love you more than anyone or anything I've ever loved in my life. I want you to know I'm here for life. Whatever we go through from this point on, I want to make it official that we'll be going through it together."

Adonis looked more serious than I'd ever seen him look, and I knew that everything that was coming out of his mouth was from the heart. I could no longer control my tears. I just let them flow as Adonis continued.

"I know this is sudden, and you're only eighteen, but I don't want to risk losing your heart to someone else. With that being said, Desireé Arie Kimbrough, will you promise to be by my side every day for the rest of our lives?"

I was still in shock. I couldn't believe what was happening. I was so mad at Adonis one minute, and the next minute, he had made my heart melt. He opened the box that he was holding, and revealed a ring that held a diamond so large that I didn't think my finger would be able to lift it.

"This is what I've been in the studio working so hard for," Adonis said, as he saw the stunned expression on my face.

Adonis did spend a lot of time in the studio, but that time was not earning the amount of money he would've needed to purchase that kind of ring. I tried to keep the negative thoughts in the back of my mind during such a beautiful moment, but it was hard. I always said that I wanted to be with Adonis, and no one else, but it just was never so real. This was such a commitment that required me to think about where Adonis' life was headed, whether it was promising or not, and what my future would be like married to him. I knew that the path he was on was not going to lead to anything good, but I had confidence that I'd be able to change that. If he wanted me, he would have to do whatever it took to keep me, and I was sure he would do just that.

"Yes, baby. I'll marry you!" I said, as I extended my hand out to Adonis, as more tears attempted to escape. I tried my best not to ruin the makeup Ess had worked so hard to perfect.

Adonis grabbed my hand, then kissed the back of it before placing the beautiful ring on my finger.

"Happy birthday, Baby," he said as he stood up. Leaving no room in between us, he held both of my hands. "Now, do you forgive me?" he asked.

Laughing through my huge smile, I said, "Of course I do."

As we headed back to the house, we walked, hand in hand. We kept glancing back and forth at each other, smiling, and both of us secretly wondering if this really just happened. Before walking back into the house, we could hear the music blasting, and everyone talking and laughing, having a good time without me. I was even more excited to make Adonis' introduction to everyone who didn't personally know him. Besides Ess, and a few of my old friends from Smyrna, no one knew exactly how serious our relationship was. I kept everything quiet because I didn't want my mom to prematurely find out too much information about Adonis.

As soon as Adonis and I stepped foot in the door, Ess came running towards me, wearing heels and all, looking extremely worried. She put her hand on my shoulder, as she tried to catch her breath.

"Dezzi. Where you been? I've been looking all over for you. We have a small problem."

I was not about to let Ess mess up my moment with something petty that could wait, so I said, "If it's small, it can wait. There's something more important that needs attention now."

As I began walking, Ess, still trying to get me to deal with whatever she had going on, said, "Dezzi. You really need to deal with . . ."

"Ess, calm down. It's her birthday. Don't stress her out," Adonis said.

Ess shook her head and didn't say another word. I walked over to the DJ's table, grabbed the mic, and told everyone to come together for my announcement. I looked around as everyone came crowding around.

"Do you see my mom and Ess?" I asked Adonis, shouting over all the noise.

He began looking around and said, "Nope."

"Well, my mom definitely can't miss this."

I put the mic up to my mouth and asked everyone to quiet down. I then said, "Has anyone seen my mom or my best friend, Essence? I really need them both to be here for what has now turned out to be an even bigger announcement than before," I said, looking over, smiling at my bae.

"I have a surprise first," my mom said out of nowhere, from the crowd.

"Oh, there you are," I said, when I finally saw my mom.

Ess came running in, looking distressed, and right after her, came one of my neighbors, Paul, running through the front door, yelling, "There's a fire in the driveway!"

"You ruined the surprise!" my mom shouted indignantly at Paul.

"Now, can it still wait?" Ess asked, sarcastically.

I could hear Adonis saying my name over and over, but I couldn't respond. I stood there confused as ever, not quite grasping the fact that someone was saying there was a fire in the driveway, and if there was, how in the world did it start? Everyone began to run outside, and I finally decided to follow once I began smelling smoke.

Once I got outside, with Adonis right behind, my heart plummeted as I saw what was burning in the middle of the driveway. All of the boxes and bags that contained dad's personal belongings were up in flames. There were even picture frames that held pictures of my dad, and us a family that my mom had thrown on top of everything. I began shaking, feeling like I was having a nervous breakdown. Most of these people didn't know my story and didn't understand what was going on, but the ones that did, stood there, shaking their heads, not knowing what to do. Even Adonis was speechless. I couldn't just stand there and watch this happen. I snapped out of it, and ran and grabbed the water hose, trying to put the fire out. Ess came to the rescue, running out of the house with the fire extinguisher.

My mom then came wobbling out of the house, hardly able to speak clearly after her obvious alcohol binge she had secretly been on for most of the day, and said, "Surprise! Out of sight, out of mind, right, Dezzi? Now we don't have to look at all this shit and be reminded everyday of how much of a liar your dad was! He said he would never leave us, and he did! You know what else? He said he would be here today, and never showed. He always made promises to me he couldn't keep, and I always forgave him! But this is how much we meant to him!"

The words that were coming out of my mom's mouth felt like they were stabbing me in my chest. As Ess and I finished extinguishing the fire, I turned around to tell my mom what was exactly on my mind. As soon as I looked at her pathetic, drunk ass, she began vomiting all over the walkway. Embarrassed was an understatement. She promised to make this day a day that I would never forget, and she had definitely kept that promise.

I suddenly heard fire truck sirens coming down the street, and they pulled up right in front of my house, where there was no longer a fire, and only remnants of some of the things my dad had touched and worn last. I dropped the water hose and began walking back towards the house as everyone silently stared. I stepped over my mother, as she laid on the concrete in her own vomit, walked into the house, and slammed the door.

<u>Chapter Five</u>

Afterhaving to end the party extremely early due to my mom's alcohol negligence, Ess and Adonis had to get my mom to bed and made sure they sent everyone on their merry way. I sat on the sofa, despondent and unresponsive to everything. I couldn't believe my mom could allow alcohol to take over her mind the way she did, knowing how much we were both hurt by what we had gone through. Her actions had been so selfish, drunk or not, and I hated her for it. We were no longer on the same side. Anyone who could hurt me so badly couldn't possibly have my best interest at heart. Everything I had left of my dad was gone except for the picture I held in my hands. It was the only one that had managed to escape the pile and blow into the yard, and happened to be my favorite picture of my dad and me. I was around six years old and my dad carried me on his back as I wrapped my arms tightly around his neck. Our smiles told the world how much we loved each other.

I rocked back and forth, staring at the picture until Essence and Adonis came and sat on each side of me. I still didn't take my eyes off of the picture.

"Dezzi," Ess said softly, trying not to startle me.

I didn't respond. I felt like if I had tried to say anything, everything that I was feeling at that moment would've all tried to come out at once. I didn't want to make myself look foolish like my mother had made herself look. I refused to be like her. I was the one who had to hold it together. I was always the one.

Ess looked at Adonis and gestured for him to give it a try, as she rubbed me on the back.

Adonis gently slid the picture out of my hands and sat it on the table. He got on his knees in front of me and held my hands inside of his.

"Baby. I need you to come out of this. I know it hurts, but remember what I told you. Whatever we go through from this point on, we're doing it together. I'm here, Baby."

Adonis put my left hand up to his soft lips and kissed it. I looked him in the eyes and saw tears, which immediately made me realize I wasn't alone. I wrapped my arms around Adonis' neck and said, "Thank you."

"You don't have to thank me. That's what I'm here for," Adonis replied.

I reached over and hugged my bestie, Ess, who had tears streaming down her face.

"You know I'm always here for you, girl, and after all that's happened, I'm not gonna make you explain that ring tonight," she whispered with a slight giggle.

Until that moment, I had forgotten all about the announcement I was so excited to make. Thinking about that just made me even angrier with my mom. My day was supposed to be special. Even more special because Adonis had proposed to me and I wasn't even able to take it all in and share it with everyone else. I wanted to tell Essence about it, but I was mentally exhausted. I guess we all were because we all fell asleep right there in the living room, in a matter of minutes.

The next morning I woke up to the smell of liquor. I opened my eyes as much as I could, and caught a blurred vision of someone standing over me. I wiped my eyes and tried again. That's when I saw that it was my mom with her arms folded, and she didn't look happy. Her eyes were bloodshot and her hair was all over her head. I tried to quickly clear my head and comprehend what was happening, but after she spoke, I remembered very clearly.

"Who the fuck is this in my house?!?!" she shouted. I had forgotten I wasn't alone. Both, Adonis and Essence jumped up when they heard her voice.

"Mrs. Kimbrough, I'm sorry. We fell asleep after cleaning up the mess from the party," Ess quickly said.

Essence had given it a good try, but that wasn't what my mom was asking.

"Who is this man in my house, and why is he here?"

Adonis was nervous and didn't know what to do or say. I opened my mouth to speak, but before I could, Ess said, "This is my friend, Craig. He was my guest at the party. I should've made him leave. I apologize."

Sternly, my mom said, "Yes, you should have! I thought you were better than this, Essence! I don't think I want my daughter hanging around with a thot like you! This is what I don't tolerate!"

I interjected, "No, Essence! I won't let you do this! It's time the truth comes out. Ma, this is my boyfriend . . ."

Adonis raised his eyebrows, and I corrected myself, saying, "This is my fiancé, Adonis, and he's here because he stayed with me, consoling me, along with Essence, after you ruined my entire evening!"

Essence stood there with her eyes big as saucers, not believing what I had just said to my mom. The entire room was completely quiet. My mom walked and stood directly in front of me. She stared at me with her glassy eyes and tilted her head to the side as if she was getting ready to apologize for what she had done. Before I knew it, she slapped me clean across my face so hard, it knocked me to the ground. I held my face and looked up as Adonis lunged towards her, but Essence pushed him back.

"Get out of my fuckin' house!" my mom screamed at the top of her lungs.

As Essence and Adonis headed towards the door, my mom walked closely behind Adonis saying, "Fiancé? Stay away from my house and my daughter, or I'll kill you!"

After Essence and Adonis sped off in their cars, my mom stood at the door, yelling, "Who made this mess in my driveway? Clean this shit up right now, Dezzi! I can't believe you! Everything I did for you yesterday, you leave this mess! Unbelievable!"

At that moment, I realized my mom didn't remember what she'd done.

I got up off the floor and said, "No, you clean up your mess for once! You're the one who always makes the messes, and I always have to clean up after you! I'm tired of it! Can I please be the child and you be the adult for once? As a matter of fact, maybe if you had been a woman with a bigger voice, Dad would still be here! Maybe if you had a backbone and said what was really on your mind and told him to keep going that day, he would've listened. I blame you!"

I ran up to my room and slammed my door. I buried my face in my pillows and cried so long and hard that I cried myself to sleep. I felt worst than I had felt in a long time. My mom hadn't allowed me to grieve and I had been holding in so much that my heart could no longer handle it. I was the one who had to be strong and carry the both of us. I couldn't do it anymore.

I awakened later that afternoon, stretching my body across my entire bed as I rubbed my hand across my satin sheets in search of my phone. When I finally found it underneath one of my pillows, it began vibrating before I could even check it. It was Adonis texting me.

"Why you ain't responding?" the text read.

From that, I figured that wasn't the first time he'd tried to contact me, and I was right. He had texted me several times throughout the day asking me if I was ok. He had even called a few times. I replied back to Adonis, telling him I was fine, and had just woken up. He asked if it was cool if we got together later on. I knew after the argument my mom and I had had earlier, she wasn't going to go for that. Especially after breaking the news to her the way that I did that Adonis and I were engaged. I didn't care. I replied to Adonis, telling him to pick me up around eight. That would give me some time to handle things with my mom.

I stayed in my room a little while longer, trying to get my mind right so that when I did finally see my mom, things wouldn't immediately go left. I just hoped that her liquor had completely worn off, because if not, trying to have a meaningful conversation with her was going to be hopeless. To mellow out my mood, I turned on some music and began cleaning my room. I felt as though I was alone in the house, but I knew I wasn't. I knew she was somewhere in the house, either passed out, or drowning in her sorrows.

While I was cleaning, my phone rang.

"Hey girl," I said in a depressing tone.

"Don't sound so sad birthday girl," Ess said, trying to cheer me up.

"Why wouldn't I sound sad? Fuck my life!"

"Don't say that! You have so much to look forward to. You'll be going to college soon, and guess what. You'll be able to do whatever you want to do. You can now if you really wanted to."

Ess paused and said, "Wait, let me take that back. I forgot who the hell I was talking to. Please don't let me give you any ideas!"

"Girl, I'm so over everything! The way my mom acted last night, I feel like she has no right to tell me anything! I'm the fuckin' adult in this house!"

"Just wait it out. You don't have long, and you'll be off to school. I know what will make you feel better."

"What?" I asked, anxious to hear what she had to say because I was truly in need of something to alleviate my anger.

"Just look down at that beautiful ring on your left hand. You have a man that loves you and would do anything for you, including wait on you. Just be patient. You've dealt with it this long. A little while longer won't hurt. "

"Yeah, you're right. I'll be ok."

"Of course I'm right!" Ess said as she laughed. I could see her beautiful smile, which always lifted my spirits when I was down, through the phone.

"You wanna hang out tonight? I know your mom said she didn't want you hanging with a thot like me, but I forgive her. I know she didn't really mean it."

We both burst out in laughter because we both knew I was the real thot . . . Well, not really a thot, but the one having sex, and Ess was still a virgin.

In the middle of the laughter, I said, "I would, but I already told Adonis I'd hang out with him tonight. I have to try to figure out how I'm gonna get away with that one."

"Well, don't use me as your alibi. I can't cover for you this time. I already have to work on getting back in good with your mom."

"Don't worry. I'm not. I'm just gonna be honest and tell her I'm going out with Adonis . . . my fiancé," I said, sounding a little doubtful, because I wasn't sure how this was going to go.

"Good luck with that one," Ess replied.

"Damn, Redbone! You can at least pretend like you have some faith in your girl."

"I do have faith in you. Faith that you can fuck some shit up!"

"Wow!"

"I'm just messing with you. Just trying to put a smile on your face. I know you'll work it out. Enjoy yourself tonight and call me tomorrow to let me know how things went."

Ess always made things sound and feel better than what they really were. I truly appreciated her for that because if I hadn't had her around, there were numerous times when I would have probably lost my mind. She was without question, the kind of friend every girl needed. After I got off of the phone with her, I took a long, hot shower to move forward in my preparation of facing whichever personality my mom would present to me this time. I was praying it was the one that kinda liked me.

Chapter Six

I slowly crept down the stairs, a little nervous of what I would encounter. As I made it to the bottom of the stairs, I noticed the aroma of a home cooked breakfast. As I walked a few more feet, before being in my mother's immediate presence, I heard laughter coming from the kitchen. Not just the type of laughter you hear when someone tells a joke, but the kind that comes from a genuinely happy person. That was the last thing I thought I would've heard after the night and morning that I'd had dealing with the foolery of my crazy ass mom.

"This may go better than I thought it would," I mumbled to myself. It was always a good day when my mom cooked breakfast in the middle of the day.

As I turned the corner to enter the kitchen, I saw my mom sitting at the table, wearing her short, blush pink robe that my dad loved to see her in, holding a cup of coffee. She sat with her legs crossed at the knee, looking as though she was purposely showing off her long bronzed legs, and voluptuous thigh. Before she notice my presence in the room, she continued to laugh hysterically, showing all of her pearly white teeth. There was no phone up to her ear, as I thought there would be. I had assumed she was on the phone with one of her friends who had magically altered her mood. I was confused by the entire episode until my attention was suddenly taken away from my mother, by the sound of a deep, male voice.

I looked to the right, in the direction of where my mom's attention was focused, which was the same reason why she still hadn't noticed me. My eyes met with those of a tall, dark, random man standing at the stove wearing nothing but boxers, scrambling eggs and frying bacon. I suddenly felt like I was caught in the middle of a scene from "Baby Boy", and my new name was Jody. This was a new all time low for the woman who called herself my mother. The person who was always supposed to be there to protect me from hurt, harm, and danger for the rest of her life, but instead she had hurt me more than anyone had ever hurt me. She had managed to destroy one of the best memories we were able to share together. That was the memory of having evening breakfast as a family, with my dad, and not some random dude. The thought that things were going to go well, and that my mom and I were going to be able to have a civil conversation and move on, had completely been erased from my mind as the anger I was feeling reignited flames within my entire body.

When my mom finally noticed I was in the room, in the middle of her unknowingly showing me what really made her happy, the laugher completely stopped, and her smile faded away. In that moment, I found out what the true meaning was of "actions speak louder than words". My mom's actions said it all. There was actually nothing else that needed to be said by neither of us. One thing she did teach me was if I didn't have anything nice to say, then don't say anything at all, and the things that would have come out of my mouth at that very moment would have sent me to hell for all eternity. Obviously, my mom didn't feel the same way. Reluctantly, she proceeded to introduce me to the stranger.

"Dezzi, this is David, a good friend of mine."

Before she could finish her formal introduction, I said, "Good friend, huh? Just how good of a friend is David? As good as all of the other "good friends" you've had?"

My mom took a deep breath, rolled her eyes, and continued as though I hadn't said a word.

Sarcastically, she said, "David, this is my lovely daughter, Dezzi. You have to excuse her today. She has some daddy issues she's dealing with." She ended by taking a sip of her coffee while giving me the side eye.

As if my mother had given him permission to speak to me, Mr. David the stranger had the audacity to talk to me as if he knew anything about me.

"Hey, Dezzi. Would you like some breakfast? I heard the two of you love mid-day breakfast, so I thought I'd come by and cook up a little something."

I tried gathering my words before they all came out at once, as I felt my eyebrows raise on their own. That was never a good sign of what was about to come out of my mouth. I walked towards David and said, "David, since you thought you would come by and try to portray what my father was to this family, and be a part of a family tradition that you know absolutely nothing about, can you tell me what you and my mom did before you decided to reenact this horrible portrayal of our past life? If you can tell me that, then that should tell me exactly what you thought you would "come by and do"! Better yet, you don't have to say a word! You're standing at my stove in boxers!"

I turned away from David, leaving him speechless, and I folded my arms, walked over to my mom, looking down at her as she still sat in her seat, and said, "So you just want to destroy every memory I have, huh? I knew you were always jealous of our relationship, but he's gone now so you could at least act like a mom and try to have a better relationship with your daughter instead of allowing some dick that probably wasn't even good, to take part in the one thing we could still share, and enjoy together."

My mom stood up, and as soon as she began to open her mouth I wanted to just walk off, but on the other hand, I was curious as to see what in the hell she possibly could've said that would make a bit of sense after what she had done, so I stayed to listen, but not for long.

"Look, David was nice enough to . . ."

That was enough right there, and I needed to hear no more, so I politely interjected.

"Nice enough to what?!?!? Fuck you?" I laughed as though I had heard the funniest thing ever, and as I laughed, she caught me off guard and slapped the shit out of me . . . once again.

I guess I had hit a major nerve for her to put her hands on me for the second time in twenty-four hours, but I just said what needed to be said. I looked at her, shook my head, and said, "Nice to meet you, David. I hope the both of you burn in hell."

I ran back upstairs to my room and manically rummaged through my closet, trying to find something to wear on my night out with Adonis. At this point, I didn't feel like I needed my mom's permission for a damn thing. She had definitely stopped thinking about me when she made decisions a long time ago, so I decided to reciprocate the same type of love she was giving me, which was none! I had no more respect for her. It was sad, but true, and I didn't feel bad about it. In R. Kelly's words, when a woman's fed up, there ain't nothin' you can do about it. Rage continued to flow through my body as my mind began to really process what had just happened. Everything my mom and I had been through together, I just didn't understand how she couldn't give a fuck, and I needed to accept the fact that I probably would never understand.

After getting dressed, I laid in my bed on my back, staring at the ceiling.

"Daddy, I need you," I solemnly said, as if he way lying right beside me.

As soon as I drifted away in a land of fantasy where everything was perfect, there was a knock on my bedroom door. Barely being able to open my eyes, I looked towards the door. I rolled my eyes, and turned my head in the other direction, not wanting to deal with what was on the other side of the door. Then there was complete silence, and I thanked God that my silent prayer that she would go away had been answered, until there was another knock at the door.

This time, she shouted, "Desireé! Open this door!" as she twisted and shook the knob of the door I made sure to lock.

I took a deep breath as I jumped up to open the door, since it seemed as though she wasn't going to leave until I did. I snatched the door open, and saw my mom standing on the other side, still in her robe.

She looked me up and down and said, "Where do you think you're going?"

"I don't think I'm going anywhere. I'm going out with Adonis. The only other person, besides Ess, who cares about me." With every word that came out my mouth, my balls became bigger and bigger. I continued with my rant. "You are so embarrassing, and don't deserve to be called a mother! I don't know what happened to you, but you're a mess! With the way you're living your life, you can't tell me how to live mine. I pray that daddy can't see you right now because he would be disgusted!"

Before I knew it, my mom had grabbed me and flung me onto my bed. I lifted my head to only see her 5'8" body charging towards me. She jumped on the bed, straddling me, and as I lifted my arms to try to swing, she grabbed both of my wrists and pinned them down to the bed.

She began yelling to the point I could barely understand her. Tears began streaming down her face, saliva ran out of her mouth as she yelled, and her eyes were now bloodshot red.

"I'm the one who's here with you, and always been here for you, but all I hear about is your daddy!" she said as her eyes became larger and larger as she spoke. She looked like she had suddenly been possessed. I felt like she had drained all the energy from my body. I couldn't move if I wanted to. I didn't know if it all in my mind, or if it was from the weight of her body on mine, but I was numb.

"If you knew half of what I know, and all of what I had to experience to get to the wonderful place our family was finally at before the accident, you wouldn't be crying about your daddy! Fuck your daddy!"

As soon as I heard those words leave her lips, I felt a burst of strength emerge from my body. That's when I used everything within me and managed to snatch my wrists from my mom's tight grip and pushed her so hard that she flew off of the bed, slamming her back so hard into the wall that I thought she was unconscious. That was, until I saw her begin to get up. I got up off the bed before she was able to plan her next attack.

Trying to catch her breath from the wind being knocked out of her, she slowly got up and said, "You are so clueless. Your daddy was my life and your life, but at the end of the day, I didn't mean shit to him, and you definitely didn't mean shit to him."

She gained her composure, and as she began to walk out of my room, she turned around and said, "Let me go get a drink real quick so I can tell you the real, unrated version about your sorry excuse of a daddy! Since I'm finally accepting the truth, it's time you do the same!" She shook her head and said, "I should've done this a long time ago," before turning back around and heading out of the door.

I suddenly couldn't control my breathing. I had never had a panic attack, but I felt like that's what may have been going on. I couldn't cry. I felt like I was having an outer body experience. The next thing I knew, I began running and screaming like a madwoman. I burst into the hallway, and ran down the catwalk like I was running a relay. My mom looked back, but didn't even have time to react because she didn't realize I was only a few feet behind her. By the time she turned around, I was gliding in the air. She put her hands up in front of her in an attempt to lessen the impact. We both fell to the ground, rolling over on our backs. She was a little quicker than I was, and before I knew it, she was standing over me. As she bent over, looking as though she was about to take a swing at me, I bent my leg, and kicked her in the stomach with as much force as I could. She flew against the cherry oak bannister of the catwalk and just sat there motionless. She had a look of panic on her face, and I didn't realize why until I saw that the railings from the bannister were falling over the edge of the catwalk piece by piece.

As I tried to hurry and get up to help her, she tried to lift her body up from against the railings that seemed to be intact, but the sudden movement caused them to loosen and fall. As they fell, my mom began to fall with them, and it was too late. We looked each other in the eyes as she fell from the second floor to the first. She hit the marble floor so hard that it sounded like every bone in her body shattered. I was in shock. I couldn't take my eyes off the gruesome sight. My mom's eyes were still open, as she lay in a puddle of blood, pouring from her head. I waited for her to say something, but it didn't happen.

Chapter Seven

I found myself sitting in the corner of the catwalk when I suddenly heard the doorbell ring. I didn't know who it could've been or how much time had passed.

"Who is it?" I said softly.

The doorbell continued to ring, but at that moment, my brain wasn't communicating with my body. I wondered if this was what it felt like when people were brain dead. The ringing at the door stopped, but then I began hearing the ringing of my cell phone. It was in my bedroom where I'd left it before I attacked my mom. What had I done? I had murdered my own mother. Those words began taking over my mind, but I couldn't believe it was true. I crawled over to the edge of the catwalk on my knees and looked down, expecting my mom not to be there. She was there, still looking right back at me. I began to panic. I quickly stood up not knowing what to do next. I looked up at the clock on the wall. It was a quarter after eight and that's when I remembered I had told Adonis to pick me up at eight. I then really began to panic and pace the floor, not knowing how Adonis would react to what I had done. One thing I could not do was open that door!

I heard my phone begin to ring again, so I ran in the room to answer it, thinking I could possibly stall for a little while until I could think of a plan.

"Hello?" I answered, trying not to sound frantic.

"Hey, Bae. Everything good? I've been ringing the doorbell. It's real quiet up in there," Adonis said, sounding concerned.

"Yeah. Everything's good," I said in a jittery voice.

"You don't sound like it. Come open the door. I'm still standing out here."

"I can't," I replied without knowing what to say next.

"Why not? She must've told you that you can't go. You sound shook, Baby. What did she do to make you so upset?"

"I'm good. Just leave!" I shouted as my voice cracked and I began to cry."

"If you don't come open this door, I'm about to open it myself! What the fuck is wrong with you?" Adonis said, now sounding more angry than concerned.

"Ok," I said as I slowly walked out of my room, towards the stairs with the phone still up to my ear.

When I finally got to the bottom of the stairs, I walked past my mom's lifeless body, trying to avoid eye contact. I focused on making it to the front door.

"Hurry up!" Adonis said loudly in my ear.

I unlocked the door, and slowly turned the knob to let Adonis inside. Once we stood face to face, he stared at me with a look of confusion on his face.

"Now what's wrong?" he asked.

I stared at him with the phone still up to my ear. He moved me out of the way and quickly walked in. As I stared outside into the darkness, I heard Adonis when he made the discovery.

"What the fuck, Dezzi!?!? What happened?"

Adonis ran back to find me exactly where he left me. He grabbed me by both arms and began shaking me.

"Dezzi! You have to tell me what happened! Talk to me!"

I finally came to, and grabbed Adonis, hugging him tight.

"I don't know what happened! It just happened!"

"She was drunk, right?" Adonis asked.

This was one time I had wished I was able to honestly say my mom was drunk, but she wasn't. She was sober, and just pissed me off! I buried my face in Adonis' chest and cried.

"Dezzi, we have to call the police."

I quickly looked up at Adonis and said, "No! No police."

"Why not? What do you plan on doing? She was drunk and fell over, right?"

"Yeah, but the police won't believe me! They'll blame me!"

"No, they won't! You didn't do this, did you, Dezzi?"

I pushed Adonis away from me and said, "See! You supposedly love me and don't even believe me! What kind of shit is that?"

"Come here, Baby," Adonis said as he pulled me close. "I do believe you. Just tell me what you want to do. You know I got you."

With puppy dog eyes, I looked at him and asked, "Do you really?"

"You know I do. Whatever you want."

"I want you to help me make this go away!"

"What?!?! How am I supposed to do that? What is really going on?"

"I thought you would do anything for me."

"Dezzi . . . Don't make me do this. You don't want to do this. You'll never be able to live with yourself. She's your mom no matter what."

I wanted to tell Adonis right at that moment that it couldn't be any worse than what I had already done, but that wasn't the right answer. I needed to get him on board with this, and I needed it to happen now! I couldn't go to jail.

"Adonis, think about it. You know how the police like to dig for stuff that's not there! They'll find a reason to think I had something to do with it. If we just do this together, it will be between the two of us. You can move out from with your mom and move with me. We have plenty of money to live off of. I'm on all of my mom's accounts."

Adonis looked at me like he was about to tell me no, but then he began rubbing the top of his head, and I could tell his brain was churning.

He took a deep breath and said, "You know I wouldn't do this for anybody else, right?"

With the lifestyle Adonis was involved in, I was pretty sure he probably wasn't new to this type of thing at all, but I continued to pretend to be naïve about it, and replied, "I know you wouldn't, and I'm so grateful for you right now."

"Let me just make a quick phone call so we can get this over with," he said reluctantly. "Do you have any thick plastic in the garage?"

"I think we still do from the move."

"Go and get that while I make this call."

As I headed towards the garage, Adonis yelled, "I'm gonna need one of these big rugs from underneath one of these table, too."

"Ok," I yelled back. I didn't know who Adonis was calling, but I was sure it had to have been someone who could help.

When I opened the door to the garage, I looked around until I found a roll of plastic high up on one of the shelves. I had to jump to reach it, but couldn't grab it. I finally hit it enough times to knock it down, and with it, down came something else. It looked like a thick book, but it was actually a photo album I hadn't seen since before we had moved from my home in Smyrna. I flipped open the first page, and saw a family picture of mom, dad, and me. I immediately closed it, but carried it with me back inside, along with the roll of plastic that I had come for.

When I got back inside, I found Adonis sitting on the couch just staring at my mom's body.

"Are you ok?"

Adonis became defensive and said, "I should be asking you that, but you seem fine. A little too fine to be perfectly honest."

"Look, I'm not fine. I'm barely holding it together. You saw the condition I was in when you got here. You helped make me feel safe and secure. That's why I love you."

Adonis rolled his eyes and said, "Let's do this."

He grabbed the plastic from me and began unrolling it. I stood there watching as he began wrapping it around my mom's feet, then continued to her legs.

He then looked at me and said, "I need you to help lift her body so I can get her abdomen."

I nodded and knelt down beside her, sliding my hand underneath her back. As I gently lifted her up, and Adonis continued to wrap, I frowned and said, "What is that smell?"

Adonis looked at me, shaking his head, and said, "It's her."

I suddenly felt sick and jumped up running, trying to make it to the bathroom. I made it just in time to kneel over the toilet and throw up the little bit of food that I did have in my stomach. Even after that, I still felt nauseous, so I sat on the floor next to the toilet until Adonis came knocking at the door.

"Hey, you ok?"

"I'll be fine."

He opened the door and said, "This is too much for you to handle. I'll take care of the rest. Go upstairs, get comfortable, and get some rest."

"You sure?" I asked.

"I'm positive. I got you."

I stood up and gave Adonis another hug. I was beginning to have mixed emotions about everything that had happened. I was trying to make myself believe that this wasn't my fault. I tried to convince myself that she provoked me and caused my reaction. If she 'd never been talking shit about my daddy, this would've never happened. I loved my mom, though, so I at least had to do one more thing.

I walked back to where Adonis had finished preparing my mom for her final resting place. I knelt beside her once more and removed the plastic from her face. Adonis had closed her eyes and she looked peaceful. I kissed her on the forehead, then the lips. Her body was no longer warm as it always was, especially from the alcohol. She was cold, and at that moment, reality had set in that I killed my mom and she was never coming back. That would be the secret that no one else would never know, and I would take it with me to my grave whenever that time came.

Before going upstairs to bed, I gave Adonis a kiss goodbye, and entrusted him with the remains of the woman who had given birth to me. The woman who no longer knew how to show me she loved me, but I still knew she did. The woman who tried her best, but her best was never good enough. The woman who died by the hands of the person she tried to protect with all she had. The woman who died disappointed at what she had created. A monster.

Chapter Eight

The next morning I woke up with the sun gleaming in my eyes. I stretched, moaning at the same time. I felt like I had been sleeping for days. I had no idea what time it was so I checked my phone and it was eight in the morning. My mom hadn't even come to wake me, which I was surprised by. Normally, she would bang on my door at seven o' clock on the dot to make sure I was up getting ready for school. *Maybe I slept right through it,* I thought to myself.

I slowly rose from the bed, stretching once more, but before I could stand, my phone rang.

"Good morning, Sweetie", I answered, already knowing it was my baby, Adonis.

"Hey. How you feelin'? he asked, sounding unlike himself.

"I'm ok. Just was about to get up to make sure my mom was up for work since she hasn't been in here yet. What's going on with you? You don't sound good."

"What are you talking about, and who would sound good after all that happened last night?"

My heart then skipped several beats. I dropped the phone, ran directly down the hall to my mom's room, which was left the same way that it was the day before. Her bed was perfectly made, and not a thing out of place. I didn't smell the beautiful fragrance of Flowerbomb, which was my mom's favorite and she never missed a day of wearing. I then ran down the stairs, hoping that maybe she was sick and was staying in for the day. Still, I found no signs of her. Her car was still in the garage.

Maybe she ended up going out on a date last night and hasn't made it home yet, I thought, which still wasn't like her. She always made sure she took care of her responsibilities, no matter what.

I then remembered I left my Adonis on the phone and quickly ran back up the stairs to continue my conversation.

"Hey, Baby?"

"Yes, Dezzi."

"I can't find my mom. Maybe she went out last night and didn't come back. What if something happened to her?" I said worriedly.

"Babe, oh my God. You don't remember what happened last night, do you?"

I began crying uncontrollably like there was something I should've been remembering, but couldn't.

"What?!?!?! Just tell me, Adonis. Where's my mom? What happened to her?"

Adonis paused, and hesitated when he said, "I took care of her," in a trembling voice.

My forehead wrinkled, and my mouth dropped slightly as I tried my best to comprehend what he was telling me. I felt like I had had a complete blackout from the night before, not remembering anything before having an argument with my mom about not being able to leave with Adonis. Maybe she had just gotten upset and left for a while.

"So you told her that we were going to be together and there was nothing she could do about it?"

"No Dezzi!" he shouted. "Your mom is dead, and I . . ."

"You what, Adonis?!?!?!

"I did what you wanted me to do! I helped you out!"

"Helped me by doing what?"

"I can't believe you really don't remember! Here it is, I haven't been able to sleep a wink all night, and you remember absolutely nothing!?!? Well, let me put it to you like this. You killed your mother before I was able to come over to prevent it, and to keep your ass out of jail, I took care of the body! Now, do you remember "Miss all of a sudden I have amnesia?!?!?"

"No . . . No. Stop lying to me."

"I'll be over in a few minutes. I'm not far from you house. We need to talk face to face before you do something stupid."

After hanging up from with Adonis, I sat on the edge of my bed and pounded my fists against my forehead, trying to dig as far as I could deep down into my brain to understand what was happening. I needed for whatever happened to have all been a nightmare.

I soon heard the doorbell , and it was Adonis. He looked terrible.

As soon as I opened the door, all of his weight fell over on me as he gripped me tightly to give me a hug. I could hear him sniffle, and I had never known Adonis to cry.

He grabbed me by my shoulders and said with teary eyes, "I can't live with this on my mind. All we have to do is tell the police your mom was drunk and attacked you, we panicked, and hid the body."

"I don't know what you're talking about," I said as I pulled away from Adonis' ole whining ass. Things were slowly coming back to me and the visuals were nothing nice. I didn't want to have anything whatsoever to do with it.

"You know exactly what I'm talking about! I told you I had your back, Dezzi, and that's exactly what I did, because I love you and I don't want anything bad to happen to you. Look, I know you're scared, and I am too, but we have to have a serious conversation about our story, and our next move. This is just not gonna go away. Questions are going to be asked, and we will have to have answers."

I plopped down on the couch and put my head in my lap. My emotions were running rampant. Even after all the things I had gone through with my mom, I loved her more than I could've ever expressed to her. Adonis came behind me and massaged my shoulders. He kissed me on the top of my head. I now definitely knew he was there for me no matter what. As he continued my massage to try to console me, he asked if I wanted to know what he did with her. I refused to know. I never wanted to know because I knew each time I came to the place where I knew she was, I would have an emotional breakdown, just as I did each time we rode that same freeway where my dad died. Adonis respected my wishes. I just hated he had to live with the thought of knowing. I knew he was strong, though, and he would be ok.

"Hey, Babe. I was in the middle of running an errand for my mom before I came here, so let's finish this conversation a little later. Just don't say anything to anyone."

"No!" I shouted in anger. I stood up, pointing my finger in Adonis's face. "We need to continue this conversation right now! First of all, we need to start being completely honest with each other if we're going to completely trust each other!"

"What are you talking about? I'm always honest with you. You know I got you. I ain't going nowhere, and that's a fact. We've definitely been through way too much now to leave each other hanging."

I pushed my index finger into Adonis' forehead and told him, "You know exactly what I'm talking about! I know what you're out here doing in these streets and I can't afford to lose anyone else. That would basically leave me by myself, and I need you! Tell me, face to face how deep are you in these streets? Be completely honest, Adonis. I'm not playing with you!"

"Let's just say I'm deep enough to take care of you and our future family for the rest of our lives. I'm not going to put you or myself in danger for something that's not worth it. I've been working hard for us, baby girl, and I will continue to, as long as you allow me. Now, if we can continue this conversation later, I'm now going to be honest with you and tell you I have runs to make so I can continue to make us some money."

I didn't quite know how to say no to that, but I didn't like him having to put his life on the line to feel like that was what was going to give us a good life, and make me happy. We would definitely have to resume our conversation later and figure out a better way. 'Til then, I let Adonis go tend to his business.

Chapter Nine

While waiting for Adonis to return, I walked around the entire house and mourned the loss of my mom. I knew now that my mom and dad were together, but I wanted to be with the both of them. This time gave me nothing but opportunity to think about my future. Specifically my full ride scholarship to Texas A&M. Adonis hadn't been honest with me, but I hadn't been completely honest with him either. He still had no idea about my plans on attending Texas A&M. I did, however, plan on telling him once he returned after "work."

The doorbell rang sooner than I expected. As I opened the front door, I said "Babe, I wasn't expecting . . ." Then I realized it was Ess. I hadn't even thought about what I was going to tell her. It definitely wouldn't be the truth because she would have dragged me straight down to the nearest Police precinct.

Ess folded her arms and said, "Oh, I guess I'm not "Babe" and obviously you weren't expecting me!"

"I'm sorry girl. There has been so much going on since last night", I said as I gave my bestie a hug.

"So, your mom still tripping about Donnie?" she asked.

"Girl, we got into this really bad argument last night when I was trying go to out with him, and you will not believe this, but she packed some of her stuff and just left!"

The look on Ess's face was full of disbelief.

"Shut up!" she shouted. "It couldn't have been that bad!"

"Actually it was. She started making comments about my dad not caring about us the way we cared about him. It really hit a nerve, and we both probably said some things we didn't mean, but now she's gone."

"Have you at least tried to call her?"

"Yeah, but she's not answering. I left voice messages, but she's not returning my calls. I'm sure she's fine. She's probably at one of her boyfriend's houses until she calms down."

"You're not worried about her?"

"Nah. She'll be fine. Don't worry so much Redbone!"

"Well, I just know your mom is very fragile. I know she can be strong, but she's fragile at the same time."

"Let's stop talking about that. Adonis was finally honest with me about his occupation!"

"Oh, really! And were you honest about your scholarship? You know that the time for you to pack up and leave is coming up real soon. It'll be here before you know it!"

"Here you go!" I said rolling my eyes.

"Well, it is reality, and I think your man should know, unless you're planning on staying here . . . You're not, are you?"

I exhaled, and said, "I really don't know what to do. I love Adonis and I really am worried about him without me being around."

"What? Cheating?"

"Noooo!"

"Ok. I was gonna say I got that on lock!"

"No, I'm worried about his safety and I know he's not going to want to come with me."

Ess grabbed my shoulders and made me look directly in her eyes. "Look! You have a whole lot going for yourself and I am not about to let you waste a scholarship on a man! They come a dime a dozen and if it's meant to be, it'll still work out!"

"Ok. I'll put some deep thought into it!

"Promise me!"

"I promise."

"I wish I did have a full ride to go somewhere, but I'm stuck here and it's definitely not by choice, and I damn sure wouldn't let a dude make me stay here if I did have a scholarship."

"Well, he's not making me stay if he doesn't even know about it."

"That's your problem. You're worried that if he knows about it, he will make you go because he loves you just that much."

I thought about what Ess said and there was possibly much truth to that. We ordered pizza and watched "Girl's Trip" until Adonis called and said he was around the corner. I told Ess we had some serious talking to do, so she understood, and met Adonis at the front door as she was leaving.

As they hugged and parted ways, Adonis looked frantic.

"What did you tell her?" he asked.

"I told her my mom and I had an argument about you and she packed a few things and left. I told her I'm sure she'll be back once she calms down. How dumb do you think I am? Don't you know if I would've told her the truth, the police would be picking me up right about now?"

"Just making sure."

"How'd things go?" I asked, trying to change the subject.

"See, that's exactly why I didn't want you to be involved or know what was going on!"

"What did I say?" I asked curiously.

"How the hell am I supposed to answer a question like that? I made it back in one piece. There are no questions that need to be asked."

"Whatever," I said sarcastically.

I sat on the loveseat and patted the seat next to me so we could have this serious conversation.

I just stared at him for a moment, 'til he finally said, "You ready to talk, or what?"

"You are so much less emotional than you were when you left earlier."

"Because what I do keeps my mind on other things."

"I don't know how to quite say this without being a bitch, and sound like I'm trying to run your life, but you already know

I don't like this street bullshit. I don't like having to worry about whether or not I'm going to see you again after you leave me. It's just too stressful."

Adonis grabbed both my hands and said, "I've been doing this for a long time now and have been doing just fine. Nothing is going to happen to me. I promise you. In addition to that, I do my music, too. Just trust me. We've been good so far, right? The only difference now is, you know for a fact what I'm out doing. I told you I'm going to take care of you and that's exactly what I plan on doing. I handled the situation with your mom, and obviously you've come up with the story we'll be sticking with, right? So we're all good."

After that spill, there was no way I was about to talk about going to Texas A&M. We had already encountered so much within the last twenty-four hours and I think at that moment, I was still in shock that my mom was gone. I decided to go a different route with the conversation.

"Adonis, you know I have plenty of money, and now it is all mine due to the circumstances. You don't have to do any of what you are doing right now to make sure we're ok. We are fine."

"I get what you're saying, but a woman will not take care of me. I'm going to continue to do what I do, and I'm sorry, but if you can't deal with that, you may be with the wrong man. I love you and don't want to lose you, but the ball is in your court."

"Don't do that, Adonis. You know I want us to be together, and we will be together."

"Ok, so that's resolved, now moving on," Adonis replied.

For some reason I felt like I had just been punked, but I guess I had. I would just wait to see where we were when it was time for me to go off to school, and make a decision from there as to what would have my best interest at heart.

Chapter Ten

After about a week of playing house with Adonis, I noticed exactly how much time he spent out in the streets selling. He barely even slept. I would feel him crawl out of bed in the middle of the night to take care of business, but I felt like I couldn't say a word. I would just say a prayer that he would return, and he always did.

Ess constantly checked in on my mom, to the point that I had to begin to lie and say that I had spoken to her just to ease her mind. Ess was always the type that always wanted to make sure everyone was cool, including my mom, who had only liked her when she was sober, which was only about half the time. Ess kept telling me while we were playing house, I was going to end of getting pregnant, but we were very careful when it came to that. Even though I was young, I knew that I didn't want kids early, if ever. Adonis and I just wanted to enjoy our time together without having any other care in the world.

After Adonis dropped me off at home after school one day, I decided to do some house cleaning. The last room I went in, that I'd finally gotten up the nerve to go into was my mom's. I slowly opened the door, and I could still smell her. Everything was dusty, which she would've never approved of. I grabbed the wood polisher and cleaned her furniture from top to bottom. I then pulled all the linen off of her bed and snuggled up in them on the carpeted floor. I felt the closeness to her, and I cried for her until I dozed off.

I didn't wake back up until Adonis called and asked if I was hungry. I was kind of hungry, but I wanted to finish cleaning my mom's room just the way she'd like it, so I told him to give me another hour before picking me up. He asked if I wanted him to help with anything and I told him I needed this time by myself. He completely understood, which I knew he would.

I thought about washing her linen, but changed my mind because that would've forever gotten rid of the scent that I loved so much. Her scent was the only memory I had left of her.

As I began putting her linen back on, I noticed something sticking out from up underneath her mattress. I pulled it from underneath her floral-printed mattress and noticed it was a journal. It looked more-so like a diary and looked old, but well-taken care of at the same time. I flipped through it, and there were several pages written in my mom's perfect cursive handwriting. The beginning entries that I began reading went as far back as before I was born.

Saturday, August 29th, 1998

I would've never thought in a million years I would've found the type of love that I have found in this man. but I have. I am so excited to be able to tell him we'll be starting a family of our own together… The most perfect family there could possibly be. I just found out today that I'm six weeks pregnant, and I already love this precious one inside of me more than I can love anything else in this world. I've decided to wait a while because I don't want to jinx anything, but I know for a fact, he will be just as excited as I am . . . If not even more.

~Carlisa

After reading what my mom had said about me and my dad, I could feel the emotions coming out of the pages. Since I had lost my mom, I hadn't felt as much sadness as I felt in that moment. In the midst of a breakdown, Adonis called me, asking if I was almost ready.

"Yeah, give me about fifteen more minutes. I'll be ready."

"You good?" he asked, sounding concerned.

"Yeah, just ran across some memories that brought a few tears to my eyes, but I'm ok."

"Ok. I'll be there soon."

I just couldn't catch a break because as soon as I hung up from Adonis, my mom's cell rang, and it was her job. I was sure they were calling to check on her and see when she'd be returning to work. I told them she was really sick and we'd follow up when she was ok to return. I didn't know how long that lie would give me to come up with something new, but I'd just have to wait and see.

I finished making up my mom's bed, vacuumed, and went to clean myself up. As soon as I finished, I could hear Adonis coming through the door.

"Baby, you ready?"

"Yeah, I'll be down in a sec."

As I walked towards the staircase wearing, distressed high-waist skinny jeans, a black bodysuit, red pumps and red leather jacket, I said, "I didn't know what to wear since you never said where we were going, so I hope this is ok."

"You could put on a trash bag and still look good, girl," he said, as he grinned and laughed.

The entire way to wherever we were going to eat, Adonis played old school music, which I could remember complaining about, and putting in my ear buds when riding in the car with my parents, but I kind of enjoyed it on this beautiful evening.

"So, you sure you're ok?" Adonis asked, referring to the breakdown I'd had before his call.

"Yeah, I'm good. You make everything good."

Adonis grabbed my hand, squeezing it tight. As soon as he did, his cell phone rang.

He glanced at it and said, "Sorry Babe, I gotta take this."

He lowered the radio, and said, " Hey, what's up?

I looked over at Adonis, and his pleasant expression completely changed to a serious one.

"Right now?" Adonis asked whoever was on the other end. "Ok. Give me about twenty minutes. I got something to take care of real quick."

Adonis hung up the phone and said, "I'm going to have to drop you back off at home real quick, but I'll be back to get you in about forty-five minutes or so."

"Why?" I asked in a whiney voice.

"Because I have to make a run, and I refuse to take you on those types of runs."

"Which means it's dangerous, and you shouldn't be doing it," I mumbled,

"What was that?" Adonis asked.

"Nothing. Just take me home."

"You wanna go? Ok. Let's go. Only because I want you to know it's not as bad as you think it is."

I smiled, just at the thought of Adonis entrusting me to be his ride or die. When he saw the smile he put upon my face, he grinned and shook his head.

"You are such a spoiled brat, you know that?"

"I'm your spoiled brat," I said lustfully.

When we finally pulled up to the spot, which looked like a large warehouse, Adonis said, "Stay in this car, no matter what. If you hear anything out of the ordinary, pull off."

"Anything out of the ordinary like what?"

"Please don't play dumb on me now, Dezzi. Gunshots . . . anything like that."

Oh my God, I thought to myself. *This was exactly why he needed to leave this shit alone!*

"Ok, but I better not hear no shit like that," I said.

Adonis gave me a kiss on the lips and said, "I'll be right back so we can go eat."

He grabbed his bag and headed towards the steel double doors of the warehouse. I attempted to listen to some old-school for a while, but then I realized around ten minutes had passed and my baby still wasn't back. I hadn't heard anything "out of the ordinary" as Adonis had told me to listen out for, but that building was steel, so if there was anything going on in there, how would I know?

I waited a couple of more minutes and couldn't resist any longer. I decided to get out of the car, gently closing the car door, and slowly walked to the doors of the warehouse. I put my ears to the door to see if I could hear any sound coming from inside. I could faintly hear voices but nothing more. I stood there for a few minutes, not wanting to interrupt the meeting. Suddenly the faint voices became louder, and then I heard what sounded like gunshots. My first mind told me to go inside to make sure my man was ok, but I heard Adonis' voice in my mind that told me to drive off. At that moment, that sounded real stupid. How in the world would I just leave my man in the middle of a gunfight?

With all the strength I had, I forcefully pulled the steel doors open, and saw as many as 20 other men up against my man, who was holding a man around his neck, with a gun to his head. He must've been with the other guys and Adonis was holding him as his hostage.

"Get out and leave!" Adonis said as soon as he saw me step into the warehouse.

As I hurriedly took my heels off, a couple of the men started running after me, and then I heard a gunshot. I slowed down, looking back, hoping it wasn't Adonis being shot at. All I saw were the men who were still after me. When I looked forward, I saw a car with bright lights flying straight towards me. It came to an abrupt stop and gunshots started flying out of the driver's side window, shooting the two guys who were after me.

"Get in woman!" Adonis yelled at me.

I hurriedly jumped in the passenger side of the car, unable to catch my breath, as we sped away.

"Didn't I tell you to stay in the car?!?!?"

"Yeah, but you were gone for so long, and I got worried. Then, when I was at the door, I heard the gunshots and really got worried. You just didn't expect me to leave, did you?"

"Uh, yes! We ain't Bonnie and Clyde! I told you I got this. Do what I tell you to do next time. This could've been really bad!"

"What do you mean by "Could've been? You shot two guys!"

"Those two who got shot could've been us, now chill out, and let's go eat!"

"You still want to go eat after all that?" I asked.

"Yeah. I'm still hungry."

"You can't do this anymore, Adonis. I just saw what can happen, and I don't like it."

Adonis looked at me and rubbed my thigh and said, "It's all part of the game, Baby. All the dude did was shoot in the air to try to put some fear in me, and I grabbed one of his men to do the same. The transaction would've gone fine if you hadn't have shown up."

"It's either this or me," I mumbled.

"What was that?" Adonis asked.

Louder and bolder I said, "It's either this or me!"

"So now you're giving me an ultimatum?"

"Basically. I can't do this with you."

Adonis pulled over to the side of the road and said, "I thought you loved me."

"I do, and that's exactly why I'm giving you this ultimatum. I don't want to live without you, but I'd prefer to be without you and not have to worry about whether or not you're coming home, than be with you and end up having the police come to my door to tell me you've been killed. I can't be stressed out like that."

"Get out," Adonis calmly said.

"What?" I asked, not believing what he was telling me to do.

"This isn't love. Love is when you will stick by a person no matter what. You evidently don't love me, so get out!"

"If that's what you really believe love is, I'll gladly get out of your car. I'm sure another nigga' would love to have a woman stand by his side the way I did tonight."

"And if he ain't a real one like me, your ass would be on the side of the road somewhere dead!"

I held my hand out before I got out the car.

"What?" he asked.

"I need my house keys that I gave you."

Adonis not so gently put the keys in my hand. I got out the car, and he sped off like I was a stranger on the street. I could not believe him. His thought process was way off, but I guess that was the exact reason he didn't want me around while he was doing that kind of work. He was a totally different person. He had shown me a side of him that I had never seen before.

After catching an Uber the rest of the way home, I just wanted to go in and relax. I ran some bath water using some of my favorite bubble bath that relaxed me the most, and while I waited for it to completely fill up, I thought about the fact that Adonis had really put me out of his car and had not a care in the world as to how, or whether or not I made it home. Was it really that serious? Did he really love me like he said he did?

After my bath water was ready, I grabbed my mom's journal from my room so that I could feel a piece of my mom and dad while relaxing in the tub. I needed them both more than ever right now Before I could even open it, my mind went into deep thought about where my relationship with Adonis was really going. It just seemed like we were on two completely different pages as to what we wanted our futures to become. When I finally came back to, I opened the journal and read the yellowish-faded page, which was dated November 26th, 1998.

Thursday, November 26, 1998

Well, today is one of my favorite days of the year . . . Thanksgiving, and I have sooo much to be thankful for! I still haven't told Babe about our bundle of joy. I'm not showing just yet, but morning sickness has been killing me! I think today will be the best day possible to break the news. I can't wait to see how excited he's going to be. I wanted to wait to tell him we were expecting until I was able to tell him the sex, but I just can't wait any longer. Holding on to this secret without sharing it with the one I love is the hardest thing I've ever had to do. We'll be hosting Thanksgiving Dinner, so the last thing I need to decide on is if I'm going to wait until the entire

family comes over to share the news, or have an
intimate moment alone to tell him. Only time shall tell . . .

   ~Carlisa

At the end of that entry, I must've dozed off for a short period because when my phone woke me up, my nose was about a quarter of an inch from the water, and my arm hanging over the edge of the tub with the journal still in my hand. I dried my hands on the towel hanging from the rack and grabbed my phone.

"Hello?"

"Come open the door," Adonis demanded on the other end of the phone.

"I can't."

"Why not?"

"I have company."

"You better not. Don't make me knock this door down."

"Ugh! I'm in the tub. What do you want?"

"We need to talk."

"We can talk when I get out of the tub, so just go sit in your car and wait patiently."

"Whatever," Adonis said with an attitude, and hung up.

When I was finally ready to get out about a half hour later, I dried off, lotioned up, and took my time doing whatever else I felt I wanted to do before letting Adonis' pathetic ass in.

When I opened the front door, I was expecting Adonis to be waiting in his car, but instead, he was sitting on the front porch.

Without turning around looking at me, he said, "About time."

"If all you came over here for was to get smart with me, or have an attitude, you can gone on back to your mama's house!"

He stood up and turned around to face me. It looked like he had been crying.

He hugged me with both arms wrapped tightly around me, and said, "I can't lose you, Baby. I love you too much. Please forgive me. I was a complete asshole tonight. I should've never taken you with me, but besides that, I should've never put you out in the middle of nowhere. Anything could've happened. Nothing that happened was your fault."

He raised my chin with his hand and gazed into my eyes.

"Please forgive me. I am so sorry."

As I gazed into his eyes, I said, "It depends."

"Depends on what?" he asked curiously.

"Depends on if you do what I asked you to do."

"What? Quit?"

"Yes. I told you we have plenty of money, and you can still do your music thing and whatever else legitimate you want to do."

"Well, I've always wanted my own record label, but it ain't that easy getting out of this game, Babe. I've been doing this longer than you know, and this is all I know."

"I understand that, but just work on the music, Baby! It's possible. You're very knowledgeable in the music industry." I then took the opportunity to sneak in, "We can even see about moving away from here. . . Maybe Texas, where no one knows us or anything about our past."

"You're so positive, but don't think I don't know what you're trying to do! I'm gonna let it slide though."

I got a little confused with that comment. Did Adonis already know about my acceptance to A&M?

"What do you mean you know what I'm trying to do?"

"I know you think I can't leave my mama. I ain't that much of a mama's boy. If I'm gonna help take care of her, I'm gonna do that regardless, whether it's from down the street or two-thousand miles away."

"I know you love your mama, Bae, and that's a good thing. That's a good sign of how you'll always treat your woman."

Adonis raised his one eyebrow and said, "Now don't forget you're my fiancé. I don't want to know what life would be without you, and you better not ever tell me another man is over here. You're trying to get someone hurt."

We laughed together standing right on the front porch, and Adonis gave me the most affectionate kiss he had ever given me since we had been together. I felt like we were finally getting somewhere.

Chapter Eleven

I had finally talked some sense into Adonis and made him make a decision between me and his street gig. Maybe now I could get him away from Atlanta. I had promised Ess we would spend some time together today and I couldn't wait to tell her about the progress I had made. She could never stand the fact that Adonis was a drug dealer and I just pretended like I had no idea.

We had planned on going out to lunch and to the mall. We didn't have much more to do since school was out. What I wasn't looking forward to were the questions Ess would have about my mom because I was sure they were coming. I wished she could just leave it alone like Adonis and I had. Of course, before I left for the afternoon with Ess, Adonis had to give me the talk he gave me every time I went around anyone who might've asked questions about my mom. He made me feel like he didn't think I was very bright. What he didn't realize was that I knew how to play things more calmly than even he did.

"Come in!" I yelled, as I heard the "Star Spangled Banner" tune of the doorbell. I knew Ess was on her was and I was busy sitting at the dining table having a cup of Butter Pecan Iced Coffee I had learned how to make on my own after Dunkin' Donuts kept discontinuing it on me, and reading a page from my mom's life.

Friday, November 27, 1998

My perfect plan wasn't so perfect. I had never experienced such a humiliating prayer before Thanksgiving Dinner in my entire life. I decided that I would lead the dinner in prayer as the entire family bowed their heads and held hands as they sat around our humongous round table. This would be the time that I would announce that there would soon be a new addition to the family.

"Thank you Lord for bringing our family together on this day of Thanksgiving. Today and every day, we are thankful for what you've continuously blessed us with, and the things that you have done in our lives to cause us to be humble. Thank you for allowing us to have breath to continue to enjoy this thing called life. Thank you Lord for the food that we're about to receive, for nourishment of our bodies, and bless the hands in which prepared the food. Lord, I especially want to thank you today to allowing me to borrow one of your children to be my own. I thank you for entrusting us with a healthy child, whether it be boy or girl, to care for, and to bring him or her up in your word."

As soon as I said those words, I could feel everyone's eyes fixed on me.

"We promise that we will not let you down." I opened my eyes, and as I said, "In Jesus' name, I pray, amen," I looked around the room for the love of my life, and he was nowhere to be found.

Everyone stood up to extend their congratulations, but the most important person who I wanted to share that moment with wasn't there. I hugged my mom and my dad. They were extremely happy to finally become grandparents. I am the only child, so I was their only hope, and they were getting up in age. After hugging my family, and accepting their love and support, I went to find the father of my unborn child.

I searched all over the house, and eventually found him in the bedroom, lying in in the bed, watching television during Thanksgiving dinner. I had never felt so disrespected in my life.

"Girl, what are you reading? You barely noticed I was even here!" Ess said, as she grabbed the other glass of iced coffee off the dining room table and began gulping it down like she hadn't had anything to drink in years.

"Now, how did you know that was yours?"

"Who else's would it be? Did your mom return yet?"

"No, but she sure has had a lot of men stopping by to check on her.

"I don't understand how you're so calm. She has been missing way too long! If you don't, I'm calling the police myself to file a missing person's report!" Ess said, as she folded her arms and shook her head, flipping the curly puff on the top of her head from side to side. "What if something bad has happened to her?"

"She's fine! She called me!"

Ess tilted her head, pursed her pink lips, and said, "When?"

"I talked to her yesterday. She said she just needed to get away for a little while. She needed to vent by herself so she went to Vegas." I said, as I came up with the lie as fast as I could. I knew Ess would be an issue because she always asked too many damn questions.

"What the hell is this?" she asked, as she snatched my mom's journal out of my hand, ripping some of the pages out.

"Look at what you did, bitch," I yelled before realizing what was coming out of my mouth.

I quickly knelt down to pick up the pages and tried putting them back in order. I started walking around in circles looking for tape so that I could put it back together.

"What is wrong with you?" Ess asked as she followed me around the house.

"Nothing! Just leave me alone!" I turned to her, and said, "Look, this is not a good time! I'll call you later. We'll have to do something another day."

Ess squinted her eyes and said, "Ok," with doubt in her voice. "You know I know you, and something's not right. I will find out so if you need to tell me something, go ahead and tell me now!"

"Nothing's wrong! Just leave!"

"What's going on in here?" Adonis asked as he walked in while I was trying to get Ess to leave.

"Oh, hey, Bae. Ess and I were gonna do a few things, but I don't feel like it anymore. I was just about to walk her out."

"It sounded like an altercation to me. Everything ok?" he asked as he put his arm around me.

"Yes. Everything's good."

"No! Everything's not good! Something ain't right! So now you have a key to the house?"

"That ain't none of your business, Ess. Dezzi said she was ready for you to go, so I think that's what's best. She'll give you a call later."

Adonis stood in front of Ess with his muscular arms folded and his legs about an inch apart until Ess savagely turned around, walked out, and slammed the door.

I took a deep breath, upset about everything that had just happened. I was upset about the lie I had to tell about my mom being in Vegas, about calling my best friend a bitch, and about her ripping the last real thing written by my mom of her early memories. I had a feeling Ess was not done yet and she was going to be the bulk of our problems. She didn't buy any of my story because she knew me so well that she almost always knew when I was lying.

I began walking around the house again, looking for some tape, when Adonis came to me at the wrong time asking me about what I had just told Ess, and talking that bullshit about keeping our stories straight. I wouldn't say much back because I was too focused on trying to find something to put my mom's journal back together just as I found it.

Finally he jumped in front of me and said, "What the fuck are you doing?"

"I need tape!" I said as I began crying uncontrollably.

"Baby, sit down. Talk to me. What happened? What's wrong?"

I put my face in my hands and said, "She ripped it! It's all I have! My mom is dead. I want my mom! Please bring her back to me! Ess is gonna tell!"

Adonis put his arms around me. "I'm sorry, Dezzi. I can't bring her back. I would if I could. I'll do anything you want me to do, but that's just impossible."

"I know! Because I killed her!"

"Baby, it's not your fault. It was an accident."

I shouted loudly, "Mom, please come back! I'm sorry for everything I did to you! I need you!"

Adonis grabbed me and held me tighter.

"Listen to me! We are going to get through this. It's gonna be hard at first, but it's going to be ok. You have to trust me. Your mom forgives you. She knows it was an accident. You just have to calm down and believe me when I say we will be ok! Don't worry about, Ess. She doesn't know anything, as long as you didn't say anything."

Adonis grabbed some Kleenex and wiped my face. He kissed me on my forehead and kept reassuring me that we'd be ok.

"Now, come on. Let me help you find some tape so we can fix your mom's book."

He helped me off the sofa and held my hand as we walked around the house looking for tape.

Chapter Twelve

After getting my mom's journal put back together, Adonis made me get undressed and get in bed. I was mentally drained and it had finally hit me that my mom wasn't coming back. I was surprised I had gone so long without truly mourning her death. After Adonis put me to bed, he said he'd be back a little later.

"Where you going?" I asked.

"I was going to the studio for a little while, and then I'll be back with something to eat."

I had been so caught up in my own emotions, I hadn't asked Adonis how he was. He was a part of this too, and I had been acting as if I was the only one going through something. He was going through an entirely different change of life after experiencing the traumatizing event that I had put him through.

"How are you, Baby?"

"I'm fine. Don't worry about me. I'm just worried about you being ok."

"Well, how's everything going with you?"

"Things are going good. Everything's coming together. Just trust me."

"That's what you always say."

"And that's what I mean. Have I given you any reason not to trust me when I say everything is going to be all right?"

I grinned as I pulled the cover up over my bare shoulders and said, "No. That's what I love about you."

"Ok. So trust me when I say I'll be back soon." He looked over at the lamp and said, "You want me to turn that off?"

"No. I'm going to do some reading."

"Ok, but don't put too much on yourself."

"I won't"

Adonis kissed me on the lips and rubbed his hand through my hair before he left. As soon as I heard the front door close, I took a deep sigh, and grabbed the recently refurbished journal off of my nightstand, and began where I left off before Ess had interrupted me:

"What is wrong with you? "I asked, not understanding why he would leave me sitting at the Thanksgiving dinner table looking like a fool.

"He sat up and said, " You're asking me what is wrong with me when you're the one that decided to make an important decision that should've been made between the two of us on your own? You know my lifestyle. It's not made for a man with a child, especially a newborn baby. Even if my lifestyle wasn't an issue, what if I wanted this to be between the two of us? Better yet, what if I just didn't want a baby right now, but now, even if I didn't want a baby I couldn't dare say that because you've told everyone you're pregnant, so it's too late to get rid of it now," he said uncaringly.

His eyes then got big as saucers and he said, "Well, we can still get an abortion and tell everyone you miscarried!"

When I heard those words even leave his mouth, my lips began to quiver and I felt like I was drowning in tears. I heard a knock on our bedroom door and I quickly ran into the master bathroom.

I could hear my mom at the door, asking if everything was ok.

"Yes, everything is great. You know, this was a surprise for me as well, so we're just both soaking it all in right now. We'll be down soon."

As I peaked around the corner of the bathroom door, I could see my nosey mom trying to peek in the room to see what was going on. She always could tell when something wasn't right. That was just the intuition of a praying mom.

"Ok, Baby. Just know the two of you are going to be excellent parents! I can't wait! We'll be down there waiting for you two so we can carve this turkey, so hurry on up!"

"Yes, ma'am!" the supposed man of my dreams said to my mom with a fake ass grin across his face.

After cleaning my face and putting on some fresh makeup, I came out of the bathroom and couldn't help but to ask why he just couldn't give up that life and raise a normal family with me.

"You really wanna know, Carlisa?"

"Yes. I do. I wouldn't have asked if I didn't."

He looked up at the ceiling like the answer was going to come down and expose itself.

As I was reading, I heard the doorbell.

"What did you forget, Adonis?" I'll be right there."

I hurriedly threw on my robe and house shoes, and ran down the stairs. When I tried to peek through the frosted glass on the door, I noticed flashing lights, which made me think something had happened that quick to Adonis. My heart wouldn't stop pounding before I was able to open the door.

I slowly turned the knob to open the door, and there was a tall white man with a crew cut standing in front of me wearing a navy blue Atlanta Police Department uniform on, who looked very familiar. From the look on his face, something definitely was wrong.

"Good Evening, young lady. My name is Officer Cavitt, and I'm looking for Ms. Calisa Kimbrough."

Trying not to show how nervous I was on the outside, I said, "I'm sorry, Officer. She's on a trip at the moment. She was going to Vegas, and maybe stopping in California for a week or so, but I keep in contact with her."

He put his hands on his hips and said, "And what is your relationship to Mrs. Kimbrough?"

"Her name is Ms., not Mrs. Kimbrough. I'm her daughter, and my dad was killed a couple of years ago on the expressway when one of those reckless truck drivers drug him all the way from one end of the freeway to the other, before bursting in flames. I'm sure you remember that if you've been a cop long enough," I said with tears in my eyes.

"Yes. I do remember. I was on site, and as a matter of fact, helped you and your mom. My sincere condolences once again."

My sincere condolences."

Suddenly, Adonis came walking through the door.

"What's going on here?" he asked.

"I'm not even sure yet, Babe. This officer rang the bell shortly after you left, and still hasn't told me why he's here."

"Can I ask how old you are, young lady?" the officer asked.

Adonis went into defense mode and asked, "First can we ask why you're here? I don't think this young lady has done anything wrong except mind her own business in her own home."

I took over from there because I definitely didn't want the police to try to find something on Adonis because he just might have found something.

"I'm eighteen. Now, how can I help you?"

"The reason I'm here is because I was requested to complete a well-being check on your mom, Ms. Kimbrough because it seems she hasn't been seen for some time and there are some people who are worried about her."

"Well, she's fine. If anyone would know if something was wrong with her, it would be me. She was sick for a while and took off work, but she had just been under too much stress and needed to get away. She's fine though."

"I believe you, but I'm going to need to see your ID, and I would like for you to call your mom for me while I'm here, just so I can feel like I'm thoroughly doing my job."

"No problem," I said, walked towards the stairs to go find my purse. While the officer wasn't looking, I pointed my index finger at Adonis, gesturing for him to sit down before he got us both in trouble. He raised both his arms to signify to me that he hadn't done anything wrong.

Once I got back downstairs, Adonis was still sitting, silently. I handed he officer my ID."

"I appreciate that ma'am."

After scanning over it to make sure everything was legit, he said, "Thanks, again. Now, can you please call your mom?"

Adonis looked at me with a concerned look on his face. He had no idea how I was going to get myself out of this one.

I looked at Officer Cavitt and said, "Better yet, here's my phone. She's stored in here as "Mom". Why don't you call her yourself?"

"Sounds like a plan to me."

As he searched for my mom's name in my phone, I looked over and winked at Adonis. He finally found it, dialed the number, and put it on speakerphone. The phone rang twice and the voicemail came on.

"Hey! You reached Carlisa. I'm busy at the moment, but leave me a message, only if it's important, and I'll return your call if it's important enough! Talk to ya later!"

Officer Cavitt hung up without leaving a message and handed me the phone.

"Those casinos are pretty loud. I'm sure she's having a good time and I'd hate to disturb her. I'm sorry for disturbing you as well."

"No problem."

I knew my mom's voicemail would pick up pretty quickly because I shut her phone completely off because I got sick of her job calling everyday.

The officer shook my hand and said, "Take care of yourself, Desireé, right?"

"Yes. You too."

The officer then went to shake Adonis' hand, and said, "Nice to meet you as well . . . I'm sorry, I didn't get your name."

"I didn't give it to you, but my name is Donnie."

"Thanks, Donnie. You two have a good night."

"Thanks, Officer," Adonis said as he closed the door behind Officer Cavitt.

"Why didn't you tell him your real name," I said, laughing.

"No one calls me by my government name except you, and you know who sent him, right?"

"Yeah, I know, but I don't even think I can blame her. Why did you come back so soon?"

"I left one of the sample tracks I needed in my nightstand drawer. I'm glad I did so you didn't have to go through that alone, but it seemed like you handled yourself pretty well. Are you sure you weren't a criminal in the past?"

"Of course not!"

"I know! No woman as beautiful as you could ever possibly be a criminal."

I grinned, and said, "You are so full of it. Before I came along, you probably had all the women that fell for all those lame ass lines you try feeding to me!"

Adonis wrapped his arms around me and tossed me on the couch. He straddled me as he put both hands underneath my robe where he felt only bare skin."

"So, you're trying to tell me I'm lame and have no game?"

"That's right!" I said, smiling.

"But look at the position I have you in right now. I can easily take advantage of you."

I pushed Adonis off me because I was pissed that he was right.

"Boy, get away from me!"

"You know I turn you on," Adonis said.

"I never denied that, but you're not about to sit here and act like you can run that lame ass game on me. Gone and take care of your business. Maybe I'll have something to give to you a little later," I said with a smirk.

After Adonis left, I took a deep breath because although I hid it from that officer and Adonis, I was nervous as hell. I just knew I was about to be on my way to jail. After finally easing my nerves and getting back comfortable, I resumed where I left off with my reading:

Finally, he said what I already knew was right in front of me.

"I 'm in love with those streets. They have satisfied me way before you came in the picture, so for that, I love them more than I love you. To be honest, I'd been planning on leaving you, not because I don't love you at all, but because I didn't want you to be part of this life any longer. It gets more and more dangerous and you don't deserve that," he said to me without any guilt in his voice.

Even though I had already known the truth, I wanted to hear it from him. I honestly thought a baby would change things. I thought it would make him realize his family was right here with me and make him go out and find something legit. I didn't care that he had just told me face to face that he was more in love with the streets than he was with me. I was still willing to stick around and pray for us to work out. I just knew this precious baby inside of me would make a difference. I was determined to make him love me and his baby more than those streets he was so addicted to, and someday he would be a husband to me and a father to our blessing. I told him I wasn't going anywhere, and he told me to do as I pleased, but he would be no part of my baby's life. I had to go back down to Thanksgiving dinner with my "man" and act like everything was ok. The sadness that I felt, I wouldn't even wish on my worst enemy. Love hurts.

~Carlisa

Tears began flowing from my eyes. I had read more than I could stand. To find out that my dad never wanted me hurt me like hell. My entire life felt like a lie. My mom was so weak. She was willing to do anything for love, including being the other woman to the streets. I couldn't understand how she could love my dad, and look at him the way she did after the way that he did her, but then I began to think about my situation with Adonis. I was no better than she was. I was sure there were plenty more answers in that book of my mom's skeletons, but I couldn't dare read one more page of my mom's misery. I always thought she had the perfect life, and she didn't. I couldn't imagine the pain she must've felt on Thanksgiving Day, to share such a beautiful surprise with a man who wasn't even worthy of her tears. Things began to click. The way my mom talked so badly about my dad before he died started to make a lot of sense, but why did it take for him to die for all of that anger to come out of her. Now, I would never know because I didn't think I could read another page of that journal. I cried myself to sleep and hoped I'd be awakened by my love to make everything better.

Chapter Thirteen

I woke up in a cold sweat, not remembering the last thing that I'd done before falling asleep. I looked to the left and saw that Adonis wasn't there, and looked like he hadn't been there all night. I grabbed my cell phone and saw that it was six in the morning. *Maybe he decided to stay over at his mom's house,* I thought to myself. Adonis cheating on me had never crossed my mind until that moment. I knew I should've known better, but I'd rather know than not know. I refused to be that chick being cheated on for years and everyone knowing except for me. I thought about calling Adonis' phone, but I didn't want to tip him off. Just in case he was out doing something he had no business doing, I wanted him to think I was in bed still sound asleep.

I threw on a t-shirt and some joggers, and quickly threw on a baseball cap. I grabbed my purse and phone and headed out the door. It was still early so I wasn't welcomed by very much sunlight. Adonis' mom lived a ways away, so I found some mellow music on Pandora, and started my journey from Buckhead to my old town of Smyrna. I swear Adonis better had been there or he was going to have a whole lot of explaining to do. As I got closer and closer to his mom's house, my nerves got worse and worse. What if I did find something that I definitely didn't want to see? I slowly drove down Adonis' mom's street and his Caddy was nowhere in sight. I didn't even waste my time stopping.

It crossed my mind again to call him, but I didn't I started feeling like the female I said I would never become, which was the stalker type. If Adonis wanted to be with me, then I was going to be the one he was going to be with. I had just wasted a lot of time, energy, and gas going looking for something that never existed. I expected Adonis to be there as soon as I woke up and he wasn't. I needed to stop being such a spoiled brat.

After my long drive back home, I found Adonis' car parked in front of my house. I pulled up in the driveway, and by the time I got out of the car, Adonis was standing outside of my car door.

"Where the hell you been?" he asked jealously.

I didn't want him to know I had been looking for him, so I just said, "I needed to go for a drive."

"You sure that's all you did?" he asked.

"Are you trying to ask me something?" I asked, sounding offended.

"Nope. Just a question. I've just never known you to be out driving around at almost seven o'clock in the morning. Were you checking up on me?"

I looked at him and rolled my eyes. "Please do not flatter yourself! I had a long night of a whole lot of stuff on my mind, and I thought you would be there to console me, but obviously I was wrong. I just needed to get out and get some fresh air since you never happened to make it home."

"I'm sorry, but I was out taking care of business."

"All night long?!?!" I yelled.

"Music never stops," but enough about that. Tell me what's on your mind."

I headed up the stairs while Adonis chased after me.

"So you're just gonna walk away and not tell me what's wrong?"

I got to my bedroom and said, "You weren't worried about me all night long! I couldn't even get a call or a text." I quickly turned around with my mom's journal in my hand, and said, "but it you're so concerned now, this is what has been bothering me! I've been spending days and nights alone reading this!"

Adonis grabbed the book and said, "Why are you reading this? This has been doing nothing but causing you to be on an emotional roller coaster. Just leave it alone! Let the past be the past!"

I flipped to the last couple of pages I had read and said, "Here! Read this!"

Adonis sat down on bed. As he read, his eyes became larger and larger.

"This can't be right," he said. "From what I do know about your dad, he would've never done your mom like that."

"That was the same thing I said, but why would she take the time to write this detail by detail. It just doesn't make sense. My dad was perfect."

"Look, Dezzi, I'm sorry for not being here with you helping you get through this, but I was doing something very important for the both of us. I just wanted to surprise you."

As depressed as I was, I could feel a little excitement come over my body. What'd you do babe?" I asked, trying to sound as enthusiastic as possible, which wasn't very much at all.

Adonis pulled a piece a paper out of his back pocket and handed it to me. He had the biggest grin on his face that I had seen since he'd proposed to me.

What I was reading seemed a little foreign, so I said, "What exactly is this?"

I did what you wanted me to, Baby! I'm leaving those streets alone and I invested in a record label and studio."

"I felt like I was about to have a panic attack. "Are you telling me you invested all of your savings in a record label you probably know nothing about?"

It's a record label I've been dealing with for a long time. I even have some talent vested in it, but you wouldn't know that because you never ask me anything about it. You only want me to do what you want me to do!"

Adonis stood up and said, just in case you wanted to know, the record label's name is Dezzigner Records . . . After you.

Adonis naming his Record Label after me didn't make me feel better about him blowing money on something that wasn't promising. He had to become much more responsible with money. We had absolutely no plan, and for him to spend his money like it was nothing did not sit well with me at all!

Adonis snatched the paper back from me, and said, "I'll see you later. Maybe when I come back, you'll be ready to talk about other things aside from what you want. As he walked down the stairs towards the front door, I followed him trying to get him to stop. I was ready to talk. I just didn't know how to take everything in. I knew Adonis had a plan, but he never told me what it was, or made me feel a part of it.

Adonis wouldn't stop, and before he walked out the door, he turned around and said, "Oh, and by the way, I didn't spend all my savings on the label. You did your part, too. Thanks for your contribution."

As Adonis walked out the door, I said, "Wait! What are you talking about? I didn't contribute anything! What did you do, Adonis?!?! As I continued to yell, Adonis drove off in his Caddy. If Adonis had done what I had a feeling he did, I was going to kill him! I continuously called his cell phone and he kept hitting "ignore". I finally did what I should've done in the first place. I called the bank.

"Good Morning. My name is Desiree' Kimbrough and I was just calling to check my balances."

"Hi Ms. Kimbrough. No, problem. I can help you with that. I just need for you to verify some information for me."

After verifying who I was to the extremely nice woman on the other line, she gave me information that I was pretty sure I had already known. Adonis had gone and emptied my entire savings account. All I had left was my $62.86 in my student checking account my mom had set up for me that I used whenever I went out with my friends and needed some cash on my debit card, and $500 in my checking account for a rainy day. The five million dollars from my dad's life insurance policy that my mom refused to ever touch was gone. Adonis had invested my dad's entire life in his own dream and left twenty dollars in the account. How in the hell could I have been so dumb to add him to any of my accounts? How could he be so dumb to take money from me that had such sentimental value? That money was never of a monetary value to me or my mom. It represented my dad and what he worked so hard for. Even though, I really didn't know how hard my dad worked for that money after reading my mom's journal, I did know that it wasn't up to Adonis to decide what to do with it. His decision was completely selfish, and showed just how much he cared what happened to me. I had made plenty of mistakes in my life, but never one that cost me over five million dollars. At this point, I considered myself done!

Adonis had said he'd be back later, but I couldn't think for the life of me what in the world he would have to discuss with me. He had messed up everything. I knew I'd told him I wanted him off the streets and we would be taken care of with the money I had, but this definitely was not what I had in mind. I had planned on him getting a real job, and I was going to do the same. That money was for emergencies only, and a record label definitely was not an emergency.

Chapter Fourteen

I had $562.86 to last me not very long. This adult thing was no joke. I still had to pay bills to keep the utilities running in the house, and that by itself was going to eat away the money I did have to my name. I could not bring myself to completely believe that Adonis had emptied my account to invest in one of his pipe dreams. I would've never added him to my accounts if I 'd thought he would've ever done some dumb shit like that. I had to think of a plan, and fast.

I couldn't even call to vent to Ess because the first thing she would've asked would've been why in the world Adonis would've had access to those accounts in the first place. My mom worked so hard not to have to touch that money, and then I do some stupid shit and the money is gone in a matter of minutes. I didn't know what to do next. I needed my mom to help me through this. If she had been here, I would've never been going through this mess!

I grabbed her journal and cuddled up on the couch, hoping I would miraculously receive some knowledge from what she had written.

December 24, 1998

When I woke up this New Year's Eve, it was so different from previous ones. I would normally wake up so excited, and anxious to give out gifts, and find out

what special thing he had done for me this year because he would always go all out for me every year. He had me spoiled, and that was part of the reason I refused to leave. I knew I had been well taken care of, and he would continue to take care of me.

This morning, I just felt sick. I began thinking about a lot of things. My baby girl would make her debut into this world in about five months, and I wanted to be able to give her a good life. A better life that I'd ever had. I didn't want her to have to worry about ever being safe. I wanted her to know she was always safe as long as I was around.

With the life her dad is living, at this moment, I know I can't promise her that, so maybe he was doing me a favor by pushing me away. I'm thinking of a plan to be able to do this on my own. I 'm intelligent, smart, creative, and know I could make it on my own and make sure my child was good if I needed to. My support system is great. If I have to go out there and get a job to take care of my responsibilities, that is exactly what I'm going to do. My child would not go without, even if it killed me, and I definitely wasn't going to stick around with a man who didn't genuinely want to stick around for me and our child. I guess I should say "my child", because he has absolutely no desire to be attached to a child right now. Money is his number one priority, so I'll let him do him, and I'm going to do me.

~Carlisa

That was when it hit me. I had everything going for myself, and I could easily take care of myself. Shit, I had a full ride academic scholarship to go away to school to complete my goal of becoming an anesthesiologist. My mom was strong, and I was too. Did she have some struggles? Yes, but she tried her best to make it through those struggles and make sure I was still good. The only difference between the situations that my mom and I were going through was that she had a child involved, and I didn't. If she overcame hers, which, evidently she did, I knew I could overcome this setback and still finish on top. I did not need a man to get me to where I needed to be. I still had the upper hand. Nevertheless, I would still listen to what Adonis had to say, which probably still wouldn't mean shit to me.

"Hello," I said as my cell phone rang with the ringtone of "Sex on the Ceiling" I had set for Adonis when he called.

"Hey. Just letting you know I'm outside if you can please come open the door."

"Oh. So now you want to be polite after stealing my money and basically leave me broke!"

"Come on. I just want to talk. Not argue. Please, just open the door."

"Ugh! Here I come."

I stuffed my mom's journal under the sofa cushions because I didn't want Adonis to think I was sitting home depressed all day reading about my mom's past. It was the truth, and it helped, but he didn't need to know all of that.

When I opened the door, I tried to quickly turn around, but he spun me back around and grabbed me around the waist to give me a hug. He wouldn't let me go.

I tried to pull away, and he whispered, "No. I feel so bad. I shouldn't have left like that after I had put your livelihood in my hands. I just want you to trust me and know I would never make a decision like that thinking it would affect you negatively in any type of way."

He pushed my bangs back and gave me a kiss on the forehead, and released me from his grip.

I rolled my eyes, and said, "I really want to believe everything you just said to me, in addition to everything you've said to me in the past, but Adonis, do you understand that is my dad's blood money you just took from up underneath me? My mom wouldn't even touch that money! Do you understand that I still have mortgage to pay on this house? My mom refused to even use that money to pay the house off! What are we going to do?"

"I know, but if I didn't really believe that I could invest it and put us in a much better situation, do you think I would've done that?"

"I looked down and twisted my legs like a shy school girl and said, "I would like to believe you wouldn't, but I don't know how I'm going to feel when this house goes into foreclosure and we don't have anywhere to live."

"Trust me. I will not let that happen. I want the best life for us that we can possibly have."

I then felt like picking Adonis' brain for a second. No parent wants their child to make the same mistakes that they made, and I had an upper-hand by knowing some of those mistakes my mom made.

"Can we sit down and talk?" I asked Adonis.

"Uh oh. This sounds serious."

"It is."

Adonis sat down in the recliner and patted his thigh for me to come sit down.

I declined. "I want to sit right across from you so I can look at you face to face. That way I can tell if you're being completely honest with me."

"So, basically what you're saying is you don't trust me."

"You can't blame me. Trust is earned, and because of what you did without giving me any type of indication of what was going on, you have a lot of earning to do."

"That's fair," he replied.

I sat across from him and said, "Adonis, what if I got pregnant right now?"

Adonis jumped up and said, "You're pregnant?"

The expression on his face made it unclear as to whether he was excited or disappointed.

"Calm down. It's just a hypothetical question. I just want to know what our plan would be, because it's not like it's impossible."

Adonis slowly sat back down in the recliner and wiped his forehead with his forearm.

"Wow. You look like someone told you it was the end of the world."

"No. You just caught me off guard, but to answer your question, we would be good. I would take care of my responsibilities and be a father to my child."

"By feeling forced to, or because you really wanted to?"

"That would be my blood. I would love my child and take care of him or her because I would want to. Why are you asking this?"

"Like I said, just hypothetical questions."

Adonis seemed a lot more calm once he realized that I wasn't having a baby, so I knew where he stood with that. I knew I wasn't ready for a baby anyway, and I made sure I took every precaution there was to make sure that didn't happen any time soon.

I did need to know Adonis' plan with this record label and studio, so that was the next line of business in conversation. Now, he should've really been sweating bullets because if he didn't have a good enough plan to satisfy me, there was going to be some trouble.

Before I began that conversation, Adonis said, "It looks like you want to talk about something else."

"Um, yeah! My five million that I invested involuntarily."

"Well, like I already told you, it's a record label. Not just something I just came up with out of the blue. I've been working towards it for a long time. The money I was getting from my "other" job was helping to fund it, but I never had enough to get it kicked all the way off. I have some excellent talent that I had been trying to manage, but they wouldn't put all their eggs in one basket with me because I wasn't established enough. I think . . . well, I know this is the beginning to something huge! Again, I apologize I did this behind your back, but I had to because I knew you wouldn't go for something that didn't seem guaranteed to you."

"Tuh. You're right about that," I said with my arms folded.

"I purchased the studio, and all the equipment was included, so I did get a good deal there."

"Ok, so you do understand we have bills, right? Money isn't going to start rolling in right away, and I only have a little over five hundred dollars to my name."

"I know that. I kept all that in mind, and yes, I do have a little money put aside that will get us by. Don't worry. I got you."

I just looked down at the floor, thinking, *Does this nigga' really got me, or is he just like these millions of other dudes who think they have a plan, invest all their money into it, and it blows up in their face?*

I'm not even going to lie. It made me nervous, but what was done was done and I couldn't cry over spilled milk.

"Well, since we're talking about everything, I need to tell you something that I've been keeping from you for quite some time now."

Adonis looked worried, and said, "What's that?"

I took a deep breath, and said, "I got a full ride academic scholarship to Texas A&M."

Adonis leaned back in the recliner. This time, he let out the recliner to put his legs up.

"I'm sure you've known about this for months now, right?"

"Pretty much."

"So why are you deciding to tell me about this now, at this moment? Is it because you were considering not going, but now that I've spent the money and told you about my plan, you realize you don't believe in me or my plan, so why not go?"

"No. That's not it. I was always going to tell you. I just didn't know the right time to discuss it because I hadn't made a decision.

Adonis stood up and walked towards me and got on his knees right in front of the couch. He put his head in my lap and said, "You know I can't live without you. I'd hate to tell you not to go follow you dream, but can't you do that somewhere around here? I need you right here with me."

"Well, I could've done it right here, nearby, with the money I had, but with that not being an option any longer, I need that scholarship."

"There has to be another way."

"Why don't you come with me?" I asked Adonis.

"I've just started all of this right here in Atlanta. I can't just leave it. Maybe if I had known about your scholarship, different decisions would've been made. We need better communication!"

I pushed Adonis up off of me and said, "No! Don't you even dare try to put this all on me! Even though that money was mine, and I didn't have to tell you if I decided to buy as many Louis Vuitton purses it could've possibly bought, I still would've told you before I did it! That's just common courtesy when you're sharing a life with a person."

"I'll take care of it, Dezzi, and not at your expense. You will go to college and become an anesthesiologist as planned. We will also have a successful business. We are going to do it all right here. We will defeat our goals! Don't worry. I'll do whatever I have to do to make it happen."

It all sounded good, but what the hell did Adonis mean by saying he'd do whatever he had to do to make that happen? That last sentence stuck with me until I went to bed that evening. I didn't like it at all.

Chapter Fifteen

I decided not to read anymore of my mom's journal until I overcame the current obstacle I was going through in my life. Although she wasn't here with me, just reading her thoughts as she was in her sober mind, helped me to get though some things. I charged my mom's cell phone up and turned it back on, just to check her messages and to see how many calls she was still receiving. It seemed that it had finally stopped ringing all day, every day. She had some messages from work, asking if she'd be returning, and of course, there were some messages from men, which I really didn't care to listen to. The few men that she dealt with on a regular basis who had still been coming by from time to time, had finally stopped coming looking for my mom. I figured they had finally gotten the hint that they had been replaced.

Adonis spent a lot of time at the studio, which I had to admit was very nice. He had five artists he was working with, and still continuing his music, but wasn't getting paid from Sound Cloud any longer. That was because he had his own record label he chose to put it on so he could get the majority of the profit. The artists that he was working with were talented, however, they were unknown. Adonis worked hard with radio stations to play their music, and trying to get as many interviews for them as possible, but to be honest, he wasn't bringing in enough money. At least not for the bills we needed to pay, and I wasn't the type to be sitting up in the dark, so I had to find a way to make sure we had at least enough money to pay the electric bill. Adonis didn't want to say it, but I already knew I needed to get a job.

He would give me money here and there. He even gave me enough money to start my first semester at Emory College. They had one of the best pre-med programs in the area. I was glad of that, but we were really struggling. I wanted to believe in this dream, but all I could see was destruction ahead of us.

I hadn't seen or talked to Ess' yellow ass since she had come by about a month ago and wasn't feeding into my bullshit, which resulted in her sending the police over to my house, which I still couldn't believe she did. It was hard going through everything I was going through without being able to vent to the person closest to me outside of Adonis. She was basically my sister, and I loved her. I was surprised she hadn't called me, but I understood, too. I had basically put Adonis before her, letting him dictate how I treated her. I felt like we needed to squash some things, and get back to where we were, so I decided to call her.

"Well, hello stranger!" she answered, immediately being sarcastic. I didn't expect to ever be hearing from you again since you had your own little family going on over there! Any little ones running around yet?" she asked as she busted out in malicious laughter.

"Ok. I deserve all of that. I'm sorry," I mumbled.

"Excuse me? I couldn't hear you!" Ess said.

"I know you heard me, but I'll repeat myself. I was wrong. We've been too good of friends to allow a man to dictate our relationship. It won't happen again. I've just been going through some things, and sista', I need you!"

"Well, even though I was treated like a stepsister, you know I'm here for you, so what's going on?"

"First off, I miss my mom so much!"

Of course, that was one thing I couldn't tell Ess the entire story about, but I tried to keep it at a minimum just so she could understand the pain and struggle I'd been going through.

"Is she still in Vegas, as you say?"

"Yes, she is. There's more, but I'd prefer to talk in person. You want to meet in a little while at Phipp's Plaza? Maybe we'll be lucky enough to run into Rasheeda from RHOA and get some selfies in."

"Sounds fun!" she replied

"Yeah, I need fun in my life right about now," I said, sounding depressed.

"Girl, It can't be bad. Things are never that bad when you at least have money!"

I didn't even respond to that comment. "Girl, I'll see you around two."

"Ok. See you there," Ess said, beginning to really sound concerned.

As soon as I hung up the phone, I heard Adonis walk into the kitchenette where I was sitting at the table having a bowl of cereal.

"Were you just talking?" he asked.

"Yeah. I was talking to Ess."

"Ess? She called you?"

"No. I actually called her." I pouted, and said, "I miss her so much. I just need her. She's like my sister."

Adonis shook his head and said, "Whatever."

"You think it's a bad idea for me to talk to her?" After I asked Adonis that question, I thought to myself, *Dezzi, you need to think for yourself. You miss your friend and you want to talk and hang out with her, so do just that. This is your life. Not his.*

He replied "I just wouldn't be talking to her ass after she sent the police to your house. As a friend, she should believe you, but I get it. Do you. Just don't talk too much, and you know what I mean."

"I know how to handle my friend. I've known her a little longer than you have. Take your own advice and trust me sometimes."

"You're right. I trust you. I know you're a smart girl."

I then had to ask an uncomfortable question, but I had to know.

"So . . . How's the cash flow?"

I already knew what his answer would be before he answered.

"We're good," he said, without an ounce of concern on his face.

"So, the mortgage and light bills are going to get paid?"

"Yes, Dezzi!" Let me be a man! Please!"

"You know, if you can't give me more money for next semester, I can sit out until we get our heads above water."

"Dezzi," Adonis said in a low tone, sounding like he was trying to keep himself from yelling at me. "Please stop. I'll let you know if things get bad."

"Ok."

That's all I could go by, and I left it alone.

"I'm going to the studio. I have a few meetings. I'll see you later," Adonis said. "Have fun, and be careful."

"Thanks, and I will. I can't wait to see you later," I said batting my lashes.

I tried to not make it seem so evident to Adonis, but I was overly excited to hang out with my sis. After I showered and got ready for my reunion, I looked through the newspaper to see if there were any places in the area hiring. There were several places looking for help, but not paying the type of money I needed. School alone was approximately $70,000 per semester. I just couldn't see Adonis coming up with that for me next semester. That's a yearly salary for most people.

When I arrived at Phipp's Tavern, I found a table, and ordered a glass of water with lemon before I texted and told Ess where I'd be. I told my waitress that I would be waiting for someone else to join me a little later and would wait 'til then to order. I had arrived a little early, so I wasn't expecting Ess anytime soon. I just wanted to sit out and enjoy the breeze on the patio just so that my mind would be clear before she arrived.

All of a sudden, I heard someone say, "Dezzi! Is that you? Oh my God!"

I turned my chair around, pulled my sunglasses up, and flipped my bangs to the side as I tried to see who was calling my name, and so excited to see me.

I didn't have to put too much effort into it because by the time I cleared my view, I realized it was Monét Anderson. She was one of those girls in high school who made sure her make-up, lashes, and hair were always perfect. She always exposed as much cleavage as possible, without being sent home from school, and every part of her body she thought she could use in a sexual manner was pierced. I could definitely see not much had changed. We were associates, and never friends that hung together, but I still stood up out of respect to give her a hug, since that's what it seemed like she was waiting for.

She then decided to make herself comfortable by pulling out a chair, and said, "Hey girl! What have you been up to?"

Before I could answer, the Redhead waitress with freckles walked over and asked were we ready to order, since my friend had made it.

"Oh, no. I'm still waiting for my friend. This isn't the friend that I was waiting for."

The entire atmosphere became uncomfortable. I did not mean for that to come out the way that it did.

"I'm sorry," I apologized. "There is just someone else I was waiting for, and I happened to run into someone else."

The waitress made things a little more comfortable by saying, "Oh yes, that does happen quite often around here since this is such a popular spot. She turned to Monét and said, "Well, since you happen to be here, would you like to order something to drink?"

Monét looked at me as though she was looking for my permission. I just shrugged my shoulders. She had already made herself comfortable, so I didn't see why she just didn't join Ess and I for lunch. I didn't know how Ess would feel about it because she wasn't very fond of her in school, so I decided to text and warn her.

Monet finally answered the waitress, and said, yes, "I'd like a Mango Margarita with salt around the rim, please."

The waitress looked at Monét the same way I did and said, "Certainly!" She then asked for ID.

Monét unzipped her purse and pulled it out with no problem. The waitress looked it over and everything was legit. I knew it wasn't legit, but somehow Monét had an ID that said she was at least twenty-one.

"Ok. Coming right up!" the waitress said. Before she walked away, she said, "Ma'am, would you like another water with lemon?"

"No, thanks!" I said with a slight grin.

My phone vibrated and it was Ess replying to my previous text.

It read, "No way! Where'd you pick her up from?"

I quickly texted back and said, "She just showed up. Sorry. See you soon. Gotta go."

I sat back in my seat and folded my arms, staring at Monét without saying a word. I was waiting for her to answer my question without me having to ask.

"What?" she asked, as if nothing was wrong.

"You already know! I lowered my voice and said, "Where'd you get that ID?

"Girl! I've had this for a while now! As a matter of fact, I've been getting one every year for the past few years. Please don't tell me you don't have one!"

"I haven't had a reason to have one. I'm not the type to just go out drinking. If I want a drink, I just go through my mom's liquor cabinet."

"Well, in my line of business, I have to have one."

"And what is that, or is it a secret?"

"I'm a dancer."

I didn't even want to continue the conversation after that because I didn't want Ess to miss any of it. This was getting very interesting. I knew Ess should be arriving any minute, so I dropped my purse on the ground, spilling everything out to try to delay the conversation. We both knelt down to pick everything up, and by the time we were coming back up, I heard a familiar voice.

"I see the klutz has struck again," Ess said, laughing hysterically.

"Awww hush, Girl!"

As we were sitting back in our seats, the waitress brought over Monét's drink.

"Thank you!"

"Oh, you're most very welcome! It looks like everyone has shown up, so I'll give you a few minutes to decide on a meal or appetizers, and be back in a few minutes. Would you like a drink when I come back ma'am?" the waitress asked Ess.

"I was gonna take a Margarita like this young lady's, but I'll just take a glass of water instead. Thanks."

"Would you like lemon?"

"No, thank you."

As the waitress walked away, Ess, already trying to let her thoughts about the uninvited guest at the table be known, she said, "Hey . . . Is it Monét?" Ess asked.

"Yes, that's right, Essence! How have you been? I don't think I've seen either of you since graduation!"

"I prefer Ess, and I've been fine. Did you graduate?"

This was not about to go well. I gave Ess a head's up so she could prepare herself before coming, but I guess I just wasted a good text. All she prepared on the way were comebacks. I nudged her leg under the table to try to get her to settle down and quit coming for this girl.

"I see you're still wearing that rusty water fro look. I thought you would've let that go by now. Your hair is so beautiful!"

Uh oh . . . Then she came for Ess, with a compliment on the end. I don't even know how to handle that.

"Look, I came to enjoy lunch with my friend. You're an add-on, so you can choose to leave or stay, but if you come with insults, that's not what we're about. We're coming in peace."

"I said your hair is beautiful. What are you talking about?" Monét replied, acting as if she didn't know what she had just done.

"Ok, whatever, Monét. Like I said, we'll have you as long as you can remain peaceful and cordial," Ess said, trying to be the bigger person.

"Of course," Monét replied.

"Good."

Although Ess did start this mess by immediately coming with sarcasm and negativity, she was my sis and I'd defend her 'til the end. I'm just glad they were able to resolve their differences on their own because I was too cute to be trying to fight.

Ess began again. "So, did you flunk a few times?"

"What are you talking about?" Monét asked.

"Well, you're drinking a Margarita." She then whispered across the table and said, "We all know we're not old enough for that."

"You're right. We're not. That was the conversation Desireé . . . "

"You can call me Dezzi," I intervened.

"Oh, sorry. Yes, but that's the conversation Dezzi and I were having before you arrived. My line of business requires that I have an ID showing that I'm older."

"And since I'm here now, can you share again what that line of business is?" Ess asked, curiously.

"I'm a dancer."

Just when the conversation was getting good again, the waitress walked over with Ess' water and sat it down, and asked if we were ready to order. We all ordered, and as soon as the waitress walked away, we resumed where we'd left off.

"What kind of dancer? I know praise dancers don't require you to have I.D. I used to be one of those," she said laughing, hysterically.

Monét couldn't help but laugh, too. "No, not a praise dancer unfortunately. I don't think they make my kind of money anyway, if any money. I'm an exotic dancer at Magic City."

"Oh wow! That's interesting. What type of income does that bring in?" Ess asked.

Ess had never been shy to ask questions if she wanted the answer.

"That's kind of personal, I interjected. You don't have to answer that, Monét."

Monét replied, "It doesn't bother me talking about it. I'm not embarrassed by my occupation, but the income really depends on the night, but I never leave with less than twenty-five hundred a night."

Both of our mouths dropped to the floor. I knew some strippers could make a lot of money, but twenty-five hundred minimum per night was beyond sufficient. If my math wasn't off, that was almost thirteen thousand dollars a week, and that's if you're working five, and not seven days.

"That's incredible," I said.

"It really is, "Monét said, and I actually enjoy what I do, but enough about me. What are you girls up to these days?"

Ess looked at me, and I looked at her. I decided to go first since everything I was about to say was going to be a shock to Ess.

"Well, I attend Emory College."

Ess looked at me with the side-eye, as Monét said, "Wow, that's a pretty expensive college. You must've gotten a scholarship. I remember how smart you were."

Ess started, "Yes, Ess, all those brains, you chose to turn down a full scholarship to Texas A&M? Please tell me you ended up getting a scholarship to Emory!"

I just looked down at the table because I had no other words. I knew she wouldn't understand my decision, because even I didn't.

"Well, this seems like an emotional conversation, so Ess, what have you been up to?"

Ess rolled her eyes at me once more and replied to Monét as the waitress placed our meals in front of us.

"Well, I definitely wasn't offered any scholarships, but I'm currently going to Atlanta Tech to finish out their Associates in Nursing program and then plan on going to a bigger university to get my Bachelors."

"That's a plan. It's so crazy how everyone is so different and has such different lives."

"That's good for you Ess. I'm so proud of you," I said.

As Monét devoured her food, she said, "Wait a minute. Weren't you two besties in high school, and you don't know what's going on in each other's lives? Ooooh, that's not good!"

"Well, if you must know, our meeting here was so that we could catch up with each other because we had lost touch, but you kinda became a distraction to what the ultimate goal was. I'm not trying to be rude, or offend you, but it is what it is," Ess said as politely as she could.

"No offense taken," Monét said. "I get it, so I'm going to quickly finish the little bit of food I have l left on this plate, and let the two of you catch up. I interfered and I apologize."

We sat there in complete silence, besides the clanking of our silverware against our plates as we finished our lunch. I was so glad that Monét didn't take offense to what Ess had said to her, but I did feel bad that we kind of made her feel like an outsider. At least it seemed like she understood.

When Monét finished eating, just as promised, she left her money on the table and bid farewell to the both of us by giving us both a welcoming hug. She also left one of her business cards for each of us before she pranced away, with her perfect body.

Chapter Sixteen

E ss had lots on her mind that she was holding back while Monét was at the table, and you better believe, she let me have it!

"I can not believe you, Dezzi. You let that scholarship go over a drug dealer? How does your mom feel about that?"

"She doesn't know yet. She doesn't even know I'm still in the area. She left right before it was time for me to leave for Texas. She had set up a U-Haul and everything for me because she said she wouldn't be able to deal with another goodbye."

"Ok, so that answers one thing, but who is paying this huge tuition for Emory?"

I took a deep breath and bit my top lip.

"I know what that look means, Dezzi. Donnie? Really? With drug money? What is wrong with you?"

Tears began flowing but I couldn't let out a cry. I felt numb.

"I don't know what's wrong with me. Maybe I just love a man a little too much. I can say that he is not a drug dealer. Not anymore. I finally got him to leave the streets after a drug deal gone wrong and I was there." I went on to tell her the story about what happened that night and the entire time I was telling her, I could hear Adonis' voice in the back of my mind saying, *"Don't talk too much"*.

Ess stood up and hugged me.

"Oh, Sis! I didn't know you were dealing with so much. I should've been there for you. I can't even imagine how stressed you've been. I'm so sorry!"

"No. I'm sorry. I'm the one who cut you off."

"So what is Donnie doing now?"

"Ess, all of this has to stay between us."

"Just don't tell me it's something else illegal."

"It's not, but he doesn't want me telling our business, so please just promise me."

"You don't even have to ask, Sis."

"He started a record label and invested in a studio. It's called Dezzigner Records and he's working with a few unknown artists, but is telling me everything is all good."

"Dezzi, how much money did he have? To be paying for your schooling, starting a record label, investing in a studio, and these unknown people, he had to have millions! Where did he get that? Hell, I don't hear any of his music on the radio!"

I was then no longer numb. I began crying so loudly that everyone at the restaurant on the patio began staring. I didn't even know how to say what I needed to say. The entire thing was just so unbelievable. I was at the point where I even wanted to tell Ess about my mom, but I knew I couldn't.

"What is wrong, Dezzi? Please tell me! You can tell me anything."

The waitress came by and asked was everything ok. Ess told her everything was fine and if she could please tell everyone else to mind their own business.

So that we could go somewhere more private, Ess got ready to pay, but when she picked up the money Monét had left, it was two-hundred dollars, which was way more than all three of our meals, so the waitress was going to get a very nice tip. Ess left it there and helped me up. There was a park nearby, so we headed there just to sit down and talk without everyone in our faces listening.

I started where we left off. Ess wanted to know how Adonis was able to pay for everything he was paying for.

"He took my dad's money, Ess."

"What? You need to go to the police. That's theft!"

"No, it isn't theft. My name was on the account. It had five-million dollars in it. It was all of the money we got from his life insurance policy. My dumb ass added his name to it, and he took it all! I never thought he would do this to me."

As we sat on a park bench under a tree, Ess rubbed my back. It was like she was speechless, and that never happened.

"I know this is hard to talk about, Dezzi, but does your mom know about any of this?"

"No. She has never had any reason to even check that account, but I have a feeling we don't have much left. I don't even think the mortgage is going to get paid, or I'll be able to go to school next semester. I'm so scared, Ess."

"I know you are, but one thing I also know is, even though I'm pissed at Donnie for doing this to you, he loves you to death and he would never put you in a position where you would have to struggle, or be without."

"I don't know. Every time I ask him if everything is ok, he's gets defensive, so I try not to say anything."

"You're going to have to tell you mom. When is she coming back?"

"I'm not sure, but what I do know is I will not let this defeat me, and I will not let my mom down."

I told Ess about my mom's journal I had been reading, and everything I had read so far. I explained to her that's why I had gotten so upset with her when she was over at my house and she ripped it. By the look on Ess' face, I didn't think she could take anything else in. I decided to leave everything at that and not open my mouth about anything else. I just didn't want my best friend to feel like I was treating her a certain way for no reason at all. I could tell that Ess had a lot of emotions stirring up inside of her at that moment. She looked like she could feel everything that I had been feeling all this time. She still tried to be encouraging and tell me everything would be ok, but it wouldn't.

Chapter Seventeen

Monday, March 1, 1999

At twenty years old, it was my first day of working my first job. Two weeks prior, I walked out on the life that I had grown to be familiar with . . . The life where I was able to have basically everything that I wanted, except for the thing I needed and wanted to most. That one thing was genuine love. I didn't want to just be someone's trophy. I wanted someone that I could spend time with, and would know without a shadow of a doubt, there would be no place in the world he would rather be. I wanted a man who would look at me like I was the most beautiful woman in the world. I didn't have that, and probably never would have with him. I couldn't waste any more time on him, and allow my baby girl to think that money was all life was about.

"Girl, you're how many months pregnant and decided to come work at Sears of all places?" the tall, slender girl with long, bone-straight hair and a Chinese bang, who was training me, asked.

"Seven months," I replied.

"Your man must've left you just like that. I see it everyday," she said, shaking her head.

I stopped folding the disorganized clothing that were once in an organized state before customers had made a mess of them. I cleared my throat, and as polite and to the point as I could be, I said, "Janae? That's your name, right?"

Before I could give her a chance to respond, I continued, "I'm not here to tell my business, or make friends. I'm here to work and make some money. As you can see," I said as I rubbed my round belly, "I have a baby girl to take care of soon, and that is my main concern. If I don't take care of her, who will? I don't mind small talk, but I would appreciate if you didn't get in my personal business. I've never been that type, so please don't take it personal."

Janae raised her eyebrows, and said, "Wow! I thought you were one of those little quiet ones. You got a little spunk in you. I like you already! I wasn't trying to be nosey or anything like that. I just be fuckin' with folks. You know how it is. I applaud you for doing it on your own. I know it's not easy."

"Thank you." I replied.

"No problem. By the way, I party a lot, so you can pick up a lot of extra shifts from me. You know how that is too, right? Those hangovers don't be no joke!" Janae said, as she laughed, but more so sounded like a scream.

After we got to learn the important things about each other, which wasn't too much, Janae continued my training session. I could tell she was a cool chick, but I was all about me and my baby. I didn't have time for no kind of drama.

As I was reading, Adonis came walking through the door at two in the morning.

I was cuddled up underneath my favorite blanket on the sofa.

"Good morning to you," I said sarcastically.

"Wow. I don't get a hug, kiss, nothing?"

"I don't get an explanation as to why you're out almost every night past midnight?"

"You know I'm on that grind! I shouldn't even have to explain that. You already know."

"Yeah, ok," I replied.

I put my mom's journal down on the cocktail table and got up to head to the bathroom.

Adonis picked it up and said, "Why are you still reading this? Doesn't it make you feel worse?"

"Why are you still even talking to me?" I asked with a serious expression. "I don't have anything else to do, and no, it doesn't make me feel worse."

"Ok. I'm sorry for coming in so late. I didn't think it would make a difference because I didn't even expect you to still be awake."

"Oh. So it would've been ok if I would've been asleep? Then there would've been no proof as to what time you really came home."

"Dezzi, why are you trippin'? You never trip on me this hard. What's going on, babe?"

I folded my arms, looked Adonis up and down, and said, "I gotta pee," as I headed upstairs to my bathroom.

I could hear Adonis' footsteps slowly coming up after me. I had closed the bathroom door, and he knew how much I hated anyone walking in the bathroom on me, so I felt like I was in a safe place. He knocked on the bathroom door without successfully receiving an answer from me. He then just came barging in while I was sitting on the toilet.

"What's up, Dez?"

"Nothing at all. I'm good. How about yourself?"

"Look, I'm not trying to play no game with you. I'm just trying to make sure my fiancé is straight."

"I think I am, but I really don't know. Maybe I can find out right now."

"What do you mean?" Adonis asked, as he frowned up.

"How much money did you make this week?"

"What? See, I knew you meeting up with that bitch, Ess was a bad idea. She been all in your ear. That's why you're acting different."

As I continued to sit on the toilet, I pointed my finger at Adonis and said, "First of all, my sister is no bitch, and she never calls you out of your name or talks against you to me, so please pay the same courtesy and don't do it to her. I've just had some time to think since I've had so much time alone, and I think I'm gonna go out and find me a job."

"A job? You don't need a job!"

"Adonis, you still haven't told me how much money you've made this week. I obviously need a job."

"A job where?"

"I'm not sure yet. Maybe somewhere in a medical office since that is the field I'm studying in, for now."

"What do you mean by "for now"?

"I'm just not sure college will be at the top of our priorities when it comes to finances, but I'm tired. I've been up all day, and I have classes in the morning. We'll talk when you're free again. Now, can you please get out so I can wipe?"

Adonis shook his head and walked out. I think I had gotten my point across to him. I was so tired of not knowing what was going on in my own house. He could think that I had to rely on him all he wanted, but I knew I could make it on my own. If I kept getting the treatment that I was getting, that's exactly what was going to happen.

Chapter Eighteen

Right after class the next day, I got to brainstorming. I needed to do something that was going to me make enough money to at least not have to worry about the household bills. No one had come and put a notice on the door yet, so I assumed Adonis was still up to date. Ess called, trying to hang out, but, unfortunately, I had to tell her I had some deep thinking to do.

I pulled out my laptop and began searching jobs in the nearby area, specifically in the medical field. I didn't see anything making more than $10 per hour, which wasn't going to get me anywhere. I looked up at the ceiling, hoping an idea would just fall onto the table in front of me. That didn't work, so since this basically seemed like a waste of time, I decided to call Ess back.

I grabbed my purse off the back of the chair I was sitting in, and as soon as I pulled my phone out, something else fell out with it. I got out of the chair and knelt down to pick it up. As I stood up, I read the business card with the silhouette of a naked woman, which read,

Monét
"It's Not a Mirage, Baby."
Come see me at Magic City
241 Forsyth St. SW
Atlanta, Georgia 30303
(404) 999-9999
Business inquiries: MonetsMagic@gmail.com

I stared at Monét's business card as I slowly sat back down in my chair. I couldn't stop looking at it, then looking back at my laptop. I looked at the email address for so long that I memorized it within seconds. *Is this the answer I've been waiting for?* I thought to myself.

I began typing Monet's email address in the "To" field, then I closed it. Stripping? How could that even cross my mind? I knew that wasn't even my type of thing. I couldn't even see myself being able to get on stage taking off my clothes in front of complete strangers. Monét had the personality for that, but not me.

Adonis snuck up on me while I was putting my laptop away. He came up behind me and kissed me on the neck, even though we hadn't made up from the other night.

"What you doing? Working on some homework?"

I saw Monét's card, and on the sly, quickly slid if from the table into my pocket.

"Yeah, I have a project I'm working on."

"Oh, yeah? Maybe I can help you."

"Nah, I don't think so."

"You don't think I'm smart enough?" Adonis asked, as he tickled my side. Now, I guess he wanted to be friends, still without having the discussion we needed to have.

"I didn't say that. You did!" I said, laughing.

Adonis lifted me up, and I wrapped my legs around his slim waist. He carried me up the stairs to my bedroom, and gently laid me on top of the thousands of pillows I had on my bed. He then caressed my arms, raising them both up over my head, then pulled my white t-shirt over my head, messing up even more, my already messy bun. He kissed my lips gently, over and over again and gazed into my eyes. I remembered exactly why I loved him so much. He stuck his arms behind me, unhooking my black lace bra, exposing my bare breasts. He grinded on top of me and sucked on my neck like he used to before he got so caught up in his sidechick . . . Dezzigner Studios. It seemed like forever since I'd felt the way Adonis was making me feel. We made love for the first time since before my mother passed. I didn't know how we were both going without, but I guess we were just using other things to keep that desire concealed.

As we laid there naked in our juices, we held each other tightly.

"I missed this about us, "Adonis said.

"Missed the sex?" I asked?

"No! Well, yeah, but not just that. Mainly the way that we loved each other. The way that we made each other feel no matter now mad we were with each other. I miss us. I just wish we could go back to the way things were, but so much has happened."

"I know," I replied, "but that doesn't mean our love can't be just as strong. As a matter of fact, it should be stronger."

"I agree," Adonis said, as he kissed me on the forehead. He then continued by saying, "You are so beautiful."

I grinned the way I always did when he said that. I actually felt like this thing was possible. I began to feel my faith in Adonis return, and then his cell phone rang.

He grabbed his cell phone, went into the bathroom, and shut the door, leaving me there naked with second thoughts, once again. I could faintly hear his conversation and could tell he was trying to talk low. I lifted up my naked body out of the bed, and crept to the bathroom door and put my ear next to it.

"This deal has to go through. My livelihood is at stake and I can't let my girl down. Just let me know where we're going to meet, and I'll be there."

I knew Adonis was lying! He was worried as hell, and now I was worried. I finally understood why he was keeping things from me. He didn't want me to feel exactly how I was feeling right at that moment. I heard him end his call and flush the toilet so I hurriedly ran back to the bed and jumped in. I tried my best to look as if I hadn't moved.

Adonis came out with a smile as if he had not a worry in the world.

"You waiting on some more of this?" he asked.

"Trying to pretend I hadn't just heard his conversation, I said, "Boy, you can't handle anymore of me!"

"You're funny," he said, as he crawled back on top of me and slid his python into my deep, warm abyss. This time around didn't feel as good as the last because now I had worry on the brain, but Adonis seemed to enjoy it just as much or more than our first session. When we were done I was shocked to see Adonis relax and turn on the television.

"You don't have to go to the studio tonight?" I asked.

"You trying to put me out," he asked. "Wait, is this your side dude's time? I'm sorry?"

"Of course not! I'm just used to you leaving me so much at night. It's become a routine."

"Well, not tonight," Adonis assured me.

I rolled over on my side and poked my butt out and backed that thang up into Adonis. I looked back at him and he grinned at me as he wrapped his arm around me. No amount of money was worth this feeling. No one could take this away from me right now. Too bad it couldn't last forever.

After falling asleep, I heard a noise outside. I slowly moved Adonis' arm from around me as he continued to snore. I looked out the window and saw that it was just the wild chick that lived across the street from me, getting out of an Uber, drunk as hell. I looked back at Adonis and he was still in a nice deep sleep. I threw on my robe and picked my jeans up off the floor. I found Monét's business card and headed downstairs to my laptop so I could drop her an email. I wasn't saying that I was going to take on a stripping job, but it wouldn't hurt to get a little more information either. I kept hearing Monét's voice playing in the back of my mind, saying, *I never leave with less than twenty-five hundred a night."*

I opened my laptop, paranoid as hell. I quickly went straight to my email, and put in Monét's email address. I then began typing. I started with the Subject Line, but didn't know what the hell to put, so I started with: Stripping with You . . . Nope. Scratch that. That sounded too desperate, although I was. After around twenty deletions, I decided on: Occupational Info. That sounded perfect.

I typed: Hey, Monét. I was thinking about our conversation at lunch the other day, outside of the little feud, but I would love to talk to you some more about some of the things you were telling me about your occupation. Please get back with me at your earliest convenience. My # is (404) 555-1234. Thanks!

"What are you in here doing in the dark?" Adonis asked, sneaking up on me, causing me to almost jump out of my seat.

"God damn, Boy! You scared me!"

"You got you a boo? Got you typing love letters and shit?"

"You sound crazy. I was finishing up that project I was working on earlier."

"Oh. Ok. You better not be lying to me. You talking about me leaving you in the middle of the night and look at you!"

"You know you don't even have anything to worry about! You got you a loyal one. You better believe that one."

"Oh, I know, " Adonis said. "Now let's go back to bed "loyal one"."

"Oh, you got jokes!"

"Girl, I'm tired as hell. Hurry your butt on up those stairs," Adonis said as he slapped me on the butt."

It felt good to sleep the entire night together for once, but I really couldn't sleep after sending that email to Monét. I was so anxious and didn't know why. Was I really considering exotic dancing, and how would I even get away with it? I'm sure someone in the club would know me and it would get back to Adonis some type of way. I definitely wasn't going to mention this idea to Ess. The only way I might mention it to her was if I definitely decided to do it because I just might've needed her services again to cover for me. The thought of what I could do with that kind of money just entranced me. I could pay for my own tuition, and pay for some of the bills around the house. We could work as a team so everything didn't fall on Adonis, although the reason we were in this predicament was because of him. For some reason, I just couldn't put all the blame on him. The temptation had been right in front of him, and he was a man with a plan. Anyone else may have taken that same opportunity if it had presented itself to them. Even me. My dad always told me to never say what I'd never do.

I kept closing my eyes and every time I reopened them, it became brighter and brighter in the room as the sun rose. I wanted to go downstairs and grab my laptop to see if I had gotten a response, but I didn't need Adonis to start getting suspicious. I looked at the clock and it was almost nine in the morning. I had gotten maybe a half hour of sleep and knew I'd pay for it later. I had class at eleven, so thought I'd try my best to get at least one more hour of sleep. Just then, I felt Adonis start moving around.

"You getting ready to go?" I asked in a groggy voice, trying to sound like I had been asleep.

"Yeah, after I jump in this shower. I can't have everybody smelling you all over me. They might try to come get some."

I giggled with my eyes still closed.

After I had finally dozed off, I felt Adonis kiss me on my forehead, and tell me he'd see me later.

"Love you, Bae," I said, as I threw the cover over my head.

"Love you, too," he said before walking out the door.

I slept until ten, as planned, showered, and got dressed for class. Before walking out the house, I checked my email, and had nothing. I began thinking, for all I knew, Monét could've been lying. It seemed to me like a person who worked nights would've responded by now. I wasn't about to keep sweating it. I was just going to keep looking until I found something that would give me some type of support.

Chapter Nineteen

A couple of days had passed, and I still hadn't heard anything from Monét, and I honestly wasn't the least bit interested anymore. During my lecture in biology class, my phone vibrated. I secretly looked down to see who it was. It couldn't have been anyone important because everyone I did talk to knew I would be in class this time of day. It was a number I wasn't familiar with, so I let it go to voicemail. A few minutes later, my phone vibrated again as I was attempting to pay attention and take as many notes as I could. Biology was the class I was struggling most in, so I needed all the extra help I could possibly get. *"This has to be something important for them to be calling back to back like this,"* I said to myself. I quietly grabbed my belongings and walked out of the lecture hall. I could hear my professor pause, like he wanted to say something, but an emergency is an emergency, and I needed to see what this was about.

When I got outside, I pressed the button on my phone to listen to my voice messages. At first I didn't catch the voice, but then I realized exactly who it was.

"Hey, girl! I am so sorry it took me so long to get back with you, but my life is pretty busy with my night job, side parties, and now I'm even doing hosting jobs. Anyway, I got back with you as soon as I could. I would've just emailed you, but it sounded like you needed to talk in person, so get back with me whenever you can. You got the number. Bye, girl!"

It was Monét finally finding time to contact me. I didn't even know how I felt about her choice of career anymore. I was giving it some serious thought, but the couple of days that had passed by had made me have second thoughts. It sounded like she was doing really good for herself, and what would it hurt to just have one conversation about it, and decide for myself what I wanted to do with that information?

I dialed Monét's number back. It rang four times, and right before I was about to hang up, Monét answered.

"Hey, girl! I was hoping you caught me in between jobs! I have a recruiting event to be at in about an hour."

"Hey! I was in the middle of class when you were calling."

"Oh! I'm so sorry. I forgot you were in school. Sorry for interrupting your education."

"No problem at all. Class was almost over anywhere," I lied. "Now what kind of recruiting event do you have going on?"

"Well, if you really want to know. I'm the host for recruiting some more girls to the club. We've lost a couple, so, it's time to find some fresh meat, you know what I'm saying?"

"I didn't even know there was a such thing as that type of event. Wow! I guess I'm just naïve to those types of things." I sat under one of the trees a little ways from my school with my back up against the tree trunk to listen to the rest of what Monét was telling me.

"I wouldn't say you're naïve to it. You're just not a part of this life, so how would you know?"

I curiously asked, "So why have you all been losing girls?"

"Girl, they get in there for a while, and find them a man who don't want them showing off those goodies anymore, so they quit and either let that man take care of them, or go and find them a regular job. Nothing else would make them leave. Honey, dancing is like a drug. Once you start, it's hard to stop. Trust me. I can't even imagine doing anything else."

I didn't want to seem nosey, but I couldn't help but ask.

"I don't like to be in anyone's business. Especially people who I'm not close to like that, but you don't have a man?"

"Hell naw! I don't need anybody messing up my money! But real talk, you should come to this event! Then you can get a feel for the type of women who are involved in this career, and if it is something you're interested in. Girl, you got the body! Them men would love the hell out of you!"

I looked down at what I had on, and said, "I'm not really dressed for anything like that."

"What do you mean? There's no certain way you need to be dressed! To be blunt, most of it just may come off anyway," Monét laughed, and said as if it was nothing abnormal about it.

"Another thing is, I have a boyfriend."

"You still with that ole street nigga'? Girl, you can do so much better, and you will in this business! I could easily have me a millionaire if I want to, but I enjoy what I do, and I'm not willing to let anyone take that away from me. At least not yet! Do you know how many proposals I've gotten since I've been dancing?"

Curiously, I said, "No. How many?"

"Girl, too many to count, and the same will happen to you! Just come on by. Don't worry! Come down to the Downtown Marriott. Just ask for the Henderson Party and they'll direct you to where you need to go."

I took a deep breath and said, "I'll think about it."

"Ok. There'll be a lot of competition there, but I know you won't have anything to worry about! You got it, Baby!"

Hesitantly, I said, "Ok. Maybe I'll see you."

"Cool. I hope so. Let me go so I can get prepared for these stankin' ass bitches," Monét said, as she hung up the phone laughing hysterically.

I grabbed my book bag and walked to the car, I threw my bag in the back, and when I sat in the front, I looked at myself through the rearview mirror, trying to make a final decision. I drove through the parking lot, and when I got to the main intersection, I sat there, motionless, not knowing which direction to go in. I sat there for about three minutes until another car pulled up behind me, honking its horn, forcing me to make a decision. I went right. Not saying it was the right decision, it was the direction to get to the Marriott.

The entire way there, I doubted myself. At every red light I stopped at, I started to make a U-turn, then I would think of all the things I could accomplish if I could just get through the initial stage presence if I did decide to go through with it. I finally had arrived and it seemed like the longest drive of my life because so many things were going through my mind. One of the major things was what if Adonis found out? Then I thought, *Adonis hid a lot from me from a long time, so even if he did find out, he wouldn't be able to say much. Plus, it was mostly his fault anyway that I would have to go to these extremes.*

I looked in the mirror once again, fixed my bun, then made it look a little messy. I then took the shirt off I had on on top of my white tank top, and found a pair of white heels in my back seat. A white tank, light blue denim capris, and white heels. That was my outfit of the day. Monét downplayed the whole situation, but I refused to look like a fool. I put a little eye shadow and dark lipstick on, and just hoped for the best. Whatever was meant to happen would happen. My mom always told me everything happened for a reason, and I truly believe there was a reason I ran into Monét the other day. She caught me at a time in my life when I needed a miracle, and she just might have been what I needed.

As I walked towards the hotel, there were orange cones, and security directing people in every direction. A black cop came behind me, startling me and asked, "Excuse me ma'am. I didn't mean to scare you. Are you one of the guest speakers for the Black Women's Empowerment Convention?"

I shamefully said, "No. I'm here for the recruiting event."

He looked me up and down, then squinted his beautiful brown eyes. I couldn't do anything but notice his long dark eyelashes.

I folded my arms and said, "Is there something you wanna say?"

"No, I just wasn't expecting that, but you should take that as a compliment. Anyway, you want to go to your left."

"Thank you," I said sarcastically.

"Good luck, " he said, and grinned with his perfect white teeth. For a minute, I almost forgot I had a man. *"Get it together, Dezzi"*, I thought to myself.

As I walked into the hotel in the direction the gorgeous cop had sent me, I ran into Rasheeda from Love and Hip Hop. I had met her plenty of times in her store, but was wondering why she was here. She then told me she was there for the Black Women's Empowerment Convention, and thanked me for coming. She was one of the guest speakers. I hugged her as I was about to let her be on her way, when Monét suddenly appeared in her ripped up apparel, looking like exactly what she was . . . A dancer!

"Hey, Rasheeda girl! You here for our Recruiting Event?"

Rasheeda looked at me again, then at Monét.

"No, sorry, I'm empowering women tonight, not the opposite," she said, as she frowned and walked away.

I was completely embarrassed. What the hell was I doing there? I felt like calling Ess to tell her what I was doing just so she could talk me out of it. The longer I was the there, I felt smaller and smaller.

Monét grabbed my hand and said, "Fuck her. She thinks she's better than everybody! That's exactly why Kirk cheated on her stuck up ass! Let me show you where to sit."

When we walked into the event, it wasn't what I had expected. I expected half-naked women everywhere, throwing themselves at whoever was going to be making he decisions. I had always thought that if you wanted a job at a strip club, you just walk in, talk to the owner, turn around, and let him decide. I guess I had watched too much "Player's Club", or maybe this was just a more prestige strip club that required more from a stripper than the norm.

Monét sat me down at one of the several round tables with three other women.

"You know what to do," Monét said to the table of the other girls.

One of them raised her index finger, and said "Fasho. You know we got you."

Monét nodded and walked away.

"So what's your name?" the girl who agreed to look out for me asked.

"Dezzi, is what everyone calls me, but my name is Desireé," I said.

"No, what is your stage name?" she asked.

I was caught off guard when she asked that, and I couldn't do anything but pay attention to the green contacts up against her dark chocolate skin. I didn't know if my mind had begun playing tricks on me, but she began looking like an Xbox.

"Hello? Did you hear me? What's your stage name?"

The other girls were staring at me, waiting for me to answer.

"I don't have a stage name."

"No stage name? Have you ever done this?"

"No, and I probably shouldn't do it now," I said, reconsidering everything. I started standing up, grabbing my belongings, and the Xbox who never told me her name, gently grabbed me by my hand and told me to calm down.

"New girls are always the best. Just sit down. I'm gonna make sure you're ok, and we're gonna get you a stage name!" she laughed.

"What's your name?" I asked.

"My real name is Deanna, but my stage name is Black Diamond."

"Desireé, how about we call you Desire?"

"That sound good to y'all?" she asked the others at the table.

"That was kinda too easy. Don't you think she needs something a little more creative?" one of the girls that had on enough make up for the entire table said.

"Um, no, Cecily. I think Desire is perfect, just like when I met you, you had all that glitter and shit on your eyes, I named you Sparkle. Was that not creative enough either? Hell, these men don't care about no names no way. All they worried about is seeing titties, ass, and pussy."

My mouth dropped, and it must've been quite noticeable.

'I'm sorry if I'm too blunt for you, but I just tell you like it is. I've been in this business for over ten years and I'm not gonna sugar-coat a damn thing. It you want shit sugar-coated, this just might be the wrong business for you.

"So you're not here to be recruited?" I asked Black Diamond.

Black Diamond looked at the other girls and laughed.

"Recruited?" she said. "Girl, I'm one of the recruiters. I'm like a trainer. I have my own team of dancers, and Monét sat you with us to see if you're a good fit."

"Well, she could've let me know!"

"Why? So you could've put on you best performance? We don't do performances here, Baby Girl. You save that for the stage. We're just here to get to know the real you. You seem a little too timid for me. Maybe you'll work better with one of these other groups."

I looked around the room and didn't see any other table that looked like I fit in.

"I'm not timid. I've just never done this. Weren't all of you nervous when you first started?"

Everyone at the table nodded their heads. Black Diamond smiled. I could already tell that she tried to act hard on the exterior, but she was a cool chick. Black as shit, but cool as a cucumber. Sparkle would make it a little difficult for me, but not too much I couldn't handle. I could maybe help her with her makeup. Candy was another, and she was gorgeous. I couldn't find a damn thing wrong with her, so I knew she made plenty of money.

"You are beautiful, Candy. I just had to tell you that. I may have to get some beauty tips from you," I said.

Everyone at the table laughed, including Candy.

"Thank you," Candy replied. Then I realized why they were laughing at me.

When Candy Spoke, I knew she wasn't all woman, or always had been all woman.

"Before you ask, I'm a transvestite. I completed all the surgeries, so I'm all woman now. I'm still working on the voice, though," she said laughing.

I thought it was cool that she could laugh about it.

After about a half hour of meeting, and talking to everyone at the table, Monét took the stage.

"Good Afternoon", Monét said with a bright smile on her face. She truly looked content with her life.

"Good Afternoon!" everyone said.

Black Diamond whispered next to me, "If you didn't know, Monét is the assistant manager of the club and a platinum dancer."

"What is a platinum dancer?" I asked naively.

"She makes the most money out of all the dancers in the club. Everyone, and I mean everyone requests her."

"We all should know why we're here today. We do this so often so that we can keep our supply of girls for Magic City at a certain number, and that number has recently dropped, but let me just stress, it wasn't for reasons we should be concerned about. I think of it as out with the old and in with the new. If this is your first time coming to one of these events, I have placed one or two of you with each table, and the leader at each table makes the decision on whether or not you're a good match for the team. It has nothing to do with what I think. I put trust in these ladies because they have the experience and expertise to know what we need in this club.

"Before we proceed any further, the leader from each table will either welcome, or dismiss the women I placed at their table, and please don't take it personal," Monét said. She began with the first table, and all of the women sitting there were beautiful. I couldn't tell which girls were being recruited, from the ones who were already part of the team.

"Ok, table number one. Are you ready, Jade?" Monét asked.

"Jade was the leader of that table. Two women stood next to her. They were both tall, voluptuous, and stunning. Jade dismissed both of them.

Monét said, "Thanks for joining us today ladies. It was very nice to meet you, but unfortunately you didn't make the cut."

The women grabbed their belongings and were walked out of the room. I was so confused about what they were looking for. Those women looked perfect for the job, but I guess it wasn't all about looks, which is what I always thought, since I had never been inside of a strip club. If I were going to go to a strip club, it wouldn't have been to see women! Three more tables were introduced, with a total of five recruits. Only three of them made it through. There were only two more tables left, which was ours, and the one right next to us. The other table went first. There was one recruit. She was so cocky. Her personality was perfect. She even gave a speech, like it was the Miss America pageant, before her leader, Ivy, revealed if she would become part of her team. She had the looks and the personality, so I already knew she would be ok.

"I want to thank you all for the opportunity to become a part of such a great organization. I know you choose only the cream of the crop, and I know I'm that and more. I will bring more money into Magic City than you have all seen in years."

Before she could finish, Monét said, "Ivy, you don't even have to decide on this one. I don't even want to take you through this torture. Guys, get this bitch out of here. She has lost her mind!"

That easily, Monét had gotten rid of one of the most perfect girls I had seen. What was she looking for?

"Next!" she shouted.

Black Diamond stood up and grabbed my hand to stand me up next to her. I was nervous after seeing everything that had occurred. I didn't even know if this was even what I wanted, but seeing how badly people wanted it, and how hard it was to get in, it made me curious to know what was so special about this group of exotic dancers.

"I would like to welcome the newest addition to our team, Desire."

Everyone clapped, and seeing the smiles on everyone's faces made me feel special and I had a feeling of belonging.

I looked up at Monét and it seemed like she was clapping and smiling harder than anyone else. I just didn't want it to be that I was chosen because I knew Monét. That wouldn't have been fair to the other girls who weren't chosen, and in my opinion, should have been.

"Ok, so now for those of you who have been chosen, it's not over yet, so don't get too excited. You still have to meet the clubs manager. His name is Deray Goodland. You will call him Mr. Goodland. If he just looks at you and doesn't like you, you are dismissed. I just wanted to give you advanced warning so your little feelings won't get hurt. If you're wondering why we make this so hard, it's because, as you can see today, there are so many girls who want to be a part of us, so we have the right to be very picky because we don't need you. We have plenty to choose from."

Monét was so different around these people. She acted so important, or maybe she was just that important. I think I liked her better when she wasn't so important.

She continued, "So right now, what we're going to do is go over to the other side of the hotel. We need to be quiet because there is another event going on, but Mr. Goodland has a room over that way and he's waiting to see us. The best advice I can give you is to just be yourself and don't be nervous. He's just a man who stands up and pees just like any other man."

As we all crowded around the exit to go meet Mr. Goodland, my cellphone went off. I looked and saw that it was Adonis. I didn't want to answer it because I didn't want him to know where I was, but if I didn't answer, I knew he would think I was somewhere else doing something I didn't have any business doing.

"Hello?" I said quietly.

"Hey, Bae. What's up?"

"Nothing much."

"Why are you talking so low?"

"I'm at this Black Women's Empowerment Convention that Rasheeda from Love & Hip Hop is speaking at."

"You never mentioned going there," Adonis said, trying to figure out what I was up to.

I heard someone clear their throat behind me. I looked back and it was Monét.

"I'm sorry, Babe, I gotta go. I'll see you a little later. There's a lot going on."

Before I could say bye or hear Adonis respond, Monét grabbed my phone and hung it up.

"We don't have time for that right now. You can call him back soon," she said.

I took a deep breath, knowing I was going to have some explaining to do that I wasn't going to feel like talking about, but I guessed I'd figure it out. Once we got from one crowded room to the next, we all found a seat or just stood around conversing with others. There was a lady walking around with hors d'oeuvres, and another walking around with glasses of champagne. I decided to take one of each, while everyone else acted as if they were watching their figure. Monét told me to be myself and that's exactly what I was doing. I walked around and found Deanna, and talked to her a little more about the club and this Mr. Goodland. Everyone made him sound so important, but then acted like it would be no big deal when we met him.

I walked away from Deanna and continued to walk around and just get comfortable with this group of people. They were people, but I couldn't say they were like me. There were a few men in the room. Why? I didn't know. Maybe they were going to have us do a sample lap dance for some of them. If that was the case, I was going to be out of there. That was not what I came out for today.

Without paying attention, I walked straight into one of the men and wasted my entire third glass of champagne on him.

"Oh my God. I am so sorry. I should've been paying attention!"

I grabbed a cloth napkin off of one of nearby tables and began trying to clean up the man who I knew nothing about.

Monét came running over in her heels in panic and said, "Deray, I am so sorry!"

Deray? As in Deray Goodland? I thought to myself

I had wasted champagne all over the manager of the club who everyone was so terrified of. I should've been real proud of myself.

"What are you apologizing for?" Mr. Goodland asked Monét.

"Well, one of our recruits did just waste her champagne all over you."

"It's ok," he said with a smirk. "We're human. Things happen. Isn't that right . . ."

Mr. Goodland said, as he held his hand out to shake mine, and waiting for me to tell him my name.

"That's right, " I said as I shook his hand. "I'm sorry, but I don't know if I should be telling you my real name or my stage name I was given today."

Monét stood in awe watching my conversation with Mr. Goodland. Her advice actually came in handy.

"Why don't you give me your real name and we'll go from there." he replied.

Mr. Goodland was around forty, but was extremely attractive. He had a head full of jet-black wavy hair that was cut short and neat. He had a mustache and goatee and his skin tone was of a golden glow. He wasn't dressed up as I would have expected him to be. He had on a white fitted V-neck shirt and straight-legged jeans. I could tell that he spent a nice amount of time in the gym.

"My name is Desireé, but everyone calls me Dezzi."

"Dezzi, huh. I like that. Let me guess. They gave you the stage name Desire."

"Good guess."

"I guess you can just say I'm good at what I do."

Mr. Goodland grinned and began looking around at everyone else who was in the room probably waiting for his attention.

I decided to let him off easy so that he didn't have to feel like he was being rude, and said, "Well, Mr. Goodland, it was very nice to meet you. I'm so sorry it was under the circumstances of my clumsiness."

"Don't worry about it. It was nice to meet you as well, Dezzi. I'm sure I'll be seeing you soon."

"Of course, I said," with a goofy smile. I really tried to smile sexy, but I could tell it came off as goofy.

After Mr. Goodland walked away, Monét headed back my way.

"Well, it looks like that went pretty well."

"I would say so. He said he's sure he'll be seeing me soon."

"Are you serious? He never says anything promising to our recruits like that. He must've really liked you! Even after spilling champagne all over him!"

We both laughed. "Maybe that's the secret", I said.

"Maybe!"

"Is it ok to go now? I have some things to do."

"Let me guess. You gotta go see that man of yours?"

"Well, you did hang up on him."

"Ok. I guess you did your thang up in here, but we're gonna need to meet up tomorrow, ok?"

"Ok. Just text me."

On my way out the hotel door, I felt like screaming. I couldn't believe how great things went and I wanted to call and tell someone, but there was no one I could tell. On my way to the car, I ran into the same officer who had scared the shit out of me earlier.

"How'd things go?" he asked.

"Everything actually went great!"

He looked bewildered, as if he was surprised, and said, "Well, that's good. I guess I'll be seeing you again, then."

"Again?" I asked

"Yeah. This is where they hold most of their meetings, and I have the privilege of making my extra side money by doing security. I don't agree with the business, but he pays well."

I didn't want to get into the conversation of what was right and wrong, so I politely said, "It was nice meeting you, and I guess I'll see you again . . ."

"Derwin . . . my name is Derwin.

"Derwin, I'm Dezzi."

"Ok, Dezzi. See you later."

As I continued to walk to my car, I could feel Derwin's eyeballs on my ass, but I refused to look back. I had other things to worry about. I had to figure out what I was going to tell Adonis when I got home, that is, if he was even at home.

Chapter Twenty

I was surprised to see Adonis' car home so early when I pulled up. As I was walking to the front door, I saw it open and he stood in the doorway with his arms folded, looking like I owed him some type of explanation.

When I got to the front door, he held the storm door open, and at the same time said, "Where you been?"

I lifted my sunglasses up and placed them on the top of my head, rolling my eyes.

"I told you when you called I was at Rasheeda's empowerment event, didn't I? If you don't believe me, Google it! It was advertised everywhere!"

"I don't care about no Google or no advertisements. What I do care about is you, and what you out here in these streets doing when I'm not looking. When I called, you were talking all low like you were on some sneaky type shit, and then hung up on me! You think I don't be paying attention, but I definitely do. Don't get your little butt caught up in something you don't want no part of."

"First of all, I'm not out here doing nothing I don't have any business doing, and it was rude for me to be on my phone during an event while someone was on stage speaking. Secondly, did you just threaten me?" I asked.

"I'm just saying, be cool," he said.

I was never really good at holding water, so I said, "What if I told you I might have a job?"

Of course I wasn't going to tell him what kind of job. I really just wanted to change the subject, and see what reaction I would get out of him if he thought I was going to work.

"I would then ask what type of job?" Adonis replied.

"Let's just say, it's in the entertainment industry."

"Well then it better be some Tyler Perry type shit or something, and didn't I tell your ass you didn't need a job?"

"I know what you said, but I need something to do outside of school."

"Whatever, girl. You just gotta be so damn difficult. You gone do what you wanna do anyway, so I might as well not even waste my breath," Adonis said, sounding frustrated with me.

Adonis didn't ask any other questions, and I sure in the hell wasn't about to offer any additional information.

"I'm about to go upstairs and jump in shower. You wanna join me?" Adonis asked with a sneaky grin on his face.

I had walked in and dropped everything on the floor, and I had OCD when it came to cleanliness, so I told him I'd be up once I finished cleaning up my mess.

"By the time you get up there, I'll be out."

"Oh, so I'm not worth waiting for?" I asked, jokingly.

"Of course you are."

Adonis gave me a kiss, and while heading up the stairs, said, "You should've asked Rasheeda for a job. I'm sure she got something for you to do, like keeping her man from making babies with other women. Women's empowerment my ass!" he continued all the way to the top of the staircase.

"Real funny," I said, as I picked up my mess off the floor.

I was actually surprised he was taking a shower so early. Normally, once he took his shower, that meant he was in for the evening, but I wouldn't believe it until I saw it with my own eyes.

After picking up everything, I glanced over and saw my mom's journal sitting on the glass table, and tried to keep walking, but just couldn't resist. Everything I had just picked up, I threw it back down in front of the sofa and sat down. I grabbed the journal, looked around as if someone was watching me, and opened the pages of the beautiful words. I slowly sat down and began my journey down my mom's memory lane.

May 15, 1999

On my way in to work today, the most amazing thing happened. Standing right in the middle of my doorway to leave my raggedy ass apartment, which was the only thing I could afford with the pay I was making at Sears, my water broke. I didn't know to do anything else except to scream. Everyone opened the doors to their apartments to see what was going on. My extremely sweet neighbor, Sheila, offered to get me to the hospital. The nice gentleman upstairs carried me to Sheila's car. I wasn't sure if he didn't realized I had fetal juices running from my vagina, or he just didn't care. I appreciated everyone's help and didn't know what I would've done without them. After I decided to end my relationship, with who was now, my sperm donor, everyone in my family disowned me, saying that was the worst thing I could've done because he gave me the best life I could've possibly ever had. If they hadn't been reaping the benefits, their opinions would've been completely different.

I prayed the entire way to the hospital . . . Not for my pregnancy, but for my life because Ms. Sheila drove like a madwoman and I was so scared. I felt not one contraction while in the car with her. She came to a screeching halt and jumped out of the driver's side door, leaving it open while she ran inside of the hospital to get help.

Within seconds, she was back with a male nurse and a wheelchair. He carefully lifted me out of the passenger's side seat. As I began to feel the pain, I began breathing heavily. Due to the condition I was in, I didn't have to wait for a room. One of the white female nurses asked was there anyone I would like for her to call.

"No, thank you," I said panting as she wheeled me into my room to get me set up on an IV before the doctor arrived.

"No one at all? I'm sure there's someone who'd want to be here to see this beautiful bundle of joy be born."

Only one name came to mind, and that was a shame. I felt sad, but honestly, there had only been one person that had been there for me through all of this.

"Yes, can you please call my friend, Janae? I know she'd love to be here."

"See! I knew there had to be someone. Now, Honey, why don't you just write her phone number on this piece of paper and I'll give her a call for you."

Before she could hand me anything, I let out a loud scream.

""I think this baby is coming!" I yelled.

The nurse put on her gloves, and me, being naïve due to never having a baby had no idea what was about to happen to me. She gently rubbed the inside of both of my thighs and pushed them apart.

She then said, "You may feel just a little bit of pressure. Take a deep breath."

I took a deep breath and said, "A little pressure my ass!"

That bitch stuck her entire fist inside of me and acted like it was no big deal that she had just raped me!"

"Sorry about that!" she said with her gleaming white smile. "I just have to keep the patients as calm as possible. You're dilated at a 6, so you have a little ways to go. Your contractions are about five minutes a part. We'll be able to give you some pain meds soon, but not just yet."

"Why not? I'm hurting so bad."

"I know, but this isn't where you're going to have your baby and we need you as alert as possible before

we move you. You're a strong woman. I'm sure you'll be ok. Now, go ahead and write that number down for me."

I quickly wrote Janae's number down, and the nurse called her on speakerphone.

The phone rang a few times and there was finally an answer right in the middle of a long, hard contraction.

Janae was caught off guard by all the screaming.

"Hello? Who the fuck is this playing on my phone? I'm sick of all y'all miserable bitches thinking you can fuck with me!"

"Janae! It's me! Carlisa! "

"Carlisa? Are you ok?"

"No, bitch! I'm in labor and I have no one to be here with me! Please just come be with me right now! Please!"

"Which hospital are you at? I'm on the way!"

I began screaming again, so the nurse had to take over the conversation.

"Hi, Janae? This is Angie. I'm Carlisa's nurse. She's doing very well right now, but she can really use your support. She's at Northside Hospital. She's not in a permanent room just yet, so just come through the emergency room entrance.

I could hear Janae going off.

"What do you mean she's not in a room? It sounds like she's about to have this muthafuckin' baby any minute now. So, what y'all doing over there now? Delivering babies in the lobby?"

Angie shook her head as she continued to talk to Janae, and said, "Of course not. She's in a room. Just not her permanent room. We're taking good care of her, so you just get here so you can help us take care of your friend."

We could hear mumbling in the background, but couldn't make out what Janae was saying.

"Hello? Janae?" Angie said.

Janae wouldn't respond. We figured she must've thought she hung up the phone when she said, "This bitch got me fucked up talking about come help take care of my friend. Ain't that what the fuck a hospital is for? They bet not get me up here having to act a fool."

I had to have just invited the most ghetto person I knew to be with me for the delivery of my first child, but what other choice did I have besides being alone?

All the pain I had endured for 6 hours straight didn't mean a thing when they put my Desireé Arie in my arms. She was beautiful. She looked me straight in my eyes wit her big bright eyes. She had a full head of black silky hair, and she watched me without making a sound. It was like she really knew me. I felt like she knew everything about me and wanted to have a conversation. I just couldn't stop hugging and kissing her. If I never had anything else on this earth, but still had her, I would've been satisfied. I had never felt so much happiness in my life. She was my life now.

~Carlisa

Chapter Twenty-One

I had completely forgotten that I was supposed to be meeting Adonis in the shower. I ran upstairs, bringing the journal with me. Obviously, I didn't realize how long I had been downstairs reading because by the time I got to my bedroom, Adonis was in the bed, knocked out, butt-naked. I cuddled up next to him, but wasn't able to fall asleep because I was too busy thinking about the immediate connection my mom and I had. Tears fell from my eyes. I missed her and wished so badly that I could change that night. I would have to live with that visual for the rest of my life, and the fact that I wouldn't have my mom to give me motherly advice as I became an adult in this world.

I cried myself to sleep, and woke up to my phone ringing. Adonis was already gone, so I figured it was him, but I was wrong.

"Hey, Diva! Rise and shine!" the voice on the other end of the phone said.

I looked at the screen to see who it was, and it was exactly who I thought I was. Monét.

"Hey, girl"

"Um, I know you're not still sleep! It's time to work!"

"Work?" I looked at the screen again to see what time it was. It was only a quarter 'til eight.

"I have class in about an hour."

"No class for you today. We have more important things to do, so call in sick, or whatever you have to do when you're in college."

I took a deep breath.

"If you don't want to do this, you don't have to. We can find other candidates, but I know you can make it do what it do in this profession. Trust me. I know a star when I see one, so give me your address. I'll be there to pick you up in exactly one hour. Oh, and make sure you wear something comfortable."

I could not believe I was about to miss class for this bullshit. What was I thinking? I rolled out of bed and jumped in the shower since I missed the one with Adonis the night before. I put on my black leggings, a black tank and white cropped, distressed tee. I pulled my hair back in a sleek ponytail, and couldn't think of any way I could've been more comfortable. Monét could've been a little more specific when she told me to wear something comfortable.

I went to the kitchen and threw a slice of bread in the toaster, and poured a glass of orange juice. I wasn't sure where Monét and I were headed, but I wanted to make sure I had a little something on my stomach.

As soon as I put my glass up to my mouth, my phone rang. I sat the glass on the counter and said, "Hey, Baby. I see you left me early this morning."

"I see you didn't make it to the shower last night."

"I know. I'm sorry, but you know I'll make it up to you."

"I know you will. What you doing?"

I hated lying to Adonis, but I had to. He would never go for what I was doing if I told the truth.

"Getting ready to go to class."

"Oh, ok."

"You still didn't give me an explanation for your early start this morning."

"I had a few important meetings this morning. Making some more money for me and my baby. Is that ok?"

His statement made me think about some of the things my mom had written. She gave up everything and didn't care.

Money wasn't important to her. She was content as long as she had her necessities and the people in her life who she loved. Adonis put so much focus on money, and that wasn't the most important thing. We had each other, but he spent more time trying to make money than spending time with me.

"Hello?" Adonis said.

"Yeah, that's fine, but you know money isn't the most important thing in the world. All I need is you and I'm good."

Adonis said, guiltily, "I know I've been neglecting you, but I'm almost where I want to be, and I'll be done. It'll just be me and you. I promise."

"Ok," I said just to shut him up, because I knew how things went. The more money he made, the more money he would want.

"I'll see you later, Baby. Maybe we can go out to dinner."

"Sounds good," I said as I told my love goodbye and hung up the phone.

I had just enough time to gulp down my buttered toast, and take a few sips of my juice before Monét showed up.

As I headed out the door, I saw Monét sitting in the driver's seat of a bad ass red Ferrari.

"Come on, Girl!" Monét yelled.

Monét had the top down so I ran down my walkway and jumped into the passenger seat without even opening the door.

Monét laughed hysterically, then became serious and said, "Girl, if you ever do that shit again, I'm gone knock your ass out with this stripper pole I got in my backseat!"

I thought she was joking, but she really did have a pole in the backseat!

"What the hell is that for?" I asked.

"You have a lot to learn, but one thing at a time, babycakes."

We drove a ways away. It was actually a part of town I had never seen before. It had to have been at least a forty-five minute drive from my house, and we finally pulled up in front of a building with a big bright sign that read "Pole La Teaz".

"Come on, girl, and open my goddamn door this time," Monét said.

As we were walking to the door, she asked, "Can you dance?"

"What kind of dancing," I asked, not positive I knew what she meant.

"Any kind of dancing. Well, maybe I should say, can you dance with some rhythm."

"I'm a Black girl. Of course I can."

Monét gave me the side eye and said, "Being Black ain't got nothing to do with it! I know plenty of Black chicks who can't dance a lick, and plenty of white chicks who will tear a black girl up on the dance floor so don't even give me that!"

As we got to the glass double doors of the building, she pushed a buzzer, as she said, don't even worry about answering that question. We'll see soon enough."

"Who is it?" a female on the other end of the intercom asked.

"Money Monét, Baby!"

I heard a click, and Monét pulled the doors open. We walked down a long hall. I let Monét lead the way. As I walked behind her, I couldn't help but to stare at her hourglass shape. I didn't sway that way, but it was perfect. As a matter of fact, too perfect. I wondered if she'd had some work done. Her ass fit her fuchsia spandex pants in all the right places. Her ass was like a perfectly shaped peach, but wasn't too big like a lot of the women in these parts would overdue it. I couldn't even say just in these parts anymore. Everyone all over the world was getting asses! I just wondered what was going to happen when it phased out.

We finally made it to another room with another set of double doors. It was dark inside, but I saw all different color lights like a nightclub before even opening either of the doors.

"Oh God!" I said, as I saw Black Diamond.

"Don't be calling on God right now," Monét said. We're about to show you some moves!"

"That's right, girl!" Black Diamond said.

"Ok. That's cool. I guess I can take a few pointers," I said, letting them know, I wasn't scared.

"First, we wanna see what you got," Monét said.

"No problem," I said, walking towards one of the poles.

I used my left arm to twirl around the pole a few times. I could see Black Diamond and Monét giggling amongst each other. They felt like they were making fool of me. After I twirled a few times, I thought I'd really give them something to look at. I 'd had a feeling where we were going today, so I removed all of my clothes besides the leotard I had underneath. The two girls began looking confused.

"Can I please have some music?"

Black Diamond walked over to the CD player and turned on Ciara's "Body Party."

I wrapped one leg around the pole, arching my back as I seductively twirled around the pole. I then put my back towards the pole with my legs spread apart. I raised my arms and pulled my body up in the air, with my legs still apart. I used my arms to twist the front of my body towards the pole 'til I could feel the coolness of the metal against my pussy. I pulled myself all the way up to the top of the pole, and before my next move, I stared the ladies face-to-face, and grinned. I flipped myself upside down, and as I slid down the pole, I did a cartwheel in the air as I held on to the pole and came down into a split. I stood up and began grinding on the pole, pretending it was the sexiest man I'd seen in my life. After my surprise audition, all I could hear was clapping.

"You tricked us, tramp!" Monét said.

"Right! What strip club you work at?" Black Diamond asked.

I couldn't do anything but laugh! I had fucked them up.

"I don't work at no strip club. I was involved in gymnastics most of my life. I guess I learned a few things that might come in handy."

"A few things? Shiiiiid! I think there's some things you might be able to teach some of us other girls! "Not me! I'm good, but maybe Black Diamond can take a few lessons!" Monét said, as she laughed.

Black Diamond playfully gave Monét the side eye, and said, "Damn, is that what they're teaching gymnasts? Gabby Douglas, where you at, girl?" Black Diamond joked.

We all couldn't help but to laugh.

"Being serious though, you're a natural," Monét said. "You knew you didn't need any lessons! Why did you even let me waste me time?"

"Hey, you told me to come on, and you're the boss, so I was just doing what I was told!"

"Well, since we have no need to be here, let's go get something to eat. I'm hungry as shit," Black Diamond said.

"Girl, you're always hungry. You better be careful before you break one of those poles." Monet said, joking with Black Diamond. "I am hungry though. Let's get out of here."

I put my clothes back on, and we headed out. We all jumped in the car with Monét. I got in the back with the pole and stretched out my legs. I knew I would be sore for the next few days because I hadn't done any of that shit in a long time. While we were on our way to wherever we were on our way to, Ess called. I hit "ignore" the first time because she didn't need to be in my business, but then she called right back.

"Hello?"

"Why you hitting "ignore" on me bih?"

"It was an accident, Redbone. What's up?"

"What you doing?" she asked.

Just chilling. Left class a little while ago."

Black Diamond and Monét began getting louder and louder in the front seat, cracking jokes and laughing.

"Who is that?" Ess asked.

"Monét and one of her girls."

Oh, you hanging with her and her and her girls now? No wonder I haven't heard from you."

"No, that's now why! Today is our first day hanging out."

Black Diamond turned around and said, "Who the hell you back there explaining yourself to? It ain't none of their business."

"This is my girl, Ess."

"Oh, that's Ess? Hey, Girl!" Monét shouted loud enough for the entire neighborhood we were riding through to hear.

"Dezzi, what's really going on? She is not your type of company. Is everything ok?"

"Yeah, everything is cool. Don't worry Redbone. I'm about to stop and get something to eat real quick and maybe we can do something in an hour or so. I'll call you when I get home."

Ess paused as if she wanted to say something else, but there was nothing else to be said, so she said, "Ok. See you later. Be careful."

As soon as I hung up the phone, Black Diamond turned around and said, "Who the fuck is Ess, and why she ask so many goddamn questions?"

"She's my best friend. She's always been there for me. I've lost important people in my life, and she's my support system." "Can she dance?" Black Diamond asked as she laughed uncontrollably. I'm just joking. It's nice that you have someone like that. So why didn't you tell her what you were really doing?"

"It's just not time, yet," I replied. "She's very protective of me. If she found out I skipped class today, she'd kick my ass."

Black Diamond was just full of questions, and she wasn't ready to stop asking them.

"So, I hear you have a boyfriend. How do you think this is going to work out? Most men don't want no woman who's everyone's property, Black Diamond said."

"She will not be everyone's property!" Monét yelled. "What she means is normally men can't handle their woman on stage taking their clothes off showing all their goodies to other men. So, once your man finds out, it may come down to choosing either him or this occupation. You just have to be ready to make that decision if it ever comes around, or you just may have one of those cool dudes who'll sit in the front row cheering you on, throwing dollar bills your way. I don't know him like that, but you do, so I'm sure you already know how it's going to go once he finds out."

It was getting hotter and hotter in that car and I was so happy we had finally pulled into the parking lot of Red Lobster. There was no wait to sit in the bar. The waitress asked if we were all 21 and Monét said yeah. I figured she must've forgotten I didn't have an ID. When we got to the bar, the bartender immediately asked what we wanted to drink.

"I'll just take a water with lemon," I said.

Monét interjected and said, "We'll all take a Malibu Coconut Rum.

"I need to see your IDs please," the bartender stated with a sly smile as if he already knew he'd caught us up. Well, he had at least caught me up."

"Let's just go," I told Monét.

"Girl, will you sit your ass down."

Monet opened up her purse and pulled out two IDs. By that time, Black Diamond had already given him her ID. The bartender grabbed the two IDs from Monét, reviewed them, then handed one to me, and the other to her. I didn't know what was going on until I looked at the ID he handed me. Monét had already gotten me a fake ID made, and I must say it was a good one. She must've used my yearbook picture, but all that didn't even matter at that moment. Tonight I was legal.

We all drank so much that night, but I was the only one with slurred speech. The other two girls were used to drinking and obviously had a high tolerance because they each had at least three drinks and a couple of shots. They were still good. I wasn't too drunk because I heard it loud and clear when Monét asked me when I was available to start. She caught me off guard to the point I had to ask for a shot of tequila, and I hadn't had a shot all night. The bartender didn't even give me time to come up with a response to that question as quick as he came with that shot.

I quickly turned it up, and said, I don't even know much about it."

"Much like what? What else is there for you to know?"

"How much will I make?"

"Girl, you can't handle your liquor at all! Did you hear what you just said?" Monét asked?

"Yes, What's the pay? I know you make a lot of money, but will I?"

"Honey, that all depends on you and how you work that stage, and every dollar that falls on that stage while you're up there belongs to you! You don't split it with anyone. There is a tip jar that's divided every night, but how much you make is completely up to you and the sky is the muthafuckin' limit!" ain't that right Black?"

"Yessir! And you better not call me Black ever again. You know I don't like that shit," Black Diamond said.

Monet continued, and said "You'll be able to pay for school and anything else you need to pay for. You see that hot ass Ferrari I got out there? Nobody bought that for me! I paid for that out of my own pockets. I don't even have a car note. With all that being said, I don't know what there is to think about."

"What about Mr. Goodland?" I asked

Monét said, "Girl, he is the coolest nigga' around. He won't let nobody mess with you and he runs a pretty classy club for the type of club it is. You got the upper hand because he likes you. I seen him all up in your face at the event. If he doesn't like you, he won't say a word to you, and from what I saw, the two of you had a full-blown conversation, so you don't even have to worry about him. Just get on stage, do you, make your money, and go home. That's it!"

I looked at Black Diamond because she had gotten kinda quiet.

"What you looking at me for?" she asked. "You waiting on me to co-sign? I agree with everything she's saying. It doesn't get any easier than this. The first couple of times, you'll need a have a couple of shots before you go out, but then you'll be fine. We have a regular crowd for the most part. Every now and then, we'll get a few newbies and they're ready to give all their money away. But for real, is your man gonna go for this? Or are you about ready to let him go?"

My eyes were so low, and my speech was getting worse and worse. I knew I needed to go home, but it didn't seem like these hoes had any alcohol in their drinks. It was like they had been drinking water the entire time. As we sat there, I continued to answer their questions.

"It's not that easy to just let him go. I waved my hand out with my engagement ring.

They both burst out in laughter.

Monét said that ring was good enough for you? It's nice, but you're worth way more that that."

It's enough for me," I said, thinking about how big my ring was, and they were acting like I had a chip of a diamond on my finger. I didn't even have it in me to argue. I was proud of the beautiful rock on my finger. "My life isn't all about things, and plus I've invested a whole lot in him," I replied, still slurring.

After I made that last statement, I shook my head thinking about my five million dollars and asked the bartender for one more shot of Tequila.

That liquor was in my head and had me thinking about how Adonis had betrayed me and I was pissed!

"I'm ready to start tonight!" I shouted, as the entire back section stared at me.

"Ok, time to go!" Monét said. "Walk her out, Deanna, and I'll pay the check."

As Black Diamond and I walked out, she tried to tell me I couldn't start tonight. I tried telling her I was ready. I had enough liquor in me to get on stage and I was ready to make some of that good money.

"You have way too much liquor in you, Dezzi! I didn't know you were a lightweight.

"I'm not a drinker," I said, "but I feel good. I know I'll be good!" I said, basically begging Black Diamond to let me work.

"Tonight would not be a good night, Bae. Trust me. Tomorrow, you can have you a couple of shots and be good, ok?"

I quit begging since it was getting me nowhere, and we finally saw Monét walking towards us as we stood next to her car. Before she could even make it there, I turned in the other direction and vomited all over the white Buick that was parked right next Monét's Ferrari.

Monet came jogging over and said, "Girl, we gotta get you home!"

She went into her trunk and grabbed a bottled water and opened it for me.

"Just lay down and relax and please don't throw up in my car!"

That seemed like the longest ride home of my life! The top was still down and the sky was spinning the entire way there. I suddenly felt the car stop and I felt even worse.

"Nice Caddy sitting out here," Black Diamond said.

"That's Donnie's Caddy. It's real nice," Monét said.

"Donnie must be her man. You know him?" Black Diamond asked Monét

"Not well. I just know him from the streets."

"Oh. Gotcha," Black Diamond replied.

I was too sick to even talk, but it had finally clicked in my head what they had just said. Adonis was home and I was drunk as hell!

I quickly sat up and said, "Y'all, I can not go in there!"

"Why not?" they both asked simultaneously.

"I was supposed to be at school. People don't get drunk at school. My fiancé's home. What the fuck am I gonna tell him?"

"You're grown, right?" Monet asked.

Without me answering, she said, "Ok, so you're gonna tell him the truth and we're going to be standing right beside you when you do."

Monét helped me out the back seat, and I staggered as I walked towards the front door.

"Where are your keys, Dezzi?" Monét asked.

They're in the bottom of my purse somewhere. Just ring the doorbell."

"Is your mom home?"

I looked at Monét in a way I don't think I'd ever looked at anyone in my life, and said, "Don't you ever say anything about my mother. Don't even mention her!"

It looked like I scared the shit out of her, but I was sure she'd never ask about my mom again.

Adonis finally came to the door looking completely confused. He looked at the two women standing next to me, and then little ole sloppy drunk me.

"What the hell happened? What is wrong with her?"

"Smell her. Can't you tell? She's wasted," Monét said with a smirk. "She probably had the most fun tonight than she's had in a very long time, so just let her get some rest. Make sure she drinks plenty of water!"

As Monét and Black Diamond began walking away, Adonis said, "Wait, don't I know you?"

"Oh, you do remember me, Donnie," Monét said as she was walking back towards Adonis. She took her index finger and pointed her long red stiletto nail into his bare chest and said, "Make sure you take care of our girl."

Monét laughed and walked away. She and Black Diamond sped off not understanding the drama they had left me in. I probably wouldn't hear about it tonight, but I would surely here about it tomorrow.

Adonis got me all the way into the house, undressed me, showered me, and took care of me the rest of the night while I vomited on almost every piece of linen, and every pillow we had on the bed. What I did tonight, I vowed I would never do ever again.

Chapter Twenty-Two

The next morning, I could smell breakfast cooking, and my stomach was still turning. Adonis had taken all the linen off of the bed and threw a blanket over me and found a couple of pillows in the guest room. I turned over to look at the time on my phone, which was sitting on the charger on my nightstand. It was only 9, and I was glad it was Saturday and I didn't have to get up for class, but I felt bad as hell for missing class yesterday. I didn't need to be getting behind in any of my classes, especially with the amount of money I was spending on them.

I then began thinking about the fact that I was supposed to call Ess back so we could do something last night, and I never did. I already knew she was pissed and I had better called her asap. Before Adonis came back upstairs to lecture me, I decided to call Ess, and try my best to make her accept my apology. I didn't have any good excuse to give her.

I dialed her number and the phone just rang and rang. Her voicemail popped on, which was unusual, because no matter the time of day, she would answer my call.

"Hey, Ess. I know you're pissed. I'm so sorry for not calling you back last night. Those bitches got me so drunk that I couldn't walk myself to my front door. You were right, once again. Call me. Love you!"

Whenever I would tell Ess that she was right, that would be all she needed to hear. I was hoping it worked this time. I didn't need to lose her. She was the next best thing I had next to Adonis.

A few minutes later, my phone rang. When I looked at the screen, I saw Ess' smiling face.

"Heyyyy, Sis! I'm so sorry."

"Yeah, you already said that," Ess said, not sounding very happy with me. "And you sound like shit. What the hell is going on with you?"

"I just got caught up. That's all. It was supposed to just be dinner at Red Lobster and they kept ordering drink after drink."

"And I guess because they kept ordering drinks, you had to drink them," Ess said sarcastically.

I knew she wasn't going to let me out of this one easily.

"I already said, you're right. I was wrong. I made a mistake."

"Does Adonis know, or was he not home when you got there?"

"He was home, but he doesn't know how I ended up in the state I was in. He just carried me in after Monet and Black . . . I mean Deanna walked me to the door. I was throwing up too much to have any kind of conversation."

"Ugh! Sloppy drunk! Where is he now?"

"Downstairs cooking breakfast."

"He's a good one. I wouldn't be cooking you shit."

"I don't want anything to eat anyway! I feel horrible. And what do you mean he's a good one? He owes me a whole lot more than breakfast!"

The line became silent, and Ess took a deep breath.

"Yeah, I guess you're right about that. I just might've murdered him for messing over my money the way that he did. How's the money situation going anyway?"

"Not good, but we'll be ok. I can hear him coming up the stairs. I'll talk to you later," I said, as I tried to quickly hang up the phone.

I heard Adonis open the door, which was partially cracked. My eyes were closed as if I hadn't been awake yet.

"I know you're not sleep. I just heard you talking," Adonis said, as he walked towards me with a plate.

I opened my eyes and said, "I wasn't trying to act sleep. My eyes were just closed because my head is pounding. I just got off the phone with Ess."

Adonis sat on the edge of the bed and said, "Here, eat this."

"I can't. I feel like if I eat anything, I'm going to vomit. . . again."

"You need to eat something because everything you did have on your stomach is gone now."

I looked at the plate and everything looked delicious. He had cooked pancakes, sausage, eggs, and also had me a bowl of fruit on the side.

"If you don't eat anything else, at least eat the fruit, and I'll go get you some Gatorade to help the hangover. First, I want to know what are you doing hanging with chicks like that?"

I already knew that was coming, because Adonis knew me, and Monét wasn't quite the type of girl anyone would see me anywhere near.

"Ess and I ran into Monét the other day at lunch. We exchanged numbers and she asked me to go to dinner with her and her girl last night. We just went to Red Lobster, but they kept ordering me drinks. I was having such a good time, but I learned my lesson."

"I hope so, " Adonis said, telling me with his eyes that this shit better not happen again.

"I'm going to get some Gatorade. Eat something while I'm gone."

"Ok, but I have a question for you," I said.

"What's that?"

"How do you know Monét?"

I was drunk the night before, but I remembered Adonis and Monét addressing each other, and I wasn't about to act like it didn't happen.

"You promise not to get mad?" Adonis said.

"Don't tell me you dated her."

"Noooo! I wouldn't date anyone like her. You should know me better than that."

"Then what?" I asked curiously.

"I know her from Magic City. I used to sneak up in there often when I was into strip clubs. This was before you. I used to request private dances from her all the time, and . . ."

"And what?"

"She used to do a little bit more than dance for me. I didn't fuck her though!"

"Oh, so what! She just sucked your dick?!?!

"Unfortunately, yes, but remember, this was before you!"

"So these bitches are laughing at me in my face!" I said, furiously.

I had to calm down because my head began pounding even more than before.

"It was really nothing, Dezzi. She had a small crush on me after that, and that was it. Don't let it upset you. Just don't be hanging with her like that."

I guess I really couldn't get mad because it was before me, but it kinda made me mad that Monét didn't tell me, but I guess I wouldn't have told me either if I got dissed after sucking my man's dick. In my petty days, I would've brought it up to her, but I was going to leave it alone unless she ever gave me a reason to bring it up. I would just keep that in my secret bag of ammunition.

"Ok. I believe you. Thanks for being honest."

"I don't have anything to hide. Now eat some of that food while I run to this store."

"Yes, Sir," I said, and gave Adonis a kiss on the lips.

"And make sure you take a shower and brush those teeth!"

"Boy, shut up!" I said as I threw a pillow at him while he walked towards the bedroom door.

He turned and gave me that playful, sexy smile I always adored, and said, "You know you stink!" as he walked out the bedroom.

I put my hands up to my nose and mouth, exhaled, and frowned. If I was Adonis, I wouldn't have even kissed me.

As soon as I heard Adonis close the front door behind him, my cell rang.

"Hello?"

"Heyyyyy Girl!" I heard Monét purposely yelling through the phone. "You don't have a hangover, do you?"

Trying to play it off like I was all right I said, "Girl naw! I'm good!"

"Girl, quit playing. I know you feel like shit. You don't have to lie! I remember those days before I started being a real drinker. Those morning afters ain't no joke! You'll be good for tonight, though, right?"

Laughing, but not too hard because of my excruciating headache, I said, girl, "You are a trip. I will be fine for tonight. You don't have to worry about me."

"You gone be able to get out the house after last night? I know Donnie grilled your ass last night. Your ass wasn't just wasted! You were white girl wasted!"

"Yeah, he did grill me, but it wasn't too bad. He'll be out doing his thing, so he won't know the difference. You know, he has his own record label."

"Oh, no, I didn't know that. That's good. So he works late hours, which is perfect for you. Maybe you won't have to make a decision after all. So I assume he ain't in these streets no more."

This bitch knew way too much about my man, so I had to ask, "How do you know Adonis anyway?"

"I just know him from around, back in the day. You know how you just hang out and get to know people, and when you're in those streets, people are going to know you."

"Gotcha, but no, he left the streets alone. He didn't even know I knew what he was into, but when I did let him know, I gave him an ultimatum. It was going to either be the streets, or me. He chose me. Trust me when I say I won't be needing to make any decisions. I'm gonna make my money, go to school, and keep my man."

I had to throw in the fact that Adonis chose me since I knew what I knew. That was only a piece of my ammunition.

"I heard that. Girl, keep that mindset, even though when you see this money coming in, you'll start wondering why the hell you're going to school. Can't no class you take help you make the kind of money you're about to make, but let me quit being a bad influence. You'll see for yourself, though! So, you want me to pick you up tonight, or you gonna drive yourself?"

"What time do I need to be at the club?"

"At least by ten. We don't open the stage 'til around eleven, but we, of course, need to go through hair and make-up. We are real live stars, you know, so start acting like one."

"Ok. I'll be there. Let me try to get something on my stomach real quick so I can get myself together."

"Ok, girl, I'll see you later," Monét said sounding excited, like she had a huge grin on her face. It made me wonder if she made commission off of this shit.

After getting off the phone with Monét, I ate the fruit bowl that Adonis had made for me, which included strawberries, cantaloupe, and pineapples, and immediately took a shower, washed my hair, and brushed my teeth. I couldn't lay there and let my man smell me like. By the time I was done, and came out of the bathroom, Adonis was sitting on the edge of the bed eating breakfast and watching TV, and I could see my Gatorade sitting on the nightstand.

With my robe on, I walked over to him, took his plate out of his hand and sat it down. I straddled him and gave him a kiss on the side of his neck.

"You are so good to me, " I said to him, as I reminded him often.

"I know I have a lot of making of to do, and I plan on doing just that. We're going to be real good. Just continue to trust me on that," he said.

"I trust you," I replied.

"Good. Now, can I have my plate back, unless you're about to give me something else to eat?" he said, as he looked me up and down.

I grinned, and lifted my body up off of his and handed him his plate.

"Not right now. I said. I'm trying to get myself back together."

"Now you know you're not a drinker like that, so I don't even know why you tried hanging with the big dogs. They get down like that. You need to continue hanging with Ess and drinking your juicy juice," Adonis said, laughing hysterically.

I couldn't do anything but laugh with him because I knew I wasn't about that life, but all of that just might've been on the verge of changing. His comment made me feel better too, because I knew he and Ess wasn't on the best terms at that moment. It sounded like he was getting over it, and hopefully she was, too. They were the two most important people in my life and I needed for them to get along.

Adonis continued, "I'm going to be leaving a little earlier than normal this evening. I'm meeting with a couple of potential artists, so we'll be in the studio for a while."

This information made me nervous. He was starting early, so did that mean he would be finishing earlier than usual? I needed him to be gone as late as possible.

"So does that mean you'll be home earlier than normal?" I asked, trying not to sound suspicious.

"Probably not. I have one of my current artists coming by late tonight, and we're working on a hot track. It's so close to being ready, I can't neglect it right now."

"I understand. I'm gonna miss you though."

"I'm gonna miss you too, Babe, but when you wake up, I'll be laying right next to you. You should hang out with Ess tonight."

"So you cool with Ess again?"

"I prefer her over them hoochies you were hanging with last night! Remember, I know about the kind of work they do."

I smiled and said, "They're not hoochies! They're just different from me!"

"Very different," he said.

It was a little disheartening hearing how Adonis felt about strippers in general. Some women just liked stripping, hence, Monét, but some women were out there really struggling, trying to make a living, which was the category I would fall under. What if he did find out about me, though? Would he feel the same way about me as he felt about them? I was praying that I would never have to explain that to him. I planned on getting in, making my money, and getting out. Then I had another thought. When this was all said and done, what if I ended up just like Monét and the rest of them?

Chapter Twenty-Three

donis and I spent the rest of the afternoon together until it was time to make business moves. The doorbell rang before Adonis left, just as I had planned. I had called Ess and asked her if she wanted to hang out. Even though I didn't have much money to shop with, I asked her to go shopping with me. I knew I was going to make it up tonight.

Adonis opened the front door, not expecting to see Ess.

I stood in the hall and just watched them in the foyer interact with one another.

"Oh, hey Ess," Adonis said, sounding disappointed. Adonis moved out the way so that she could come in.

"Hi, Adonis," Ess said, which made me realize she still wasn't over her anger she had with him. I could tell, first of all by the tone in her voice, then by the fact that she called him Adonis, which she never did. She always called him Donnie.

I had to then intercede.

"Come on you two. We are all friends, and we need to just move past the pettiness. Get over it. Tomorrow's not promised and if something happened to one of y'all, you'd feel horrible. Just hug it out."

Ess stood there with her arms folded looking stubborn with her mouth turned up. Adonis took a deep breath, not knowing how to react to her stubbornness, and make things right between the two of them for me, so he did what he did best . . . Made the best out of the situation.

He picked her up and hugged her, spinning her around. She tried her best to keep her beautiful smile from appearing on her face, but she couldn't. He put her down and she was so dizzy she could barely stand. He grabbed her arm and held her steady. Once Ess regained her composure, they both apologized to each other, which is all I wanted. I didn't want to have to feel uncomfortable around the two of them, and they shouldn't have wanted me to have to feel uncomfortable.

We all left out together. Adonis went in one direction, while Ess and I went another direction. I wanted to make sure I didn't let this new venture of mine come between me and Ess, which was part of the reason I wanted to meet up with Ess earlier in the day, so I would still make it to the club on time. I completely refused to tell Ess what I was up to.

After shopping, we went to dinner.

"You set me up, didn't you?" Ess asked.

"Set you up how?" I asked, sounding dumbfounded as if I didn't know what she was talking about.

"Set me up so I could make up with Donnie. Don't act dumb!"

"Well, at least you're calling him Donnie again, and not Adonis."

"I'm still mad at him for what he did to you regarding the money situation, but being your friend, I'm not even going to bring that up to him, so we're cool. I know you love him, so I can't do anything but love him. You're still my sister."

I was happy that Ess and I had that conversation. I knew she would always have my best interest at heart, but sometimes, I would have to handle situations on my own.

"So what's up for the rest of the night?" Ess asked.

"Nothing. Probably, just lounge around and watch TV. Really nothing more to do," I replied, trying to make it sound like I was going to have a dull night alone, but that may have been a mistake.

"I can hang with you if you want so you're not lonely."

"Thanks, but not tonight. I'm gonna probably do some reading and get some rest. Monét and her girl wore me out last night."

Ess' whole expression changed, and she said, "Oh, I forgot, you did hang with them last night and got sloppy drunk."

Surprisingly, she didn't ask anything about it. Instead she changed the subject and asked, "Have you heard from your mom?"

I think I would've preferred the drunkenness conversation and lecture.

"As a matter of fact, I did. She's enjoying herself by her lonesome self. I just think she needed to get away from everything that reminded her of my dad. She's ok."

"Well, at least you talked to her and know everything is good. I know that had to have made you feel better."

"Yeah, it did," I said right before taking a sip of water.

The waitress came with the check and I looked at my phone. It was going on seven o' clock, meaning I still had a couple of hours to get where I needed to be.

"So, any new men on the radar I should know about?" I asked Ess, hoping there was someone to keep her occupied.

"Girl, hell naw! Who wants this wild-headed chick?"

"You're beautiful. Stop acting like you don't know it."

"Well, there have been a few, but not my type. I'll know it when I meet him. Our spirits have to connect."

"There you go with all this spiritual talk. If you like a dude, you like him!"

"I know, but I want him to be right! I have to feel that spark! My time is too valuable to waste even just a month on someone."

"Girl, you sound like you're forty years old. You have plenty of time! I feel you, though. I wouldn't want to start all over. Adonis and I have been together too long," I replied.

"Yeah, what has it been? Two years? That's like forever!" Ess said sarcastically. "Enough of this relationship talk, though. Let's get up out of here. I got some homework to do, since you refused to have a sleepover with me."

"Girl, don't act like that!" I said, feeling bad.

"I'm just messing with you. I know sometimes we just need some time alone."

We left the money for the check on the table and walked out holding hands looking like dikes, but we didn't care. I couldn't care about any other chick any more than I cared about her. We listened to a few songs and sang together word for word until she dropped me off at home. I gave her a great big hug and told her thank you for always being such an awesome friend, even when I'm a bitch.

She laughed and said, "Girl, get out of my car! A little bitchiness never bothered me!"

I smiled as I slammed her car door, and intentionally threw my little hips from side to side all the way to the front door of my house.

She rolled down the window and said, "Gone Girl with yo sexy ass!"

"Quit looking at my booty!" I said, laughing until I turned the key to get into the front door of my empty home.

I still had time for a hot bath to calm my nerves. I was beginning to get a little nervous, but I knew if I didn't do this, I would always wonder in the back of my mind, what if I had. I always said I would never live with "what ifs", and I didn't plan to start on it now. If I wanted to try something, that's what I was going to do.

I ran a nice hot bubble bath, and grabbed my reading material before getting in. As I eased in, I exhaled. It felt like I released so much stress after I got in. I turned on Pandora, and began my reading.

June 21, 1999

It has been rough being a single parent with a newborn baby, with my only income being from Sears. My hours have been cut because I can barely afford daycare and they feel I'm not reliable enough to work full-time. My mom tries to help as much as possible, now that she's decided to be a part of my life again, but she works, too. My Dezzi doesn't deserve this life. I don't understand why God is putting us through this. I just want her to have everything her heart desires, and first and foremost, a real family with a mom and a dad. She's a little over a month old now, and still doesn't know who her dad is. I don't want her to go not one more day without a dad. I just knew he would come around when he found out she was born, but he didn't. Every little girl needs a father in their life, and I will not keep that from her. No matter how much he hurt me, he's still her daddy, and I know when he sees her, he will fall in love with her just like I did. Even if we can't have a relationship, he will have one with his child, and I'm going to make sure of that.

~Carlisa

November 25, 1999

This Thanksgiving is so much different than last Thanksgiving. Not just because my Dezzi is here with me, but also because I'm actually genuinely happy and everyone around me is happy. We have Brandon here with us, and there is nowhere else he'd rather be. Dezzi loves him. Every time she sees his face, she smiles, and that makes me smile. I prayed and prayed for us to have a family again, and God listened. He heard my cries and felt my tears. The part I was most happy about was that Dezzi would never have to remember the time in our lives when her daddy walked out on her and we had to struggle. We made it through, and nothing will ever come in between me and my family again.

~Carlisa

I sat the journal on the floor, and thought to myself, why would my dad ever leave us in the first place, and how did my mom get him to come back? I always thought he was the best dad ever, but after reading what I'd read, I just didn't know. Something wasn't adding up. One Thanksgiving, he leaves my mom pregnant, and the next Thanksgiving, we're one big happy family again? I continued to think hard about that, as I listened to my music and dozed off. When I woke up it was a quarter after nine. I jumped up out the tub, almost slipping on the ceramic tile floor. Water dripped on the journal that I had forgotten I'd sat on the floor. I hurried and picked it up and laid it on my bed to dry.

I dried off, and put on some of my best smelling lotion and body spray from Victoria's Secret. I put a little baby oil on, figuring that should help me slide down that pole a little easier. I put on some of the sexy lingerie I'd bought today while Ess was at the food court getting a Cinnabon. I just threw on some jeans and a t-shirt on top of the red lingerie, and brushed my hair into a low ponytail. I couldn't think of much more to do, since Monét said we would be having a hair and make-up session. I put on a pair of heels, grabbed my purse, and headed out the door. When I got in the car, my heart was beating like it was going to jump out of my chest. Leaving my purse in the car, I grabbed my keys, and went back into the house. I grabbed a shot glass, went into my mom's liquor cabinet, and took two shots of Vodka to calm me down and get me started. With each shot, my body cringed and I almost gagged, but I had to do something to take the edge off. After that, I left the house for the second time, got into my car, and headed to my new place of employment, Magic City.

Chapter Twenty-Four

Wthen I pulled up into the parking lot of Magic City, there was a long line of both men and women, but mostly men, waiting to get in. Right before I got out of the car, I got a text from Monét telling me to pull into the parking lot in the back of the building. I put my car back in drive and headed to the back. It was completely dark besides a small light above one of the doors on the back of the building. I assumed that was the entrance for the dancers. I parked as close as I could to the door because I didn't want to have to walk too far. It didn't look too safe out there. I took a deep breath before getting out the car, grabbed my purse, and walked towards the lit up door.

When I reached the door, I turned the knob and it was locked. I then saw what I thought was a doorbell, but it was obviously a buzzer to get buzzed in.

"What's the passcode?" I heard a man with a deep, raspy voice say.

"Passcode? I don't have a passcode," I said not knowing what in the hell he was talking about. Monét had never mentioned that I would need a password.

"Well, I can't let you in. Please move away from the door," the rude man said.

I walked back towards my car, while at the same time trying to call Monét.

"What's up, girl! You made it yet?" Monét asked, sounding like she was already tipsy.

"Um, yeah, I made it, but can't get in. Your ass didn't tell me about a passcode!"

"Oh, girl, my fault. Before I give it to you, you better not share it with anyone. Not even your man, or your girl, Ess!"

"I'm not! What is it? I'm standing out here in the dark and it doesn't feel real safe back here!"

"Safe? Girl, look around you! There are cameras everywhere. Deray keeps his girls beyond safe. You have nothing to worry about. The passcode is "Make that Money", and don't let Byron scare you when he opens the door. He's a big teddy bear when it comes to us girls, but he won't let nothing happen to us."

"Ok. Where are you?" I asked Monét, since it definitely didn't seem like she was already in the building."

"I'm about five minutes away, and Deanna should be on her way. Go on in and Byron will lead you to hair and make-up."

"Ok. See you soon, then."

I began walking back to the door because I didn't know what was going to happen if I stayed too close. Byron made it sound like I was about to be attacked if I didn't get away, but I guess that was his job. I rang the buzzer again, and heard Byron's voice once again. It didn't scare me as much this time since Monét had given me a little background about him.

"You better know the passcode this time!" he yelled.

"Make that money", I said with confidence, like I had known it all along.

Byron buzzed me in, and when I saw him, my mouth dropped to the ground. He looked to be about seven feet tall and I'm sure he was over three-hundred pounds. He was light-skinned with freckles, and had some big ass lips.

"Now that's better, but next time, don't say it so loud," Byron said to me with a small grin.

"Got it," I said, feeling more safe already.

"Come on. I'll show you where the girls get ready," he said as we walked down a long hall. "You're Desireé, right?"

"Yes."

He suddenly stopped and said, "Don't be nervous. I got you."

I didn't know what it was about those words, but they always made me feel like everything was going to be ok. They were the words Adonis always used when he knew I was worried about something.

I smiled at Byron and said, "Thank you for that."

Byron nodded, but no grin this time. We finally reached a door with pink and silver glittery letters that read, "Dressing Room".

"Here you go," Byron said. "They should be waiting on you."

"Do I need to knock?" I asked.

"Nope. Go on in. I gotta head back to the door to let the other ladies in, so good luck," he said as he winked, and walked back in the direction from where we had just come.

"Thank you," I said as I turned the knob to walk into the dressing room.

When I entered, all I saw were lights, stools, mirrors, clothing racks, and an entire team. Mr. Goodland treated these girls like movie stars for real.

"And you must be one of the newbies," a lady in a catlike suit said as she came from the back. She was wearing a long black wig that had to have been as least thirty inches, with Chinese bangs. I assumed she had to have been the make-up artist because hers was perfect.

"Yes, I'm Dezzi," I replied.

"Hey, Dezzi! I'm Jalisa, but just call me Lisa," she said with a smile. "I'm gonna have fun with your cute little face. I won't have to do much, though. You have natural beauty. Some of these chicks that walk through here make me work miracles!" she said with uncontrollable laughter.

We then heard the doorknob turning, and I could hear Monét's loud mouth before the door even opened.

"Hey y'all!" she said, loud and obnoxiously.

"Hey, Miss Monét!" everyone said in unison.

The pretty man who was twisting in one of the styling chairs said, "Girl, are you ever gonna come up in here sober?"

Monét looked at him and said, "No ma'am!"

Everyone in the room burst out in laughter, including myself. She walked over to me and gave me a hug and kiss on the cheek.

"Hey, Sis! Have you already been introduced to everyone?"

When Monét hugged me, all I could smell was Tequila. Her party had obviously already begun. I felt some type of way when she called me "Sis". That was a word that I didn't use freely, and only Ess and I used it amongst each other because I could really consider her my sis. Monét was cool, but I didn't trust her like that. Upon arrival, Monét's face was clean, without a touch of make-up, which was probably the first time I'd seen her that way. I could understand why. She barely had brows, and she had absolutely no lashes. The bags under her eyes were atrocious. I was thinking to myself that Monét must've been one of the women Lisa had to perform miracles on because every time I'd seen Monét outside of here, she was absolutely gorgeous.

"I've only officially met Lisa."

"Ok, well that's really the only person you need to meet."

Everyone in the room looked at her like they were ready to whoop on her ass.

"Well, I guess you don't need your hair done this evening," the pretty man said sarcastically, so I took him as being one of the hairstylist, or at least Monét's hair stylist.

"You know I'm just messing with you, Kelsey!" she said as she walked over and gave him a hug.

"Ooh girl, you had way more than enough to drink. How did you even make it here?" he asked in a concerned tone.

Monét pulled Kelsey up out of the styling chair and said, "Don't worry me and my Tequila. Just get this face and hair together. " Kelsey rolled his eyes, as Monét plopped down in the chair.

Obviously I was wrong when I thought that Lisa was going to do Monét's make-up. I assumed Kelsey must've been assigned strictly to Monét.

"Dezzi, this is Kelsey, as you've heard. He does my hair and make-up. He is my personal stylist," Monét said, confirming my assumption.

I thought to myself, *So, Kelsey is the miracle worker.*

She then pointed to the left at a woman who was on the heavier side, with a beautiful round face, wearing blue lipstick. She was already working on one of the other dancers and doing a damn good job. I was hoping she would be the one to do my hair and make-up.

"That's Britt over there. She's also one of our stylists."

Britt looked a little shy, as she smiled, waved, and continued working. I could tell she was all about making her money, and that was it.

As Kelsey began on Monét's face, she continued to try to talk, telling me that there were others in the back who would be getting our attire together for the night, so I would have to get fitted since this was my first time.

"First, you better go ahead and hop in Lisa's chair and get that face beat before all these other heifa's start rolling in," Monét said.

She was right, too. They started running in fast, including, Deanna, Cecily, and Candy. There were plenty others too, but I didn't know them by name. I then realized why the dressing room was so big. I just hoped none of the women had a problem with hygiene because that was way too many women in one room for someone's ass to be stankin'.

As Lisa worked on my face, I spoke to everyone, and realized everyone came in the same way that Monét came in . . . Tipsy. I can't even say that Monét was tipsy. She was full blown drunk! I didn't even know how she was functioning, but I guess she was used to it. As soon as I began thinking that maybe I should've drank something stronger, or taken a few more shots, A woman with sparkly purple pasties on her nipples and purple panties came walking around the dressing room with a tray full of shot glasses. When she held the tray in front of me, I grabbed one.

Lisa stopped with what she was doing and said, "Dezzi. This is your first time, right?"

"Yeah," I said naively, not knowing what she was getting at.

"Well, honey, believe me when I say, you're gonna need more than one."

"I looked back at her and said, "Well, I took two shots of Vodka before leaving home."

Lisa shook her head and said, "Let me help this girl out."

She grabbed three more shot glasses. She tossed one down real quick and put the other two right on the side of me.

"They're right there when you're done with that one," Lisa said as she pointed to the counter that was within arm's reach. She then dismissed the purple lady.

By the time Lisa was done with my make-up, I was in a totally different space. I didn't know what was in those glasses, but I was having conversations with everyone in the room like I had known them all my life.

I was so tore up, I looked over at Monét who was still sitting in Kelsey's chair, and said, "Oh my God. You are gorgeous! I got up out of Lisa's chair, went over and straddled Monét, and kissed her in the mouth. What was crazy was I didn't think anything of it. It just came natural.

"Does this mean I'm a lesbian?" I asked.

Everyone in the room burst out in laughter.

"No. That just means you're ready," Black Diamond said.

"That also means I have to fix your lipstick again," Lisa said, not looking too happy.

"Oops. Sorry," I said, as I gently touched my lips.

"Well, since you're already over here, let me get your head together," Kelsey said.

"What?!?!? Now you know that's not happening. You do my hair, and my hair only!" Monét said.

"Ok," Kelsey said. "Get up then and let me sit down so I can get paid for nothing," he continued.

Hesitantly, Monét got up and said, "Gone and get my girl together since this is her first night, and since she just got me wetter than a bitch been in a long time." She then looked at me before walking to the back to get dressed, and said, "Don't get too comfortable in my seat.

After I sat down, "Kelsey whispered in my ear, "Don't worry about her. That bitch drunk as hell. That's how she gets. Very territorial, so you better not give her too many more of those kisses. She might try to claim you."

Chapter Twenty-Five

After watching a few of the other girls work the stage and get their money, my turn was finally coming. I'd had a couple of more shots while I was waiting because I didn't want the others I'd already had to wear off before it was my turn. I was dressed in pink sparkles, which matched my sparkling pink eyeshadow and lipstick. I wore a short, blush pink sparkly robe, but with the sheerness, much of what was underneath wasn't hidden. I also wore pink, glittery, five inch Red Bottoms. The girls had put something on my legs to make them look edible, and pushed up my titties to make them look more pronounced.

I could hear the DJ as the stylists were perfecting me behind the stage.

"I don't know if y'all ready for this one!" the DJ said, as if he knew they were about to get a treat.

The crowd was screaming and I was getting pumped just thinking about the fact that was all for me.

"DJ Rome got something for you! Something new and fresh! Something y'all then all DESIRED for a long time!" Don't blame it on me when y'all don't want to go home to your wives or whatever you got after this one!" DJ Rome had to laugh at himself, and he had the crowd going. "Ok. I guess y'all makin' enough noise! Y'all earned this one! Let's meet Miss Desire!"

I could hear the music beginning to play. I thought I would be able to pick my own music, but DJ Rome, who I hadn't even personally met yet, decided to play "Earned It" by The Weeknd. I heard Monét behind me, saying, "You got this girl."

The curtains opened. I hadn't stepped on stage yet, but the crowd was already praising me, not even knowing what to expect. They couldn't see me, but I could see them. The crowd was full with young, middle-aged, and old men. There were also the few women I had seen standing in line.

The spotlight came on, and I began my sensual strut across the stage, which was covered in glitter. I eyed the audience and batted my long lashes that were perfected by Lisa. As both the spotlight, and the crowd's eyes followed me, I felt sexy, like I was the most beautiful woman on the planet. As I got closer to the pole and swayed my hips from side to side, two very sexy men came up behind me and removed my robe, each kissing me on my neck and shoulders. They then exited the stage. I raised my arm, and snatched the pole as if it was my man, jumped, and twirled all the way down, wrapping one of my legs around it until I reached the bottom and heard my ass clap against the floor as I went into a Chinese split. The crowd was excited. I stood up and walked down the center of the stage until I was almost to the edge. Money was flying everywhere, and the more I saw, the more I was willing to do to get the crowd to give me more.

As I began unbuttoning my pink bra top, at the same time, eyeing and blowing kisses to the audience, I saw Mr. Goodland sitting right there front and center. When I saw him, something just made me want to do more. In my mind, I said, *Fuck these buttons!* I ripped off my top and put on a performance by teasing the crowd as I turned backwards, but still looking over my left shoulder, directly as Mr. Goodland, as I removed my thong. I was holding him captive with my eyes. It was like he couldn't take his eyes off of me. Someone from behind the stage swung a chair out onto the stage, and I knew exactly what it was for. It felt like I had done this before, or maybe it was the alcohol.

I finally took my eyes off Mr. Goodland and walked towards the other end of the stage. I reached my arm out and grabbed one of the younger men out of the audience. Everyone began cheering him on. I held his hand as I walked him across the stage to the chair and gestured for him to take a seat. As I gave him probably the best lap dance of his life, he grabbed my ass. I removed his hands and put my index finger in his face, telling him no touching. I could feel his freaky friend between his legs get harder and harder, so I took him out of his misery, got up, and walked my prop back off stage. He had a smile on his face, I'd never forget, not even thinking about the fact that his friend wasn't ready to go back into hiding yet. He didn't seem embarrassed by it at all. At the end of my performance, I looked down and the stage was full of money. I put on my robe, picked up what I'd definitely earned, blew a kiss, and walked off stage. I could hear my name being yelled by the entire crowd.

"Desire, Desire, Desire!"

I couldn't believe how much fun I'd just had. I honestly didn't think I would be able to go through with it, but I did.

"Now I know that is something we all desire, so she definitely has the right name!" DJ Rome said, as the audience continued to cheer.

Monét and Black Diamond came and gave me a hug.

"Awesome job, girl!" Black Diamond said.

In the middle of me saying thank you, I suddenly felt queasy and had to hurry and find the bathroom. When I finally found it, and ran into one of the stalls, I had to vomit. I heard someone running after me, but I was too much in a hurry to see who it was. I just figured it was probably Monét. I heard someone outside of the stall running water. After the water shut off, someone entered the stall in which I was still on my knees, and my head hanging down.

"Here. Put this across your forehead."

It was the sound of Lisa's consoling voice.

"Don't worry. You're not the only one this has happened to. Don't tell them I told you, but this same exact thing happened to Monét and Deanna the first time they got on stage, so don't feel bad. The drinks did help though, didn't they?"

I nodded my head as Lisa held a cool towel to my forehead. I was glad she was there for me. She seemed like a cool chick who would definitely look out for you. Monét then walked in and said, "Is she ok?"

"Yeah, you know how it is," Lisa said. "She'll be fine."

Suddenly, I thought about the time, and I said, "Where's my phone? What time is it?"

"Your phone is on the table by my styling station. You want me to go get it?" Lisa asked.

I jumped up, and said, "No. I'm good, but thank you so much."

I ran out of the bathroom, into the dressing room, and saw my phone sitting exactly where Lisa said it was. As soon as I got into the dressing room, Kelsey began applauding me.

"Girl, for your first time, you did better than some of these bitches who been doing this shit for years!" Kelsey said with a huge smile on his face as he tried to fix the curls he had put in my hair earlier.

I saw that I had a few text messages and got a little nervous.

"Lord, please don't let Adonis be at home and see that I'm not there," I said under my breath.

"Hey girl! Just checking on you! I'm over here bored as hell! We should've had that sleepover," the first text from Ess read.

Ess then texted again, like twenty minutes later. "Dezzi! I know you're not sleep already. You're just not gonna respond to me, huh?"

Thankfully, the third text was from Ess too, which read, "Maybe you are sleep. You did say you were a little tired. Goodnight. Call me tomorrow."

I looked at the time and it was almost one o'clock in the morning. I had no idea what time Adonis was going home, but I knew I had better been there whenever he got there. I started to call him just to see how long it was going to be before he left the studio, but it was way too much noise in my background for me to get away with that.

I washed all the make-up off my face, but unfortunately couldn't get the eyelashes off without yanking out my own, so I was just going to have to tell Adonis I was trying something new. I brushed my hair back into the ponytail I had before I got there, and put my clothes back on.

"Uh oh. Somebody must got a man at home," Kelsey said.

"As a matter of fact, I do, and he's not home yet, so I have to make it there before he does."

"You better gone then, girl, even though I'm mad you then messed up all those pretty curls! I understand though."

"Thanks for everything, Kelsey. Tell everyone I said bye, and I'll see them later. Wait. Where is everyone else anyway?"

"Girl, these bitches greedy! They out in the audience doing lap dances, or in the VIP room trying to get them some more money. You'll see if you stick around long enough. The other stylists are gone except for me and Lisa, but I'll tell everyone what you said."

"Thanks. Have a good night."

As I walked towards the exit, I saw Byron standing guard.

"You leaving already?"

"Yes, Sir. Unfortunately, unlike the other girls, I have curfew."

"Ok. Well, be safe out there."

"Will do. Thanks."

Byron watched me halfway to my car, and then I saw Mr. Goodland walking out, gesturing for me to wait. He then turned around and obviously told Byron to gone about his business because the door shut right afterwards. As Mr. Goodland walked towards me, he slowly clapped until he stood directly in from of me.

"What a dynamic show you put on here tonight. I just had to give you a personal applause, Miss Desire."

"Thank you, Mr. Goodland," I said nervously.

"Call me Deray, and there's no need for you to be nervous. Now, if you weren't out there doing what you're getting paid to do, then you should be nervous, but I don't think I'll have that problem with you. Monét did a good job scoping you out."

"Thank you . . . Deray."

"No. Thank you, Desireé. Now, where are you going so early?"

I was reluctant about answering that question because I wasn't sure what the right answer was, but my parents always taught me that honesty was the best policy, although, I hadn't been too honest lately with some of the most important people in my life. For some reason, I felt like I couldn't lie to Mr. Goodland . . . Well, Deray, so I told him the truth.

"I have a fiancé at home. He's not home yet, but he can't find out what I'm doing. I just know we're having some financial issues he's not being honest about and I'm school. I have to have a way to at least pay for that."

"I understand. Well, hopefully this helps, and maybe we'll be able to find some extra things for you to do in the future."

Deray grabbed my hands, looked me in the eyes, and grinned. "You know you have a way of putting a spell on people with those eyes, right?" he asked.

"Really? No, I never knew that."

"Well, now you know, and that talent will help you make a lot more money than the other girls. You have a good night, and make it home safely."

Deray released my hands and walked back towards the building as I told him thank you, and got into the car. I watched him as he walked to the door. He didn't have to ring a buzzer. He had a key. He was the big man and was intrigued by me. Before he walked in, he looked back and waved. I was embarrassed because I was actually still sitting there watching him. I had already wasted too much time to even worry about it. I had to get home, and that was about a twenty-minute drive.

When I finally pulled up at home, Adonis' car wasn't there yet. I was thanking God all the way to the front door, until I got all the way in and closed the door behind me. I could finally breathe. I hurriedly ran up the stairs, took off my clothes, took my hair down, and got in bed, trying to fall asleep as quickly as possible so I didn't have to fake it when Adonis got home. I was the worst at faking being asleep.

Too bad for me, Adonis walked in about twenty minutes after I did, and I was still awake. I still attempted to fake like I was sleep. I heard him open the bedroom door, and begin moving around the room as if he was looking for something. He then pulled the cover back.

I jumped up and said, "What are you doing?"

"It smells funny in here. What you been doing?" he asked.

"Trying to sleep until you came up in here at . . ." I looked over at the time, and continued, "almost two o' clock in the morning waking folks up for no reason!"

"I'm sorry, Bae. I guess I'm just paranoid."

He just didn't know how paranoid I was at that moment. Adonis had never come in the house and done that in the past.

"What are you paranoid about?" I asked.

"You. Feeling like you might get you someone else. Somebody better than me, who can treat you better."

"Awww. Come here," I said, opening my arms to Adonis. "There is no one who can treat me better than you do. I know you'd do anything for me."

Adonis laid on top, then raised his head up and said, "You been drinking?"

I hadn't even thought to shower and brush my teeth. I was just trying to get in bed before Adonis got home, but I was quick on my feet.

"Oh yeah. A little bit. I was doing some reading, and had a couple of drinks out of the liquor cabinet."

Then he looked at me and said, "What's that shit on your eyes?"

"Just some eyelashes, Bae."

"You know how I feel about all that fake shit. You don't need that."

"Well, I can't take them off without getting something to get them off with. They're glued on, and if I try to take them off right now, my real ones are going to come off with them. You don't want me walking around looking like Kermit the Frog, do you?"

He grinned, and said, "Well, make sure you get them off tomorrow. I don't like it," he said loud and clear.

"Yes, Sir," I replied sarcastically. "And how did your night go?" I continued.

"It went pretty good, actually. I have some real talent on my hands. Just wait. I'm going to give you everything you ever dreamed of. I want you to be proud of me."

"I'm already proud of you," I assured him. "Now take off those clothes and turn off these lights so I can go back to sleep," I demanded.

"Yes, ma'am," he said as he laughed.

Chapter Twenty-Six

Weeks went by, and I became more and more comfortable with my hustle, and I was loved by everyone that came through the club. No one there called me by my real name. I was "Desire" to everyone. I still lived my normal life, hung out with my girl Ess as much as possible, and Adonis seemed like his business was on the up and up. He would come home with gifts for me from time to time, so I knew he had to have a stash somewhere. He also had begun putting money back into the account that he had taken everything out of. One thing I had been neglecting was my reading. Once I read in my mom's journal that she had her family back, it made me feel content. Yes, I still had questions, but when I left off at that particular part when my daddy came back and she was happy, I felt a little happiness that I didn't want to dissipate. My mom must've felt content after that too, because her next entry wasn't until October of 2002 when I was three years old.

October 3, 2002

Dear Lord,

I'm stuck between a rock and a hard place. I know I prayed to have my family, and to be happy again, but I should've prayed that you do your will in my life. I truly thank you for revealing to me what was going on in my house last night, but what do you want me to do with this revelation? I love my husband, and I love my daughter. Seeing him fondle her last night with my own eyes hurt my heart. I don't understand how he could do this to our daughter.

As I read, tears began flowing from my eyes. My daddy was the perfect dad. These had to be lies, but why would my mom write lies in a journal. That just didn't make sense. My dad fondled me? Why? Why didn't I remember? I then remembered the words my mom said to me that hurt and upset me so much. She said, "If you knew half of what I know, and all of what I had to experience to get to the wonderful place our family was finally at before the accident, you wouldn't be crying about your daddy. Fuck your daddy!"

Those words were what caused our fight, and the reason she was dead right now. I couldn't stop crying. I didn't want to continue reading, but I wanted to know why she stayed. He had already hurt her once and abandoned us. This was far worse, and she stayed? I just couldn't make sense of it all! I continued to read. There had to be something more. Maybe she realized he wasn't fondling me, and it was just a huge misunderstanding.

She is only three years old. I know he knew he was wrong by the way he looked at me when he saw me standing in the doorway . . . the way he threw the covers back on top of her as she slept peacefully. I wonder how long this has been going on, but I know I will never know. He'll never be honest about this. It shouldn't even matter to me how long it's been going on. Just knowing it happened once should be enough, but I love my husband, and I know he loves me. He made a mistake and I have to forgive him. His promise to me to never do it again sounded so sincere. I know we've all done things that weren't right, and if you can forgive us, we should be able to forgive each other. That is what I'm going to do. I'm going to forgive my husband. Dezzi is too young to know anything, and I'm just grateful that it was revealed before she was at the age that she would remember. I wouldn't want anything like this to affect her future. I know he didn't mean it, and it won't happen again.

~Carlisa

I balled up and cried like a newborn baby. Adonis came running from downstairs watching the game to see what was going on.

He grabbed me and said, "Baby! What's wrong?"

"She let him hurt me, and just let him get away with it! Why would she do that?"

I cried on Adonis' shoulder for hours. While I cried, he read what I had read and couldn't believe it either. Everything seemed to be going perfectly, and then I find out the man in my life, who I loved most molested, me. My own daddy molested me! I cried until I fell asleep thinking about the fact that my mom could forgive someone who molested her baby girl. That was just sick and I hated her for it, but I had to do as she did for my daddy. I had to forgive her.

That night, Adonis asked if I wanted him to stay home with me. I would've loved to just stay home and lay up under him, but I had business to take care of. There were some special VIPs that would be at that club, and I couldn't miss that kind of money. Deray would've been at my front door if I didn't show up. I didn't know how long I would be at the club, but I was going to get that money as long as I could. Deray was clearly showing favoritism between me and the other girls. It was very evident, and had started driving a wedge between me and the others. I tried telling him, but he didn't care.

That night, when I got to the club, I was a little late because I had to get another cry out before I left home. I was the last of the girls to get their hair and make-up done. Everyone wasn't scheduled to come in tonight due to the crowd that was going to be there. Only the best of the best dancers were invited, which, of course, included me. The few that were in the building were already either on the floor or on stage. While in the dressing room, Lisa, Kelsey, Britt, and I could hear a bunch of "Boos" out in the audience. We decided to go see what all the chaos was about. All we saw was Monét performing, but obviously, because they hadn't seen me yet, they were quite disappointed. I had become the one to get the crowd going and that hadn't happened. Suddenly, the crowd started chanting my name, and I felt so bad. I didn't want anyone to think this was intentional, because it definitely wasn't.

"Come back to the dressing room so we can hurry up and you dressed. You're going out there with her," Lisa said.

We all ran back to the dressing room and everyone helped me get out of my clothes and get into something sexy as quickly as possible. We couldn't let Monét go out like that. After getting me dressed, Lisa ran over to DJ Rome and told him to play "Location" by Khalid.

"That ain't what Monét got me playing for her! Y'all know she chooses her own music!"

Britt pushed Lisa out the way in a not so shy fashion, got all in DJ Rome's face and said, "Do what she told you before I throw your lanky ass over in the crowd and play it myself."

Of course, DJ Rome did what he was told. When the music stopped, Monét first began looking around, not knowing what was going on, and the crowd became silent. "Location" began playing, and I slowly began walking out onto the stage, gesturing with my index finger for Monét to come towards me. She slowly began sexily walking towards me. She stared at me, batting her fake lashes, giving her thanks. Once we reached each other, I grabbed her by the waist, and lifted her up on the pole. As I lifted her, I licked her stomach and had the crowd going wild. As I danced for the crowd, and teased them a bit, Monét came sliding from the pole with her legs straight up in the air. To make things even more interesting, I did the unimaginable. When she reached the floor, I got on my knees, pushed her thighs back with all my strength and licked her pussy. I had never heard so much noise in my life.

Monét raised herself up and fondled herself for the audience as I did some tricks of my own on the pole. At the end of our spontaneous performance, Monét and I wrapped our arms around each other, and we gave each other a sensual kiss. We kissed so long, the lights came on. We then both blew kisses to the audience, which I must add was my trademark, and ran to the dressing room!

"Now that was hot!" Kelsey said.

"Sure was!" Lisa and Britt agreed.

"You sure you're not a lesbian, bitch?" Kelsey asked with a serious face.

"No, I'm not a lesbian! I am happily engaged to a man!"

"Well, whatever you are, thanks for helping a sistá out. I've never had the type of response I was getting before you came on stage," Monét said.

"No problem. Anything to help another sistá."

At that moment, Deray walked in. He never came into the dressing room so it must've been something serious.

"Desire. Can I see you for a moment? After you get dressed."

"Girl, what you then did?" Kelsey asked.

"I don't know, but I guess I'll find out."

I hurriedly got dressed, and grabbed my purse, keys, phone, and everything out of my locker because from the look on Deray's face, it didn't look like there was any coming back.

"I guess I'll see y'all soon," I said as I headed towards the dressing room door.

As soon as I stepped outside the door, Deray was waiting on me.

I jumped when I saw him and said, "Oh, hey! You scared me."

"Sorry. Didn't mean to scare you. Come walk with me."

I began to get nervous and said, "Is everything ok?"

Deray had his hands in his pockets and a serious look on his face. We walked towards the doors that led outside.

"Things aren't horrible, but they aren't great either," Deray replied.

"Hey, Byron!" I said as we walked out the door.

Byron nodded.

Deray began talking again once we made it to a place where no one could hear him, except for me.

"You know, this was a very important night for the club, right?"

"Of course I do. You and everyone else made that very clear."

Before I realized it, we were at Deray's pearl white Lamborghini. He hit a button and the doors opened.

"Get in," he said. "Let's really talk."

I sat in the passenger's seat and he got in the driver's seat.

"You don't mind if I drive you around for a minute while we talk, do you?"

I looked at the time on his console, and said, "Not at all".

Deray shook his head, looking as if he wasn't pleased at all. He hit a button to close the doors and began driving.

"I'm going to begin with saying I don't care for all the time constraints. I'm the boss around here, so you need to make some decisions. If I need you, I need to come first. I noticed you were late tonight, which caused all the commotion. People were there to see you first. Anyone blind would know this."

"I'm sorry. I had something . . ."

Deray stopped me and said, "I don't do excuses very well, so please don't give me any. Yes, you fixed the problem, but you put your industry reputation on the line."

"I'm sorry. I don't follow."

"Let me help you understand. These men don't want "lesbian" Desire. They want the Desire that only wants them . . . A man. Now, without my authorization, you're out there on my stage eating pussy."

"I didn't think it was that much of an issue. It won't happen again," I replied.

"It's too late, but I like you, Dezzi. I like you as Dezzi, and not Desire. You're one of the only girls who has come in here and I can still see their innocence. There's just something about you. I want to take care of you."

When Deray stared me in my eyes and grabbed my hands as we pulled over into an empty school parking lot, I knew he was serious.

"When I first met you at the event and you clumsily wasted your champagne on me, I knew I wanted you," he said as he laughed.

I couldn't help but to laugh. Everything that Deray was saying at that moment was so endearing. It seemed like he had been around me more than Adonis had been lately, and to be honest, I did feel close to him.

Deray continued, "That first performance you gave was hypnotic. No other woman has ever been able to get my attention and keep it the way that you did that night. That's when I knew for sure, you were the one. I know you have a fiancé, but I guarantee you he can't take care of you the way I can. We need each other."

After Deray finished his spill, I didn't know what to say. He stared at me for a moment and I just looked in front of me at the school at which we were parked. Deray then turned on the music and began driving. I had no idea where we were going, but we rode around for about an hour.

I finally decided to speak, and said, " So, if I don't accept your offer, does that mean I no longer have a job with you?"

"Can I ask you something, Dezzi?"

"Sure," I replied."

"Why do you even want this job? You are so much more than this."

"I need to help pay for college."

"Where's your parents, or what about student loans?"

"My dad is dead and my mom is not around. I don't believe in loans."

"I hear you about the loan thing. The worst two things you can get into are some bad pussy or some bad debt!"

We both laughed.

"Seriously though, Dezzi, I'm not trying to force you into anything. You're always welcome to work at the club, as long as you follow the rules. Shit, you're the one who people are now coming to see. You're the star, but I want you to know you have options. Imagine not having to get on stage and take your clothes off for strangers, and being able to not have to work and just focus on school. Imagine being loved like no one has ever loved you before. I got you."

As soon as I heard Deray say that, I saw Adonis' face in the back of my mind, and knew I had to get home.

"I'll have to sleep on this. Can you please just take me to my car so I can get home?"

"Yes, I can do that."

Deray headed back to the club. As he headed that way, he asked, "Did you get any money for that performance tonight?"

"No. It was actually Monét's performance. I just helped her out a little bit. I was late, so I basically missed my time to perform."

"You helped just a little bit, huh?" Deray chuckled.

We finally pulled back up at the club, and I was a little sad to see the ride end, but I knew I needed to get home.

I was waiting for Deray to open the car door, but he was still sitting in the driver's seat pulling out his wallet.

"Can you open the door, please?"

He looked at me and said, "Can you be patient, please?"

Deray pulled out a wad of money, counted it and handed some over to me.

"I can't take this," I said.

"Yes, you can. You provided services for me tonight and didn't get paid, so I'm paying you out of my own pocket. Take it."

I hesitated, but I slowly reached for the money. As my hand got closer, Deray pulled his hand back further, until our lips met, and I felt a spark. It was something I had never felt before.

"You felt it too, huh?" he asked.

I didn't say anything.

"You don't have to say it. I can tell in your face," he said as he handed me the money and opened the car door. "I'll see you later, Dezzi."

I still couldn't say a word. I just walked to my car, got in, and headed home. I didn't know what had just happened, but I had a lot on my mind to begin with, and now I had some extra shit to deal with. It didn't look like it was ending there. When I pulled up to my house, not only was Adonis' car there, but Ess' car was there, too. When I saw both of their cars, I assumed they had tried to call me. When I pulled into the driveway, I looked all over the car for my phone and found nothing. It wasn't in my purse, nor any of my pockets. How else could this night go absolutely wrong?

Chapter Twenty-Seven

As I walked up the walkway, the front door opened, and there was Adonis standing there with a stern look upon face. Once I reached the door, he opened the storm door for me, welcoming me in, without a word. I then saw Ess sitting on the couch with her legs crossed and armed folded. They reminded me of a mother and father waiting on their teenage daughter to get home, and they were obviously upset because she was late.

I sat my purse down on the kitchen table and said, "What's going on, y'all?

Ess was the first to speak, which I wasn't surprised about at all.

She stood up with her arms still folded and said, "What the fuck do you mean? What's going on with you? We've been calling and texting you all night, and you didn't have the decency to answer neither one of us? I thought we were better than that! Anything could've happened to you, and you walk in here all nonchalantly like you ain't did shit! That shit hurts!"

Adonis paced the floor, and whenever he did that, I knew he was pissed. That let me know he didn't have any words to say. The resolution he had in mind was taking action.

"Look, I'm sorry. I've been going through a lot and just needed some time away. Where my phone is, I don't know. Y'all know if I knew you were calling I would've answered." I figured playing the victim role would help get me out of this mess, so I turned to Adonis and said, "You know all about what I'm going through. You were here with me today and know what I found out! My mind is just all over the place right now!"

Adonis finally decided to speak. He first took a deep breath and said, "Dezzi, I asked you if you wanted me to stay with you! I knew you were hurting. I could've been right here with you, but you chose to make your face up like a clown and put that shit on your eyelashes again that I told you I didn't like. That doesn't look like someone who's hurting to me. That just looks like a person who's looking for a way to get out and do whatever the hell she wants to do!"

Ess walked up closer on me and said, "I hadn't even noticed! What is up with that shit on your face? You're looking like Monét and her girls! Are you hanging out with them?"

"No! I'm just dealing with some things, so let me be!"

"Adonis showed me what was in your mom's journal, and it is fucked up, but whatever you're doing is not the way to deal with it! You need to talk to someone, right along with your mother because I know this has to be eating her up, too! I know the therapist you two were seeing wasn't helping, so find another! You can't live life bearing all of this on your shoulders. You know I'm always here for you! I can't believe you didn't at least come to me. It should not have to come down to your man calling me to come over after one o' clock in the morning to help try to find you, or wait for you to get home."

Adonis intervened and said, "I came home early to try to surprise you and take you out to dinner to find you not even here. I know we don't do a lot together because of how busy we are, but I honestly wanted to surprise you tonight. I waited here for hours before I even called Ess. I didn't want to put anyone else in the middle of this."

As Adonis spoke, he continued to pace the floor. I felt bad, but I didn't know what to say. I had never thought about what I'd do if I ever got caught. I guess I should have.

"Y'all, all I can say right now is I'm sorry. I wasn't trying to worry anyone, and I definitely wasn't trying to mess up any plans you had for us, Adonis. Please accept my apology. Both of you."

"So that's it?" Ess asked. "You're not even going to tell us where you were?

I knew Ess wasn't going to give up that easily. That was just not her style.

"Ok. I was out with Monét. I know I should've called you before her, Ess, but I just wanted to be around someone who doesn't know my history. I don't like to always talk about what I've been through. I just wanted to go out and try to take my mind off of everything."

Ess walked over to me and gave me a hug, as she whispered in my ear, "Don't you ever do this shit again! You know I'll whoop yo ass!"

I looked over, and Adonis had finally sat down. I went over and sat on his lap and hugged his neck.

He wrapped his arms around my waist and said, "You just don't know how worried I was. After everything you've been through, I didn't know what you might've done, or what might've happened to you." He lowered his voice and said, "I thought we already had a discussion about Monét. She is not your girl for real."

I whispered, "I'm sorry, Baby. I know not to trust her, but I have to admit she's fun to hang with" I said, as I kissed him on the forehead.

Ess cleared her throat and bucked her eyes to remind us she was still in the room.

I looked over at her and said, "It is so nice to know that I have people in my life who care so much about me, and willing to come together to find me. I appreciate the both of you."

"I even tried calling your mom. I thought maybe you had gone out to Vegas wit her," Ess said.

Ess just couldn't leave shit alone.

"You didn't tell me you had called her," Adonis said, looking at me as if he was trying to tell me I need to get my shit together because this was the type of shit that happens when I decide to go missing.

"What happened when you called her?" I asked Ess.

"No answer. It went straight to voicemail, but I did leave a message that I couldn't find you, so don't be surprised if you get a call."

"Ok. Thanks for the heads up. I don't know about y'all, but I'm tired as hell, and ready to go to bed."

"Me too, Ess said. I guess I'll head home."

"Girl, it's late. Don't even think about going out there right now. You can sleep right here on the sofa sleeper. I'll bring some blankets and pillows down."

"Ok. If that's all right with the both of you." Ess looked over at Adonis and said, "Donnie, is that ok?"

"Of course it is. I'm the one who called you over here all late."

"Good, because I shole didn't feel like driving home! Thank God for good friends!" she said, as she yawned in the middle of her laugh.

"I'll worry about finding my phone tomorrow. It's probably in Monét's car somewhere. I'll be right back down with blankets," I said as I headed upstairs with Adonis right behind me, holding on to my hips.

When I came back down, Ess had already let out the bed and was laying on the bare mattress. Just when I thought she was done preaching to me, she started up again.

"Dezzi, I know how you always had me defending you with your mom. This better not be one of those types of ordeals. Please tell me you weren't out with another man."

"Girl, now you know how I feel about Adonis."

"I know, but look at you! You look like you were out trying to impress someone."

"Adonis and I are good. Don't you worry about that. I'm not putting you in the middle of no kind of mess. Trust me."

"Ok. I'm gonna trust you on this. I just hope I don't regret it."

"You won't," I said as I threw some pillows and covers over Ess and gave her a kiss on the forehead.

"Goodnight, Sis," I said to my best friend.

"Goodnight," she replied.

My next dilemma was trying to figure out where the hell my phone was. I knew it wasn't really in Monét's car because I hadn't been in her car, and tomorrow was Sunday, so I couldn't get into the club to see if it was there. My memory may have been a bit clouded, but I could've sworn I grabbed by phone with everything else when I walked out with Deray. As a matter of fact, I made sure I grabbed everything because I wasn't sure if I was going to be allowed back into the club once Deray came to the dressing room to get me.

I could've called Deray and asked him if he could check his car, only if his phone number wasn't stored in my cellphone which I didn't have. Everyone's number was in my cell phone, but one thing I did have was Monét's business card with her phone number. The only thing with that was it wouldn't look too good if I were to call her and ask her for Deray's phone number because I possibly left my phone in his car. I didn't need to add any fuel to any fire, so I thought of another plan. I would wake up bright and early tomorrow morning and dust off my laptop and find Mr. Goodland's address. I'm sure he wouldn't mind a short visit for a good reason, but for now, I was about to go upstairs and give my man the type of loving he deserved after the night he had because of me. This would be a night he would never forget, and it would definitely end on a good note.

Chapter Twenty-Eight

As the sun rose, I crept out of bed, jumped into the shower, and hurriedly threw on a pair of jeans and a tank top. I quickly brushed my hair back into a low ponytail and put on a baseball cap. I put my sneakers in my hand before I tiptoed out the bedroom door and headed down the stairs. I was trying my best not to wake Adonis because I didn't feel like answering any questions as to where I was going. When I got to the foyer, I held on to the wall as I put on my sneakers, and I suddenly heard the clearing of one's throat. I looked up as I finished getting the heel of my foot in my last shoe, and saw Ess standing a few feet away from me with her arms folded and head tilted to the side. Her curly, brown hair was all over her head.

"And where are you sneaking off to so early? It's only seven a.m.!" she asked without any sound of humor in her voice.

"I was just up laying in the bed, staring at the ceiling, so I thought I'd go by Monét's place to see if I can find my phone." I said, hoping that Ess didn't keep asking questions, or even try to go along.

"And you think Monét is already up? You know the work she does! This is her time to sleep. By the way, I was actually thinking about that before I went to sleep last night. I'm sure she had to work last night. Were you at the strip club with her?" Ess asked.

"Monét never sleeps, and no, she took the night off last night Inspector Gadget!" I said, laughing. She's a party girl, but she is always going, so I'm sure she's up. I'll be right back. I promise. I just feel so lost without my phone."

Ess looked at me as if she didn't believe me. She pursed her lips to the side, and turned around, walking in the opposite direction with her arms still folded.

"Whatever you say, Dezzi. Don't get yourself into any trouble because I'm not bailing you out!" she said as she walked away.

"Don't worry about me. I'm all good."

To be honest, I didn't know where I was going. I didn't know where Deray lived, and had no idea how to find out without people asking a million and one questions, or people thinking something was going on that really wasn't. As I drove around thinking, I found myself in front of the club. I was hoping that for some strange reason, Deray would be there, but I didn't see his car. I did, however, see Byron's car. I pulled around and parked my car in the back parking lot next to Byron's black Escalade. I quickly jumped out of my car and ran to the door and rang the buzzer. I heard some scuffling inside, but no one came to answer. I tried to peak through the tiny window and didn't see anything. I tried the buzzer again, and I finally heard Byron's voice. Instead of asking for the passcode, he just said, "Who is it?"

"It's me, Byron! Dezzi! Can you open up for a second?"

"Hold up a second, Dezzi."

What the hell is he doing in there? I thought to myself.

A couple of minutes later, Byron opened the door, but without moving to the side to let me in. He stood in front of me and said, "What's goin' on? Did you forget something?"

I looked around curiously, trying to see what Byron seemed to be trying to hide. Byron had a towel and kept wiping his face. I knew he was a big guy, but I didn't understand why he would be sweating so profusely if he wasn't doing some major work inside.

"I didn't forget anything here, but I was trying to find Deray," I said softly. "Are you ok, though?"

"Yeah. Why you ask that?" Byron asked.

"You're sweating like crazy."

"I was just in here doing some cleaning, but forget about that. What you need to find Deray for?"

"I think I left my phone in his car last night, and I need to get it back asap."

"In his car, huh?"

Byron shook his head.

"It ain't nothing like that. He just wanted to give me a talk last night, and we sat in the car and took a drive."

I didn't even know why I was explaining anything to Byron. I didn't care whether or not he thought anything was going on between me and Deray. Who would he tell, and why would he even care?

"Byron! What are you doing? Did you forget about me?" I heard a familiar voice say in the background.

I put my hands on my hips and said, "And who is that?"

"Uh, that's one of the housekeepers who helps me keep the it clean up in here."

After Byron told that big bold-faced lie, all of a sudden I saw Britt standing behind him.

"So you're just gonna stand here and lie to me, Byron?"

"What I gotta lie to you for?"

"I don't know. You tell me, or the housekeeper standing behind you," I said sarcastically.

Byron turned around and immediately wiped his forehead with the towel he was carrying around. Now I knew why he was sweating so much.

"Baby, you didn't have to come back here. I was on my way back," Byron said to Britt.

"Baby?" I said surprisingly.

"Dezzi, this ain't nobody's business, just like you and Deray ain't nobody's business."

"Wait a minute! Her and Deray?" Britt said. "Well, well, well. I guess we all have our secrets, huh, Dezzi?" she continued.

"Look. There is nothing going on with me and Deray! I just need to get my phone I dropped in his car. Y'all don't have to worry about me saying anything. As far as anyone knows, I didn't see y'all today. Byron, can you please just tell me where Deray lives?"

"Now what if I tell you that, and when you get over there, he has his woman friend or someone there?"

"I don't care who's there. This is a matter of life and death. I need my phone!"

Britt then put her two cents in and said, "Oh, Byron! I know why she's so desperate. She got a man at home and she can't tell him where she left her phone!"

I thought Britt was the quiet one, but I guess I was wrong. That was a front she just put on in front of the other girls. She was one of those that was a sponge that sat in the room and soaked up all the info she could and talked about us later. I knew all about that kind, but now I had figured her all out. It was ok, though. I now had something on her, too.

"You're right, Britt. I do have a man, and it is detrimental that I get my phone back and get back home before he wakes up and realizes I'm not laying next to him. I'm sure Deray wouldn't like what was going on around here after hours either. I'm sure he's pretty strict about this kind of thing, but your secret just might be safe with me, if I can get the information I came for."

Britt rolled her big, almond shaped eyes and said, "Byron, give her the damn address."

She then turned her pretty, fat ass around and walked back to wherever she came from. Byron took a deep breath and gave me the address.

"You better not say nothing about what you just saw or where you got his address!" he threatened.

"I got you, Boo! You just better be glad I like y'all. Y'all kinda make a cute couple!" I said as I laughed and ran back towards my car.

I had wasted way too much time messing around with Britt and Byron trying to get some information that Byron could've given me right away. I was just glad that I caught Britt there or

I probably would've never gotten the address. Deray lived about forty-five minutes away from the club. I knew for a fact that I would never make it back home before Adonis woke up, but I would just have to face the repercussions when I got home. I would call him as soon as I got my phone to make things go a little smoother once I got home.

As I drove, I listened to the Goapelé station on Pandora. I was praying I didn't run into a bad situation once I got to Deray's house. I didn't want to intrude on him and any woman. I know how women can be, but by the way I was dressed, any woman should've been able to tell that I wasn't trying to impress any man.

When I finally made it to the address that Byron gave me, my first thought was that he had messed me around just to get rid of me. My GPS had led me to a small brick building with an entrance on one side and an exit on the other. There was a gate, which made me feel like I was at a tollbooth, so I just couldn't enter. I stopped at the building and there was a white older woman with a short red haircut.

She slid open the glass window she was behind and said, "Hi, can I help you?"

"Yes. I don't know if I'm at the right place. I was given this address, but maybe I was given the wrong address."

"Who are you looking for?"

"Deray Goodland."

"And what is your name?"

"Is this where I can find Deray?"

"Name please," the woman stated, sounding as if she was getting frustrated with me.

I didn't understand why she just couldn't tell me if I was at the right place.

"Dezzi Kimbrough," I said reluctantly.

The women said, "Give me a minute," as she slid the glass window closed.

I sat at the gate for about three minutes, and just as I was about to go in reverse to go back home phoneless, the gate began to open.

The red-headed woman opened the window, and said, "Mr. Goodland has given me permission to let you enter. Go right ahead. Sorry for the trouble, she said as she smiled, and all the wrinkles around her eyes appeared.

"No problem. I know you're just doing your job," I said as I drove through the gate.

As I drove further and further down the road, I began to think I was being punked. I had to have driven at least a quarter of a mile before I began to see a house, and it wasn't just a house. I thought I had just reached the Playboy Mansion. I then saw Deray standing in front in a navy blue robe, pajama pants, and house shoes, with his hands in his pockets. He gestured for me to park in the driveway on the left side of his huge mansion. Maybe Deray was a pimp. I didn't know any club owner who could've afforded something even close to equivalent to what I was seeing with my own eyes at that moment.

I parked, and by the time I was getting out of the car, Deray had made it halfway there.

"I see you slept on it and made your decision pretty early, huh? You even did your research to find out where I lived, because I know I didn't tell you. I don't tell anyone where I live unless either, I trust them, or they've made a commitment to me, and you don't qualify for either," Deray said.

"Ouch, that hurt!" I said, as I stood in front of him.

"Well, did you want me to lie? How can I trust a person I barely know?"

"But you were willing to "take care of me" last night," I replied.

"Yes, and I still am, but that doesn't mean I have to trust you. Trust comes eventually, but am I really this easy to find, or did Byron's soft ass give in to you?"

"Can I just get what I came for?" I asked, trying not to have to answer that question.

"Yeah, it must've been Byron. You must've caught him and Britt, and this was his way of hushing you up."

I had to admit, Deray was a smart man. He already knew what was going on in his club, but I still wasn't answering that.

"I just came to get my phone. I think I dropped it in your car."

"Oh, is that the only reason you came to see me?"

"Yes, unfortunate for you, it is."

Deray laughed and said, "I love your sarcasm. It's really a turn on. Follow me. We'll go look for your phone."

I followed Deray to one of his five garages, and he opened the one that had his white Maserati in it. I was curious as to what other cars he had hidden away. Deray opened the passenger side door and I immediately saw my phone on the floor in between the door and the seat.

"And there it is, thank God," I said, as I bent down to grab it.

As I came back up and turned around, Deray was directly behind me, standing so close, we almost kissed for the second time.

"Well, I'm glad you found what you were looking for," Deray said. "Now why don't you come in and have breakfast with me? My chef was just finishing up cooking me an omelet. It's not two, but I'll be more than willing to share," Deray said, sounding very persuasive.

"I really have to go. I left while my boyfriend was still asleep, so I know he's already up looking for me."

"He's already gonna be pissed, so what's a little more pissed gonna hurt. By the way, I thought he was your fiancé," Deray said.

"He is my fiancé," I said with a confused look on my face.

"You just called him your boyfriend," Deray said, as he told me to follow him inside. "Don't worry so much. I'll give you your space to think of something creative to tell him when you call him in the next five minutes. You don't want him to worry too much."

Deray was smooth as hell and had a whole lot of swag. I followed him. as I was told. When we got inside, I was scared to touch anything. Everything looked expensive. Even the ashtray I seen sitting on the dining room table with a cigar sitting in it.

Deray looked back at me as I followed him to wherever he was taking me, and said, "You started thinking of something yet?"

"Yeah, I'm thinking. Thinking I should be getting in my car going home."

"If you really thought that, you would be in your car on your way home. I didn't put a gun to your head."

"Whatever," I said.

"Here. Go in there and think of something good to tell him that will give yourself a little time to enjoy yourself," Deray said, as he opened the door to a room that I didn't even know what to call. Let me just say that if I was a guest staying there for a while, I wouldn't have had any reason to leave that room, or whatever it was, because it had everything that I would've needed during my stay.

Deray closed the door, and as soon as he did, I sat on one of the sofas as I looked around trying to figure out what the hell I was doing. I had to think of something believable to tell Adonis and I had no idea what that was going to be. I thought to just call him and let whatever came out of my mouth flow, but then again, I was afraid of what might've come out of my mouth.

After about five minutes, I dialed Adonis' number. It rang one time and he immediately answered, sounding wide awake.

Before I could say a word, he said, "I see you found your phone."

"Well, good morning to you, too," I said, trying to throw the guilt off of me onto him."

"Good morning. Now where did you find your phone, and where are you now?"

"I went to Monét's house, thinking it was in her car, but Deanna had accidentally grabbed it, so it was at her house all the way across town, so that's where I am now. She wants to go to breakfast, so I'm waiting on her to get out of the shower so we can grab something to eat and I'll be on my way home."

"I can't believe you trust them like that. Breakfast, Dezzi, and that's it! No alcohol." Adonis said, sounding stern.

"I promise. I love you, Baby."

"I love you, too, but about this breakfast thing, so you're just gonna leave Ess here hanging out in the living room, huh? I thought that was your girl!"

"Oh shit! I forgot Ess was there. Never mind. I'll tell Deanna another day."

"Don't worry about it. Ess went home a little while ago. Go ahead and have your little breakfast. I'll be here waiting, unless money calls."

"Ok, Baby. I'm so sorry about last night."

"I'll forgive you . . . eventually," Adonis said, jokingly. "See you later."

My heart was beating fast as hell. I couldn't believe I had just gotten away with that lie. I guess I was real creative, just like Deray had told me to be. I still felt bad about leaving Ess at the house, so while I was still alone, I decided to call her to let her know I was ok.

"So you got your phone back, I see."

"Dang, I can't get any slack!" I replied to Ess.

"Slack for what? Leaving me at your house with your fiancé who woke up looking for you, grilling me like I knew where your ass was? Girl, I know you, and I know you're up to no good, but like I already told you, I'm not covering for your ass anymore!"

"You don't have to, because there's nothing to cover up. I was just calling you to let you know I had found my phone. Deanna had accidentally picked it up last night, and I already called Adonis and cleared everything up with him. Everything's good, but thank you so much. I appreciate you."

Deray walked in holding a glass of orange juice, and tapping his watch as I was talking to Ess.

I put my finger up to my lips, gesturing for Deray to remain quiet. I could tell by the look on his face that he wasn't very fond of that treatment. I continued my conversation with Ess anyway.

"Yeah, yeah," Ess said.

"You know I do. You've done a lot for me."

"Yeah, I know. Gone and get home to your fiancé. I'm in the middle of a project for school since you woke me up all early. I'll talk to you later."

When I hung up the phone, Deray asked, "Did you just tell me to be quiet in my own house?"

"Um, yes, I did, because you know if you said something you could've really caused some chaos."

"Ok, don't let it happen again," he replied.

The thing about Deray was that he was so smooth, even when he was being obsessive and domineering. It was sexy, and I could tell he knew it. That's why I couldn't even take him serious.

"Come on to the dining room with me," he continued.

When we arrived in the dining room, the chef was setting two places at the long table.

"I wanted you to have your own omelet, so I had him to cook another one while you were making your call," Deray said, as he pulled the chair out at one of the places the chef had set for me to sit down. He sat in the other seat catty-cornered from me. Deray put the glass of orange juice he was holding in front of me.

"Thank you," I said appreciatively.

"You're very welcome."

I took a sip and asked, " What is this, because it's definitely not just orange juice?"

Deray laughed and said, "It's a Dreamsicle."

"Um, the Dreamsicle I'm familiar with comes on a stick and is frozen."

Deray squinted at me and asked, "How old are you?"

Trying not to sound nervous because I had used my fake ID to get the dancing job, I said, "Twenty-one."

Deray shook his head, and said, "You're still a baby. An adult Dreamsicle is Sunny Delight mixed with a little Pinnacle Vodka. Don't worry. I'm not trying to get you drunk. I'm trying to get to know the real Dezzi, and not Desire, a little bit, if that's ok with you."

I remembered my promise to Deray that I wouldn't drink any alcohol, but I took a sip of the Dreamsicle, and it was so good, I really didn't think it could be considered alcohol.

"I don't see a problem with that, but next time you want to serve me any amount of alcohol, please let me know first."

"No problem. I just thought it would be something light and refreshing for you, but I understand. You don't have to drink it."

"I actually like it. Thank you," I said as the chef sat our plates in front of us that contained our omelets that looked absolutely delicious.

"I hope you're not a vegetarian," Deray said.

"No, not hardly."

"Are you saying that because you love meat, or you dislike veggies?"

"Neither."

"Ok. Good. So you don't mind the mushrooms, spinach, and peppers? I probably should've asked what you liked, first."

"No. I'm fine. Everything looks great. I'm not much of a picky eater."

"How long do I have you?" Deray came out of nowhere and asked.

I tried to act dumb and said, "What do you mean?"

"Exactly what I asked. How long can you stay here with me today?"

"Not long," I said, even though I kinda wished I had all day to spend with him. He was mysterious, and just as much he wanted to find out more about me, I wanted to find out more about him, too.

"That's not good," he replied, right before putting a forkful in his mouth. After he finished chewing, he said, "I wanted to show you around this place and do some more talking."

"Speaking of this place . . . This huge place . . . Is this really how strip club owners live?" I asked.

"Yeah, if you're business oriented. You have to know how to run your business, and create other businesses out of that main business."

Being nosey because I have no shame, I asked, "So what other businesses have you created?"

Deray looked at me as if he was surprised that I had enough nerve to ask him that.

"As I told you when you first got here, I don't trust you yet, and we're not committed to each other. As a matter of fact, you're committed to someone else, so I doubt that we will ever be on that level."

"Ok. That's fair enough. It didn't hurt to ask."

"I can tell you, I'm legit."

"You didn't even have to tell me that," I replied.

"I know, but I decided to because I wanted to."

It seemed like my question irritated Deray so I decided to finish my meal and drink in silence. He kept looking at his phone, which kept vibrating. I started to tell him how rude he was being, but I kept it to myself.

When we both finished, he stared at me and said, "Girl, I wish we had more time, but we don't, so I'll let you leave with the phone you came to get. Thank you for having breakfast with me, though. It gets depressing eating alone sometimes."

"Well, maybe we can do it again some day," I said with a grin.

Deray stood up and pulled my chair out so I could stand. He gave me a hug and he smelled so good. He actually smelled so good that I couldn't let him go. He was the one that had to pull away from me, which was a little embarrassing.

"You ok?" he asked.

"I'm good. You smell very nice."

"Thanks. Let me walk you to your car."

I followed Deray to the front door, admiring the beautiful, exotic hardwood floors throughout. I was feeling a way I had never felt before and I didn't know whether I liked it or not. When Deray opened the front door to let me out, he first looked into my eyes as if he was asking me if I was really ready to leave. I looked away to disengage the connection that was quickly forming. We walked slowly to my car, making small talk about how nice the weather was. When we got to my car, I told him thank you for everything, especially for allowing me into his home without notice. He told me I was welcome any time, and gave me his cell phone number as we talked so I didn't have to go on a wild-goose hunt the next time I needed him. Deray opened my car door as we said goodbye. As I was getting into my car, Deray attempted to kiss me, but it didn't work out after the bib on my baseball cap hit him in the forehead.

Deray looked embarrassed and I couldn't do anything but giggle. He didn't give up that easily. He removed my cap, grabbed me by the waist, and kissed me. I kissed him back and it felt so good. It was one of those kisses that made your clit throb. When I came to, and realized what I was doing I pushed him away, took a deep breath, and exhaled.

"Deray, we can't do this. I'm engaged and in love with my fiancé."

Deray replied, "Listen to me. That's the second time we've kissed, and both times I think we both felt something strong. You know what that means, Baby Girl? You're not as "in love" as you say you are."

"I gotta go," I said, as I jumped in my car and sped off, leaving Deray standing in his driveway. I stopped at the gate and waited for the woman to allow me to leave. She slid open her window and told me to have a good rest of my day. I told her thank you as the gate opened, and I headed home to Adonis . . . my fiancé who I was in love with, no matter what Deray had just said.

Chapter Twenty-Nine

All the way home, I couldn't help but to think about the life Deray was living, and the life I could be living if it wasn't for Adonis. I had a man who was offering to take care of me and was asking me to do nothing for it. My mind was in shambles. I loved Adonis so much, but the more I thought about what he did with the money my mom had put away for us, the more it seemed like I disliked him. I started wondering if I could love and hate someone at the same time. I really didn't think I had any hate in my heart for Adonis. I just resented what he did.

When I pulled up at home, I assumed money had called Adonis because his car was gone. I felt a little relieved because I really needed some time alone. When I walked in the house, I could smell the scent of Adonis' cologne, which meant it hadn't been long since he'd left. I ran upstairs and grabbed my laptop and a blanket so that I could relax on the sofa while I reviewed my finances. I could see what was in the bank, but I had no idea of what Adonis had on hand. He kept telling me we were good, but I needed to see it, meaning, I was going to have to talk to him about depositing some of the money he was making into the bank so I wasn't worried all the time. If he was allowed to make withdrawals, he needed to be making deposits as well. He had started off making deposits, but that started becoming less and less, until they were non-existent. I assumed the mortgage was getting paid since we hadn't gotten a foreclosure notice.

I logged into my bank account, hoping I didn't have to have that talk with Adonis, and he had suddenly begun making deposits, however, that wasn't the case. It was the same that it had been. Adonis hadn't deposited not one dime. All I could do was shake my head. While sitting there, staring at the computer screen, I decided I wasn't going to have that talk with Adonis. I didn't even want him to have access to my accounts any longer. Instead, I decided to take his name off of everything since he had taken what he wanted anyway. I would just deposit my money that I was making into my account instead of hiding it around the house. The last thing I needed was for Adonis to find that money and ask where I was getting it from, or even invest it in his "business".

I couldn't take care of any bank business today since it was Sunday, but that was number one, next to class, on my agenda for the next day. After making those plans, I went upstairs, took a little nap, and cleaned myself up to make myself more presentable. I hadn't been to see Dezzigner Records yet, and I thought it was about time that I did. I put on a black, mock-neck sleeveless bodysuit, my dark-blue low-rise skinny jeans, and a pair of black, Red Bottom heels. I put my hair up in a cute Chinese bun and pulled down a few pieces on the side. I didn't do much to my face, besides put on some nude lip-gloss, and a little mascara on my fake lashes that Adonis had finally gotten used to.

When I pulled up to the studio, everything on the outside seemed very nice, but I didn't see a sign that signified in any way that it was named after me. As I was getting out of the car, I saw Adonis' car parked a few cars ahead of mine, so I knew he was inside. A few females were also walking towards the door as I was on my way up the stairs to where the front door was. As I was about to pull the glass door open, a male wearing sunglasses came and pushed the door open from inside.

"Damn girl! You sing, too?" he asked as he held the door open for me.

"No. I'm looking for Adonis."

"Oh. My badd. I wasn't meaning to disrespect my boy. You must be Dezzi."

"Yes, I am, and no disrespect taken," I said as I shook the dude's hand.

"I'm Cameron, but you can call me Cam."

"Nice to meet you Cam."

"I ain't never seen you around here. Do you know where you're going?" he asked.

"No, not really," I said. "Actually, this is my first time being here."

After I said that to Cam, I thought about the fact that Adonis had never even invited me to the studio. My first-time should've never had to consist of me just popping up unexpectedly.

"Damn!" Cam said, with surprise. "Let me take you to where Donnie's office is. I don't think he has a client right now."

As Cam took me to Donnie, I asked, "Who were those women walking in?"

"Oh. They're a singing group we're working with. I recently discovered them singing on a street corner."

"So what do you do around here?" I asked Cam, as we walked down the long hallway.

"I do a little bit of everything. I work in the A&R department, which is still under development, so most of the talent that comes through here, I bring in, and I work with them in the actual studio."

"So the business is doing pretty good financially, huh?" I asked trying to be as nosey as I could to get as much information as I could.

"It's doing ok, to be a new business, but this isn't the only job I have. If you have a family, this right now is not gonna keep food on the table, but it'll pay out in the end."

That sounded like some bullshit that Adonis had fed him, like the bullshit he was feeding me, and was all the information I needed. Cam didn't know just how much he had helped me out. We finally made a left, and went halfway down the hall, and Cam knocked twice on the door and walked in.

"Hey! Look who I found," Cam said as we walked into Adonis' office.

He was sitting at his desk, trying to look important, and a woman was sitting right across from him with her back facing us, but as soon as we walked in she turned around and stared me up and down.

Adonis quickly rose up, and said, "Hey, Bae! What you doin' here?"

"I realized I hadn't been by to see what my money paid for, so I thought since I didn't have anything else to do, I'd stop by and check it out."

Cam took that as a sign to leave, and said, "Nice to meet you Dezzi! See you later Donnie. I'll probably be back later after I get off."

"All right man. I'll see you later," Adonis replied.

I waved as Cam ran out the door.

"Dezzi, this is my client, Toi. Toi, this is Dezzi."

Toi stood up and shook my hand, and told me it was a nice to meet me.

"It's a pleasure to meet you as well," I replied to her.

"Well, we were just finishing up here, so I can show you around if you want, Baby. I don't have to be in the studio for about another hour to work with an artist."

With my arms folded, I said, "That would be nice. I don't plan to stay that long anyway."

There were a million things going through my mind at that moment. I couldn't stop thinking about what Cam said regarding his money situation. Adonis handed Toi a folder full of documents and shook her hand. It seemed like this was his first time meeting with her. I just hoped she didn't portray what all of his female artists were like because she looked pretty rough around the edges.

Before walking out of the office, Toi told me bye, and told Adonis that she would have her lawyer to go over everything with her and would be getting back with him soon.

I was thinking to myself, *Lawyer? Girl, bye! It don't look like you can even afford a place to live!*

After the door shut behind her, Adonis said, "See, girl! I got it going on around here," as he gave me a hug and swung me around.

Once he let me go, I folded my arms and said, "So why does Cam have to work another job?"

"Because he chooses to, and that's his business. Come on. Let me show you around," he said as, he opened the door for me.

Adonis took me straight to the studio, which was very nice. I saw quite a few people walking through the halls before we got there. I was confused as to whether some of them were artists or actually worked in the building, which caused me to have more questions. If all these people worked in the building, and Adonis supposedly owned the place, who was paying all these people? Adonis seemed to be real short with me when I asked him about Cam, so I chose not to ask him any more questions. I knew how irritable Adonis could get when he felt like I didn't trust him. After the entire tour of the place, I still hadn't seen any sign that read "Dezzigner Studios". I wondered if it even existed. That was one thing I would ask Adonis about, but right now wasn't the time nor place, so I would wait until we were in the comfort of our own home.

"See you later! Love you, Babe," I said as I got into my car, and Adonis leaned in to give me a kiss as he closed my car door.

I sat there with my car running as I watched Adonis walk back inside "Dezzigner Studios" and get back to work. I stared at the large, stone building, making sure I wasn't missing anything. I felt like I should've been more impressed after seeing what Adonis invested in and was so proud of, but I wasn't. I felt like I was more impressed just by hearing about it. I felt like a kid who had just been told there was no Santa Clause. After that visit, I honestly believed that I was the breadwinner in the household, and that scared me.

I drove around the city in circles, not knowing where to go or what to do next. I picked up my cell to call Ess, but I didn't even want to talk to her about what I had just encountered. I didn't even know what I had encountered, so how would I explain it to someone else? I needed someone to make me feel some relief, and make me feel like everything would be ok, so I called someone who I felt could do just that.

"Hey, Love. You miss me already, huh?" the voice on the other end said loudly over the music playing in the background.

"You sound like you're having a good time," I said to Deray.

"I am, but I'd be having an even better time if you were here with me."

"Where are you?" I asked curiously.

"I'm at this Jazz club called Café 290 on Hildebrande. You're probably too young to appreciate a place like this though."

"I know of the place. My mom used to go sometimes, so yeah, I think I'll pass."

Well, you want me to meet you somewhere, or I can pick you up? I know you called for something . . . Not just to see where I was."

"I was just cruising around, and thought of you."

"It's nice to know I'm on your mind. Is everything ok? It's Sunday, you have the night off, and you want to be driving around talking to your boss on the phone?"

"I wish I did have to work tonight. Maybe it would keep my mind off some things that I'm stressing out about," I said, sounding pitiful as hell.

"Dezzi, don't stress over things you can't control. You'll kill yourself doing that, and you're way too young to be stressing out about anything. Is it school? Got finals or something coming up?"

"No. Other things. You're right though, I'm too young to be stressing over this kind of stuff, but I made my bed, and you know the rest."

"I don't like the way you sound right now. I'm about to get up and head home. You meet me there. Ok?"

"No, Deray. I'm good. I don't want to bring down your mood."

"No one has the power to bring down my mood, but I guarantee you that I can make you feel better."

I had driven so long that I was only about ten minutes away from Deray's home.

"Ok. I guess."

"I'm walking out right now. I'll be home in about twenty minutes."

"Ok. See you then," I said, already feeling better, but knowing I was doing something I had no business doing at all.

Since I was closer to Deray's house than he was, I didn't head straight there. I went to one of the local liquor stores and bought a bottle of wine. I just wanted to take a few sips out the bottle before meeting with Deray, just to calm my nerves a little. I found a little secluded street, and did just that. I was starting to understand why alcohol had become my mom's best friend. It gave me such a calming sensation, and I could feel comfortable doing and saying almost anything. It took me away from reality temporarily when I needed it. I regretted ever judging her, and began to feel like I was more like her than I thought. I leaned back in my seat and closed my eyes as I took my first sip of Moscato. As I sipped, I felt my phone vibrate. I thought it may have been Deray making a change of plans, but it was Adonis texting me, just to thank me for stopping by to show him some love, and that's why he loved me so much. I put the bottle of Moscato back up to my lips, but this time took much more than a sip. I replied to Adonis and told him it was a pleasure, and of course, told him I loved him, too, as I got ready to pull off and meet with another man.

I had perfect timing because as I was driving down the road to Deray's secluded home, I saw lights in front of me, and his gate opening up. He saw me coming, and waited to let down the gate until after I pulled through. The booth was empty, so I assumed he didn't have anyone working there all day. I pulled into the same parking space I had been in when I was at his house earlier. Before I could grab my purse, he was opening my car door letting me out. I stood up and he immediately gave me a hug.

"I'm so glad you decided to come back. I was a little disappointed when you left earlier, but I did enjoy our breakfast together."

I smiled as I said, "I enjoyed it, too."

I could tell Deray was old school, as he grabbed by hand and walked me to his door. He only let it go to unlock the door and welcome me back inside. I stood in the foyer, where there hung a huge chandelier above us, until he told me in which direction to go.

"Follow me," he said, as I followed him up the spiral staircase.

I hadn't been upstairs earlier because I didn't have a lot of time for Deray to show me around. Once we got upstairs, he went to the left. I continued to follow him, but I did look back and saw several doors at the other end of the hallway. We got to a set of double doors and when he opened them, I saw the largest bedroom I had ever seen in person. My house was pretty big, but was absolutely no comparison to what I was currently experiencing. His bed was larger than a king-sized, and the television on the wall spread from one end of the wall to the other end. He didn't just have a sitting area in his bedroom. It was an entire living room. The entire thing was just crazy. I couldn't believe my eyes.

He turned towards me and said, "You like?"

Cheesing, I said, "I love it! You have great taste to be a man."

"Well, I had a little help from my interior decorator."

"Well, both of you did a good job."

"Sit down and relax," Deray said.

"Where should I sit?" I asked.

"Wherever you're comfortable. I'm not here to make you do anything that you don't want to do."

As I walked over and sat on the edge of the bed, Deray grabbed the television remote and turned on the TV. He then walked over and stood in front of me. He knelt down on one knee as if he was going to propose, and lifted my legs up, one by one, and took my heels off.

"Beautiful feet," he said, as he kissed both of them.

He walked over into the living room area, putting my shoes out of the way, and came back over to sit next to me.

"You look different from how you looked this morning. What did your afternoon consist of? It looks like you went and took care of some business."

I looked at him and said, "I guess you can say that. I went home first and took care of some things online, then went and visited my fiancé at work."

I was sure to say "fiancé" that time because Deray was sure to let me know the last time when I didn't refer to him as that.

"Oh, ok. Doesn't sound like much fun, but ok," he replied.

Sarcastically, I said, "Let me guess. We could've had more fun."

"Sure could've."

I crawled to the top of the bed and leaned up against the leather headboard, and said, "So, tell me, Mr. Deray, if I would've stayed earlier, what would we have done?"

Deray followed me up to the top of the bed and said, "You seem to be getting comfortable."

"Don't worry about me," I replied. "Just answer the question."

"You know, that's no way to be talking to your boss."

I looked around, and said, "Um, I think we're way beyond a boss/employee relationship right now."

"Oh, so does that mean I'm getting somewhere with you?" Deray asked.

I folded my arms and said, "Can you please just answer the initial question?"

Deray grinned, and looking directly in my eyes, said, "We would've done whatever you wanted to do. I have an inside Jacuzzi and pool, and I take a swim daily. You could've taken it with me today. I like to horseback ride and today was a perfect day to do that. I have two horses out back."

"Oh really?" I said, sounding extremely impressed. Now this was a man who had made things happen for himself.

"Yes, now did that sound more interesting than your day?"

"I guess it did, but it is what it is. I don't have it like you."

"But you could," Deray said, as he straddled me, and began kissing me.

I didn't attempt to stop him because I didn't want him to stop. Everything about it felt so right, even though I knew it was so wrong. Deray got up and slid my body down so that I was laying flat on the bed. He then grabbed the remote, turning the TV off, and hit a button on the wall by the headboard, which caused music to begin to play. He bent over and gently kissed me again on the lips. This time, without tongue. He then began unbuttoning my jeans. He suddenly stopped, and looked me in the face. I didn't know what he was thinking.

He then said, "Before I continue, tell me to stop if you want me to stop."

I thought about it for about ten seconds, and I said, without a doubt in my mind, "I don't want you to stop."

Deray pulled my jeans over the heels of my feet, and I bent my knees so that he could unbutton my bodysuit from in between my legs. His hands were so soft, and felt go good gliding across my body. After unbuttoning the three buttons keeping my bodysuit intact, he raised it up over my head. I had decided to go braless today, so I was completely naked. As my knees were still bent, Deray pushed my legs back even further, and I could feel his entire tongue enter my moist place of pleasure. He teased and licked until I came, screaming so loud that if he'd had neighbors, they would've called the cops. He then climbed on top of me and kissed me so I could taste my own delicious juices. As he stood up, I held on to his waist, and he stood in between my legs as I unbuckled his belt, and undid his button to the black slacks he had on with a white fitted V-neck shirt. His pants dropped to the floor, exposing his boxers, which his very friendly partner in crime was poking through.

I gently pulled down his boxers, and lowered my head just enough to put all of him in my mouth. Deray put one hand on the back of head as he moaned. I gagged, but kept bobbing my head up and down as I massaged his balls. He sounded like he was about to cum, which I was not ready for him to do, and apparently we were on the same page. He lifted my head up by my chin, and lifted me up by my arms. We wrapped our arms around each other as he kissed me all over my neck. I turned us around as if we were dancing, so that he was backed up against the bed. I pulled his shirt up over his head and admired his muscular physique. I then pushed him in the chest with the palm of my hand so that he would fall back onto the bed. I then crawled on top of him as he waited to feel me from the inside. To be honest, I couldn't wait to feel all of him inside of me, and just as I'd expected from the looks of things, it was the best feeling in the world. We both moaned simultaneously as I felt his python reach every sensitive spot within my warm, snug secret place. I fit him like a glove. Perfectly. We fucked so long and so hard, I had multiple orgasms, which I had never experienced before.

Chapter Thirty

After the lovemaking that I had just experienced, I hated to have to bid farewell to Deray for the evening. Adonis was good, but he was still young and had some learning to do. I just hadn't realized how inexperienced he was because he was my one and only. I was sure that Deray was very experienced. He was old enough to be my father, but I didn't think of him that way because he didn't look nor act his age of thirty-eight.

We laid together, cuddled up for about an hour, and I told Deray I had to go.

He held me close, and said, "You don't have to go. You want to go."

"No. I really don't want to go. You just don't know how much I don't want to go, but I have obligations at home. I really enjoyed myself though."

Deray sat up, and said, "I really hope you come to your senses soon, and realize where you belong."

"I guess you think that's here with you."

"I don't think. I know," he replied. "You'll realize it though. I've been waiting on a woman to give all of this to. Someone who would deserve and appreciate it."

"How do you know I deserve it?" I asked.

"Because I can feel it."

"Let me ask you something." I said.

"Go right ahead."

"You don't think I'm too young for you?"

Without hesitation, Deray said, "Not at all." Age ain't nothin' but a number. Is that what's bothering you? You think I'm too old for you? Age is all in the mind, and I could see if you were underage making me look like a pedophile or something, but that's nothing I should be concerned about, right?"

"No. I just know we don't know each other like that, so I don't want you to get to know me and realize I'm not at all what you want."

"Well, let's just enjoy what we're doing, get to know each other, and see what happens. No one has to know a thing." Deray replied.

"That's fair."

"Good."

After our little talk, we showered together, I got dressed, and went home as if nothing had happened. I hadn't heard from Adonis, and he hadn't made it home by the time I got there. Deray was still on my mind, so I sent him a goodnight text, and he replied right away with a heart.

Adonis finally made it home that night, telling me about his long day, and how one of his artists was working on a track and just couldn't get it right. He seemed frustrated, but I still needed some questions answered.

As we laid in bed, I said, "Baby?"

"Yes, Dezzi?"

"I didn't see any signs today when I came by the studio that said "Dezzigner Studios". That is the name of it, right?"

"Yeah. Signs are expensive, Bae. I just haven't been able to get that part taken care of."

I rolled over from my side, and laid on my back, and said, "So you're telling me out of the money you've made out of this and the five million dollars you took, you weren't able to get, let's just say, a two thousand dollar sign?"

Adonis quickly sat up and said, "How long am I gonna have to hear about that money. Is money more important to you than us?"

"No, but you did do what anyone would call some shady shit."

"So now you don't trust me and believe me when I say the name of the studio is "Dezzigner Studios?"

"To tell you the truth, talking to Cam today, it doesn't sound like he's making much out of this studio thing. He said it's doing ok for being new. Have you even been paying the mortgage? I don't want to wake up one day with a foreclosure notice on the door."

Adonis sat there shaking his head. "I feel it's some fucked up shit that you don't believe in your man. I'm not gonna let anything happen to you. I've been there for you and I'm not going anywhere. I got this. Let me be a man!"

"Ok, but I have one more question."

"What?" Adonis said, sounding even more frustrated.

"Who were all those people walking through the building? If you're the owner, do they work for you, and if so, who's paying them?"

"Hold up. You said one more question and that was like a ten in one."

I rolled my eyes and said, "Can you just please answer?"

"Yes! They all work for me and I pay them a lil somethin'."

"Ok. That's all," I said as I rolled back over, with my back facing Adonis.

I could tell that he was still sitting up, and then I felt him get up out of bed. He went in the bathroom, and when he came back, he got all up behind me and started grinding.

"Now what am I gonna get for answering all your questions?"

I closed my eyes and said, "I'm not feeling good. I have a headache."

"All right. I got you," Adonis said as he rolled over and went to sleep.

I felt bad for not satisfying my man when he needed me to, but I had just been with Deray, and I felt that would've just been nasty. I couldn't do it. Adonis would get over it, just like I guess I would get over his lies, because I knew he wasn't telling the entire truth with the questions that I asked him tonight. He just didn't want me to worry, as always. I just tried not to think about it, and went to sleep so I could be prepared for class the next morning.

The next morning, Adonis woke up bright and early, grinding up on the back of me once again, massaging my clit.

"I let you get away last night, but not today," Adonis said, as he was behind me kissing me on my neck.

He pulled down my thong, and forced his rock hard dick inside of me. I moaned as he slid inside of me, and began massaging my nipples. His thrusts became harder and faster, and he groaned as he worked hard to satisfy me at the same time he satisfied himself. He acted as if he knew he was in competition with someone, when in my mind, there was no competition. We both came at the same time and breathed heavily as we continued to lay in our mixture.

Adonis kept his arm around me and said, "See what you missed last night?"

I giggled and said, "Yeah, I see."

"I had to catch you before you went to class. I took your tuition in last week. It was lower than what I thought it was going to be."

My heart started beating so hard, I thought it was going to jump out of my chest. My tuition was lower because I didn't think Adonis was going to have the money to pay it, so I had been paying on it. I guess I did need to trust him. Obviously he was making money if he could afford to pay my tuition. If he paid my tuition, I was sure he had paid the mortgage. That's if he had his priorities right, but I wasn't even going to bring it up anymore.

All I could say was, "Thank you, Bae."

"You're welcome. I told you I got you."

"I know you do. I don't know why I doubt you," I said, as I got up to get in the shower.

My cell phone vibrated, and I picked it up wondering who was texting me so early in the morning. It was Deray sending me a good morning text. I saw that I was going to have to get him in check and tell him no more morning texts.

"Who was that?" Adonis asked, as I walked towards the bathroom.

"It was a group text from my professor, telling us that class would be in a different lecture hall this morning."

I couldn't believe how fast that lie came into existence. I was already beginning to become good at it. Adonis followed me into the bathroom, as I knew he would.

"Please don't get that water steaming hot! You be trying to boil my balls!"

I laughed as I turned on the water and said, "Well, you can always wait until I'm done and take your own shower."

"Then I'll have to wait for some more hot water. I lose either way!"

I stepped into the shower and said, "You better come on in then!"

While we were in the shower, Adonis said, "I'll probably be real late tonight. I'm going to see my mom after I leave the studio. I haven't seen her in a while. Then, I have a group performing at one of the clubs tonight, so of course, I have to be there."

I hadn't heard Adonis mention his mom since everything that had happened with my mom. I didn't know if he thought it would cause me to feel some type of way, but I knew he was a momma's boy. I knew he was probably taking money to her, too, because he was always sure to take care of her. Shit, she was the main reason we were still here in Atlanta! The group he was talking about had to be the three girls I had seen the day before who Cam told me hadn't been around long. Adonis was probably trying to get some exposure for them.

"That's fine. I'll be ok. Maybe Ess and I will do something."

"Or you and Monét?"

"Maybe! And If I do decide on Monét instead of Ess?"

"All I have to say is you better not be out there doing no Monét type bullshit. Don't forget, I know her."

"I'm my own person. I just may pop up where you are, so be careful!"

"I have nothing to hide! You're certainly invited to come" Adonis said, and I believed him, but I had a whole lot to hide.

He didn't know how much of a favor he was doing for me by working late, and hopefully he never found out.

After my shower, and getting dressed, I left Adonis at home still relaxing. He didn't have to rush and be anywhere. On my way to class, I called Deray.

"Hey, Beautiful," he answered.

"Hey," I said sounding not so excited.

"What's wrong?" he asked.

"I'm not trying to be rude, but you can't be texting me early in the morning. He got to asking me questions."

"Questions like what?" Deray asked.

"Who was that texting me, of course."

"Tell him none of his business!"

"Now you know . . ."

"I'm just playing. I know you know how to lie because I know you had to tell at least one last night. My fault, though. I didn't mean any harm. I'll just wait 'til you text me in the morning. Don't make me wait too long, though. "

"I won't," I replied.

"I couldn't stop thinking about you last night," Deray said."

"I thought about you a lot, too, but we'll have to talk later. I'm about to walk into class."

"Ok, sweetheart. I'll see you later."

I had three classes today and they were all long and boring. I didn't think I learned one damn thing or took any notes. All I could think about was Deray. It was just something about him. I couldn't get him off of my mind. When it came time to go to work that evening, I felt different heading in. Deray's car wasn't outside yet, and I hadn't talked to him since before I went to class. I saw Byron at the door as usual, and knowing we both had secrets about each other made things feel very strange. When he let me in after I said the passcode, he just nodded his head at me. I couldn't even get a hello.

When I walked into the dressing room, the normal people were there, which was everyone who was always on time.

When I walked in, Britt looked at me with her pretty smile, and said, "Hey girl!" as if I didn't know the real deal.

"Hey, Britt," I said.

"Since when do you speak to people when they walk up in here?" Lisa asked Britt.

"I guess I'm just in a good mood today, and Dezzi cool people."

Lisa and Kelsey looked at each other with a confused look on their face. Other than that, everything else about that night at work seemed normal besides the fact that Deray was not in the front watching me as I performed, and when I got ready to leave, he texted me, telling me he was leaving too, and to meet him at his house. I did as I was told and we had another enjoyable night. He must've had everything planned out and knew I would do as he asked because he had the chef to have dinner ready for me. We had a delicious steak dinner, and our own dessert afterwards.

That went on almost every other night as Adonis worked his late nights. No one knew a thing. Byron and Britt probably had an idea, but even they didn't know for sure. None of the other girls noticed anything, and I knew not to mention anything to any of them. I knew how women were, and if I didn't even tell my best friend, Ess, what would make anyone think I would tell anyone else? Monét never even had the decency to tell me the real deal between her and Adonis' past. I thought she eventually would have, but she didn't. My sex life with Adonis did begin to suffer due to what was going on with me and Deray, and I was going to have to quickly find a way to fix it. Deray was slowly reeling me in, but I hadn't lost all feelings for Adonis. I couldn't just leave him like that. I had to have a good reason, and that was what I didn't have. Others probably would say I had five million reasons, but for some reason, that just wasn't a good enough reason. I felt like he had good intentions, so maybe that was the reason I didn't feel like that would've been a good enough reason to leave.

Chapter Thirty-One

I waited for Adonis to leave the house almost every evening, and this evening wasn't any different. Well, it was a little different. He was leaving a little early because he wanted to stop by one his cousin's houses to check on his aunt before he went in to work. His mom had told him she was sick. I had been searching all over for my ID, hoping Adonis hadn't found it, but I'm sure if he had there would've already been a million questions asked. I was pretty sure I had left it over Deray's house the last time I was over there. I actually didn't know when I had lost it, or even the last time I had seen it.

I had begun just popping up over Deray's house at if it were mine, and he didn't mind. Cathy, the lady at the gate, and I had become good friends since I was at his house so much. At the beginning, I wondered if there were any other women Deray wined and dined, but I no longer wondered about that because it didn't matter what time of day I went over Deray's house, there was never anyone else there. The only way he was wining and dining someone else was if he never invited them to his house.

"I was just making sure you were home, " I said while driving and talking on the phone to Deray one evening before going in to the club. "I'm on my way over there. I think I might've left my ID over there because I can't find it anywhere."

"Yeah, I'm here, and you know you don't have to explain why you're coming by."

"I know, but I don't want you to think I just be trying to check in on you."

"I know you just wanna see me. That's fine!" Deray said, laughing. "I'll look around for your ID before you get here. Park your car in the middle garage. I have one of my employees coming by from one of my other businesses, and I don't need him in all my business. You understand, right?"

"Of course I do. I'll see you in about ten minutes."

"Ok," Deray replied.

Deray would sometimes have me park in the garage when he was doing business at his house. I wasn't sure, but I sometimes thought he might've been doing something illegal and didn't want me to be in the middle of anything. I could've been completely wrong, but if I wasn't, it was a very familiar situation. He didn't seem like the type to be doing anything illegal, but I never put anything past anyone. I was ok as long as I knew he was looking out for my best interest.

When I got to Deray's house, Cathy opened the gate and waved, and I waved back. I used the garage opener Deray had given me to open the one he had told me to park in. I pulled in, and as soon as I did, he opened the door that led from the garage to the inside of the house. I waited for him to open my car door, as he always did. I had become extremely spoiled, and he knew it. I knew it was all a part of his plan to get me to stay with him, but I think it was harder than what he thought it would be.

"Hey, Babe," he said, as he gave me a hug and kiss.

"Hey!" I said, happy to see him. "Did you have any luck finding my ID?"

"Nope," he said. "You sure you left it here?"

"Honestly, I don't even remember the last time I saw it."

As we walked into the house I began looking around. I could tell Deray had looked under sofa cushions in the family room, but there were so many rooms in that house that I had been in, if it was there, there was no telling where it was.

While Deray continued to help me, I asked, "What time is your employee coming?"

"He'll be here in the next twenty minutes. He just called not too long ago, so I'm just gonna need your little pretty self to go in the bedroom and relax 'til we're done. We'll be done before you have to be at the club for showtime."

"You act like I don't know the routine by now. I know you don't like to conduct business around me."

"That's not it. I'm not trying to hide anything from you if that's what you think. I just don't like to mix business with pleasure, and you're my pleasure . . . Desire," Deray said, smiling and winking at me.

"Desire? Really? I've never heard you call me Desire."

"Because I don't like it," he replied in a serious tone.

"Why don't you like it? And you're the boss, so if you never liked it, why did you approve it when it was given to me?"

I don't like it because it's a stripper's name, and I don't like thinking of you as a stripper."

I was so confused at that moment. I didn't want to sound stupid with my response, so I thought real hard on it.

"But I am a stripper, right?" I asked, sounding not so sure anymore.

"You are, but that doesn't mean I like it. I already told you that you don't have to do this anymore. I'll provide everything you need or want. Just know you can stop anytime you want. You don't have to go get on that stage tonight if you don't want to. I know you've noticed I won't even watch you on the stage anymore. I can't stand being in the audience seeing those men enjoy you in a way that only I should. You'll always be Dezzi to me."

I was so flattered that Deray cared so much, and I could tell I was blushing. I understood exactly where he was coming from, but unless I was committed to him, I wasn't giving up my only method of income. Yes, he bought me things, and gave me money, but it would never be like my own. I didn't feel secure enough to depend on Adonis completely.

"You know I just like to have my own. I can always go find another club to work at so you don't have to see it," I said with a grin on my face.

"Now you know that definitely ain't about to happen!" Deray said, laughing. "You know if you're mine, everything that is mine is yours."

"You say that, but . . ."

"But what? You said earlier on that we didn't know each other like that so you really didn't trust me like that, and let's just see what happens. You know me now, so now what? What are we waiting for now?" Deray asked, with one eyebrow raised.

I was at a loss for words, and that rarely ever happened.

"Nothing to say, huh? I'm just saying because inquiring minds would like to know, but it you don't know, it's ok. I'll just continue to wait," he said and smiled.

Just then, Deray's cell phone rang. I was saved by the bell, because I still didn't have any intentions on leaving Adonis to be with Deray.

"Go ahead and let him through," I heard Deray say, which meant his employee was on his way through the gate.

Deray looked at me and I said, "All right. I'll be upstairs."

I ran up the stairs to the bedroom, and shut the door. I began looking all over for my ID while I was up there. The bedroom was where I was the majority of the time, so I was hoping it was someone in there. I would keep it in my pants pocket sometimes, so I was thinking maybe it had fallen out when I took them off one day. I pulled the sofa cushions off and found nothing. I looked under the bed, and in the walk-in closet. Still nothing.

I remembered a few times we had been in one of the other bedrooms down at the other end of the hall because Deray refused to let me lay on sheets if he hadn't gotten around to washing them. I knew better, but I opened the door and figured I could just creep down the hall real quick without anyone seeing me. As I opened the door and began walking on my tiptoes, I heard a familiar voice, which stopped me in my tracks. I slowly peeked over the staircase and saw Deray sitting in the living room with Adonis.

"What the fuck?" I whispered.

Was this some kind of joke? They were chatting it up more like friends than boss and employee. I knelt down to try to hear the conversation more clearly. That's when I realized it actually wasn't a very friendly conversation I was hearing.

"I paid you the five mill back, so now can I just get back to where I was with you. Everything was going good 'til I made one small mistake. I apologized and I gave it back. You know I was good for it anyway. You know I was always one of your best," Adonis said, sounding like he was trying to plead his case.

"You stole five million dollars from me while I trusted you with everything I had and thought I wouldn't notice? Now you want me to trust you again and put you back in the position you were in when you stole from me? That record label that you were starting must not be going too well," Deray said, looking at Adonis sternly.

"Not well enough for my style of living."

So, let me get this straight. You were eating and living real good off of me, steal from me to start something to make more money, you get yourself demoted, and you're still not making more money than before you got demoted?" Deray began laughing, and said, "That's some fucked up shit right there. If I told somebody that, they'd call you a dumb ass muthafucka. You must've been smart about something though."

"What's that?" Adonis asked with the dumbest look on his face I had ever seen.

"How the hell did you get that five million back to me so fast?"

Adonis held his head down in shame.

"You don't have to tell me, but I know you must've done some reckless shit to get that money within twenty-four hours of me finding out it was missing."

"I'm gonna tell you, because I look up to you, and it's been killing me inside."

Deray looked up at him, waiting to hear what he had to say. I knew what he had done, but I couldn't wait to hear him admit it to someone.

"I stole from my girl's bank account that she put me on. It was from her dad's life insurance policy. "

Deray's mouth almost hit the ground.

"I know. I'm pathetic."

"How did you explain that? I know she got rid of your ass," Deray said, sounding like he had no sympathy whatsoever for Adonis.

"No, she didn't. I told her I invested in the record label, which I did, but it was initially the money I took from you. I just paid it back out of her money. Now I can't even pay her back. I'm struggling trying to make sure we're ok, so I'm not just asking you to do this for me. It's for her too, and I know you don't know her, but she didn't deserve this. I've been lying to her ever since. I even told her the label was named after her, but it's not because I don't even own the entire label. I'm just an investor, and my dumb ass invested the most out of everyone."

Tears began running down my face. I couldn't believe how badly I had been deceived by Adonis. I had given him opportunity after opportunity to just be honest with me, and he still wasn't. He jacked off my money and left me with nothing!

"Is this the same girl I sent one of my guys to meet you to help clean up the mom's body?" Deray asked.

"Yes, Sir," Adonis said.

I couldn't believe Deray knew about my mom, and didn't even know he knew about my mom. I could tell Adonis had a lot of respect for Deray, but Deray no longer had much trust or respect for him.

"What kind of girl is this? Didn't she kill her own mom?"

"She's a good girl . . . A real good girl. She's just been through a lot and that was a complete accident. She freaked out, and because I love her so much I helped cover it up. She even gave up a full scholarship to Texas A&M for me. Now, I've done this to her, and she has nothing."

Deray shook his head in disappointment and said, "I'll be right back."

I watched Adonis as he sat there waiting for Deray to come back. He had his face in the palm of his hands and began pounding his fists into his face, which he should had. I wished I could have at that moment! I didn't feel sorry for him. He was sorry, and I couldn't live like that any longer. I couldn't trust him and trust was everything for me.

Deray returned a couple of minutes later with a bag. Adonis looked up at him as Deray stood over him.

"I'm not doing this for you. I'm doing this for the girl because she was dealt a real bad hand of cards when she ran across you," Deray said, as he handed the bag over to Adonis.

Adonis opened the bag and said, "Thank you for helping me help her."

He stood up. Deray put his hand out and Adonis shook it.

When Adonis got ready to turn around to walk towards the front door, Deray said, "Donnie."

Adonis turned around to look towards him.

"Be a man, and let me see what you can do with that. Turn it around and don't disappoint her or me. She's had enough disappointments in her life."

"I promise you I won't disappoint you again. Thank you for giving me a second chance."

"Get to work, Donnie," Deray said as Adonis walked out the door.

Deray slammed the door behind him, and I stayed exactly where I was with tears rolling down my face. When Deray began walking towards the staircase, shaking his head once again, he saw me at the top crying. He stormed up the stairs and wrapped his arms around me.

"I'm sorry, Dezzi. I'm so sorry. I didn't want you to find out like this, but I didn't know how to tell you."

I was confused about what Deray was apologizing to me about, but I was crying so hard at that point that I couldn't get the words out to ask him. He picked me up and carried me to the bed, laying me down. He then went in the bathroom and I could hear him running water. He came back and wiped my face with a warm towel as I tried to calm myself down. Deray kept whispering that he was sorry.

"What are you sorry about?" I was finally able to get out in a whimpering voice.

"I'm sorry for not telling you what other type of business I was in. You should've never been in this position without knowing the atmosphere you were in. Would I let you ever be in danger? Of course not, but you still should've known," Deray answered.

"Thank you for apologizing for not being honest with me, but you never lied to me. I just never asked. That's not what I'm so upset about."

"What is it then, Baby?"

"That was him!" I shouted, and began crying again.

"Him, who? Him, your fiancé?"

"Yes!"

"And he was talking about you?"

"Yes! He took all my money and lied to me about everything! I trusted him!"

"Oh my God! I cannot believe this! And I gave him more product, calling myself being nice, giving him another chance? How could I be so stupid?"

"It's just in your nature. He's a good guy. He's just made some bad choices."

"So he's the reason you had to resort to stripping. Son of a bitch! How could he put you in this position? You're not going to that club tonight. That's not even where you belong. Grab one of my t-shirts out the drawer and get comfortable. We have some talking to do."

Deray left out of the room and closed the door. I didn't know where he went, but I knew he was hot, so I assumed he went to let off some steam. I got undressed and put on one of Deray's tees. When he came back he seemed a lot more calm.

"Sorry. I had to go take me a shot of something. This shit just blew my mind."

"I know, and I know you have a lot of questions for me."

"I do, but I also know you've been through a lot, and I only know some of the things from the things Donnie told me about you in the past before I knew it was you he was talking about. I just don't want to ask the questions because I don't want to overstep my boundaries and ask the wrong thing. Turn off your phone and I'll turn off mine. We don't need any interruptions. Let's have a heart to heart, if you don't mind."

"I understand that, I said." I turned off my phone as I watched Deray turn off his.

"Ok. Let's see. Where do I begin?" I said, looking up at the ceiling.

I decided to begin with my dad and how he died. I then went into my mom with her drinking problem, and since Deray already knew about the accident with my mom, I told him the entire story of how that occurred. The entire time I was talking to him, his eyes became bigger, and his mouth opened wider. When I got done talking to Deray, I don't think anything he had ever seen or heard could beat anything I had just told him. He was speechless. He could do nothing but hold me in his big strong arms, and I let some more tears out until I fell asleep. I had held so many things in for so long, I completely broke down. I felt safe and secure where I was currently and didn't have any desire to leave. I didn't care if Adonis would be waiting up or looking for me. None of that mattered to me in that moment. I wasn't worried because I felt like I had nothing to lose. I had lost everything except the person I was with right then, and my best friend, who I had been neglecting again. My life was a mess this entire time. I knew it was a mess, but I found out just how much of a mess it was tonight. One thing that I did see for myself tonight was that karma is really a bitch. The man that Adonis stole from basically stole his girl. Now that's karma!

Chapter Thirty-Two

I woke up the next morning to breakfast in bed. I could tell my eyes were puffy, but Deray still looked at me like I was the most beautiful woman he'd ever seen.

"Hey, Sweetheart. How you feeling?" Deray asked, as he sat the large tray of food down beside me.

I put my hand up to my head with my eyes still squinted from just opening them up, and said, "I have a slight headache, but I guess, I feel ok considering everything that happened."

Deray went into the bathroom and came back with a bottle of Advil.

"Here. Take these," he said as he handed me two Advil and the glass of orange juice from the tray.

I threw the pills in my mouth and swallowed them down with the juice. I looked at the abundance of food, which included pancakes, eggs, bacon, sausage, ham, grapes, strawberries, toast, and hashbrowns.

"I'm not very hungry," I said, trying not to sound ungrateful.

"You don't have to eat a lot, but you need to eat something. You didn't eat anything last night before you went to sleep."

"I know. You're right," I said as I sat up in the bed.

Deray put the tray right in front of me so I could grab whatever I wanted. I first thanked him for everything before grabbing a slice of ham from one of the plates.

"You don't have to thank me for anything. Thank you for allowing me to be here for you right now."

Deray began cutting up the pancakes for me. He treated me like a queen, even though he knew what I really was. My mind began to wander as I sat there. *What in the world do I do next?* I thought to myself.

After Deray got me situated, he walked over into the living room area and began watching TV. I began looking around the room trying to figure out where my phone was. I didn't even know what time it was.

"Everything ok over there?" Deray asked.

"Where's my phone, and what time is it?"

He got up and took my purse from off the recliner and brought it to me.

"I don't like to go in people's purses, but I did throw your phone in there last night so that didn't get lost, too," he said with a slight smile. "It's almost nine o' clock, but rest however long you need to."

"I have to go home," I said, as I hit the power button on my phone to turn it on.

"And then what?" Deray asked.

"I really don't know," I replied as my phone began beeping like crazy with notifications.

"I have an idea."

"What's that?"

"I can take you home to pick up just the things you need, and bring you back here with me. To stay."

I was reading through the text messages as Deray was talking, so it seemed as if I hadn't heard what he said.

"Hello?" he said, attempting to get my attention.

I looked up at him, and said, "I'm sorry. I heard everything you said, but . . . "

"But what? He's worried about you, so you have to let him know you're ok?" Deray replied, trying to predict what I was about to say.

"No. I was actually about to say my friend Ess is worried. Adonis must've called her, and she's been calling and texting me all night, and morning."

"Well, call her and let her know you're ok, and you can get ready so I can take you home."

"I was going to say, I don't need you to take me home. I can take myself home, but I do need to get away for a minute 'til I figure things out as to what my next move is going to be, so if it's ok, can I just come back here for a few days?"

Deray looked confused, but said, "Yeah, you can stay however long you need to, Dezzi."

"Thank you," I said as I attempted to smile. I just couldn't make the drastic decision to move in with Deray in the state of mind that I was in.

I finished eating as much as I could, got up to shower, and got ready to head home. I had no idea what I was going to run into once I got there, or the mindset Adonis was in, but from the text messages, he didn't sound good. In one of the messages, he even said that he was going to kill whatever nigga' I was out with. That was part of the reason I told Deray that I'd take myself. Even though I was beyond pissed at Adonis, I wasn't about to flaunt Deray in his face, especially knowing what their relationship was.

On my way home, I called Ess. I couldn't allow her to worry any longer than she already had. Monét had also called and texted, but all she was probably concerned with was why I wasn't on stage when I was supposed to be. I didn't consider her a real friend, so she wasn't even worth calling back. At least, not right now.

"Where the hell are you?" Ess said angrily as soon as she answered the phone.

"Calm down. I'm ok. There is a lot you don't know, Ess, and evidently, a lot I didn't know about Adonis. He's been lying about a lot of things, and I just don't think I can do this with him any longer."

"Honestly, I don't believe it's just him, Dezzi. You've been acting so different lately. I barely see you or talk to you, and when I do hear from you it's because your fiancé called me because you've been missing for hours. I don't know what's been going on with you, but I wouldn't blame Donnie if he did feel like there was someone else in the picture. He may have not been completely honest with you, but you need to be honest, too."

I had to take the phone away from my ear and look to see who I was talking to. Ess sounded like she was more on Adonis' side than mine. This was the same girl who was pissed at him about the money situation.

"Are you serious right now?" I asked her. "I understand you being mad because I haven't really been including you in things that have been going on, but trust me when I say, Adonis has been telling me a bunch of bogus bullshit."

"I believe you when you say that, but tell me this, Ess. Do you have someone else?"

I hesitated, and cleared my throat.

"I know you enough to know the answer to that after that hesitation," Ess said. "Is this new guy the reason you're willing to give up on Donnie that easily? You've been dealing with the bullshit, so what's so different now?"

"No, Ess! I make up my own mind, and my mind is still not made up! I just need a few days to myself to think about some things after finding out the things I've learned. I want my mind to be completely clear when I make a decision. I just wanted to let you know I was ok, and if you don't hear from me for a few days, don't worry. I'm good."

"Ok, Dezzi. Whatever you say. Just be careful, and can you please at least leave your phone on? I'll feel a little bit better if I know I can get in contact with you if I need to. I know your mom probably would, too."

"Ok, Ess. I can do that."

After getting off of the phone with Ess, and allowing her to cloud my mind even more, I began thinking about my mom, and let out a few more tears right before making it to my house. I pulled up in the driveway, next to Adonis' car, and wiped my eyes with the back of my hands. I took a deep breath before grabbing my purse and getting out of the car. The front door was already open, so I walked right in. Adonis was sitting on the sofa, looking a hot mess like he'd been up all night, which he probably had.

"Well, hey there," he said sarcastically.

"Hi," I said, dryly, as I stood there waiting on him to go in on me.

As he stood up, and walked towards me, he said, "I'm gonna ask you where you've been, and I don't want to hear anymore lies like you've been telling."

Is he really going to talk about me telling lies? I thought to myself, but I didn't want him to know I was at Deray's house the night before when he stopped by.

"I'm not gonna lie, and had no intentions on lying," I said.

Adonis folded his arms and cocked his head to the side and said, "So where were you?"

I took a deep breath and said, "Adonis, there's someone else I've been spending time with, and that's who I was with."

"Who is it?"

"That's not important," I replied.

"I thought you said you weren't gonna lie."

"I'm not lying. I told you I've been spending time with someone else. I'm just refusing to tell you who it is right now."

"So is it a man or a woman?"

I became extremely offended, and said, "Are you kidding me? I'm not even going there with you! I just came to get a few things so I can take a few days to clear my mind, so that's what I'm about to do."

As I headed up the stairs, Adonis followed me, still talking.

"So you think you can just go stay with another dude and come back whenever it's convenient for you? I've been taking care of you! I've been paying this mortgage and your tuition!"

Adonis just needed to quit talking because he sounded like a straight up fool!

I turned around and said, "You stole five million dollars from me! You haven't been taking care of me, or any other shit around here! You've just been slowly paying me back!"

Adonis became quiet for a moment, as I grabbed a suitcase and overnight bag out of my closet.

"I apologized for that, Dezzi!" Adonis began again. "I promised you I'd make all that shit up to you. I just need a little time. You just couldn't wait! What can this other nigga' do for you that I can't?"

As I threw clothes and shoes in the bags, I said, "More than you know, but this isn't a competition of who can do more for me. It's about me feeling safe and secure, and feeling like I can trust what someone is telling me. I don't feel that with you right now."

Adonis sat on the edge of the bed shaking his head.

"I can't believe this shit right now," he said.

I finished packing, and almost forgot one thing. I opened my nightstand drawer and threw my mom's journal inside the suitcase on top of my clothes.

I took off my engagement ring, and put it in the palm of my hand, holding it out in front of Adonis as he sat there looking pitiful.

"I'm not saying never. I just can't wear this right now," I said.

He wouldn't take it, so I gently grabbed his hand, opened it, put the ring inside, and closed it. I put his hand up to my mouth and kissed it.

"Please don't do this, Dezzi. We've been through too much together," Adonis said softly.

"I gotta go," I said, as I grabbed by luggage and walked down the stairs, out the door, and to the car. As I drove off, I felt a sense of relief and sadness at the same time.

Chapter Thirty-Three

I headed back to where I'd be staying the next few days or so, constantly wiping tears from my eyes. I didn't know why I was crying, but the tears wouldn't stop coming. I didn't know whether the tears represented my entire past, my mom, Adonis' lies, my dying friendship with Ess, new beginnings with Deray, or a combination of it all.

When I got back, Deray helped me into the house with my luggage, and said he had a surprise for me.

"Look at what I found while you were gone," Deray said, as he held up my ID.

"Thank you so much! Where was it?"

"It was underneath one of the couches in the bedroom, but is there something you want to tell me?"

Hesitantly, I said, "No. Why?"

"You don't have to lie to me," Deray said. "I know this is a Monét ID."

Trying to act stupid, I said, "What do you mean by that?"

"Come on, Dezzi! You know that ID isn't real, so you must not be twenty-one. I know an ID that Monét had made when I see one. So how old are you?"

"I'm sorry for trying to continue to lie about it. I already know you're a smart man, and I understand if you want to leave me alone right now. I should've just been honest upfront.

"No you shouldn't have. Then you wouldn't have been old enough to work in the club, meaning I would've never met you."

"Well, I should've at least told you the truth once I saw things progressing the way they did, so I do apologize."

"Like I said before, age ain't nothin' but a number. As long as you're legal, I'm good, so please tell me you're at least legal?" Deray playfully got on his knees and begged.

He lightened the situation a little bit, so I felt a little better when I told him I was eighteen.

"You are so much older than your years," Deray said.

"Did you just call me old?" I giggled.

"No. I'm just saying you're very mature for your age. There aren't many eighteen year olds, if any, I would've ever thought I'd be with in this way. You're actually a woman and not a kid."

"Well, I kinda had no choice, but to grow up fast with a mother who was always drunk."

"I'm sorry."

No. It's ok, but lets not talk about that.

"Ok. We won't. Finding your ID actually wasn't the surprise. Let me show you what the surprise is."

We walked to the back of the house where his stables were. While I was gone, he had prepared his horses so that we could go riding. I was so excited because I had never been riding before.

We walked to the back of the house where his stables were. While I was gone, he had prepared his horses so that we could go riding.

"I think horseback riding is the most relaxing thing you can do when you have a lot on your mind," he said, as he helped me onto his white horse, which he had name Eva.

He jumped on his other horse with such ease. "You ready to go, Ninja?" he said, speaking to his horse.

He gave me instructions on riding as we headed along a trail that I had never seen before. Once I kind of had the hang of it, Deray and I began talking about how my trip home went. I told him how torn apart Adonis was.

"I would hate to lose someone like you, too. He knows he messed up, but he'll be ok. I decided I'm going to still help him out because I always treated him like a son, but now he's disappointed me, so he'll have to work harder."

I was surprised when Deray said he was still going to help Adonis after how angry he was the night before about how he had done me.

"Well, I didn't tell him we would never be together," I said to Deray to make it clear that I hadn't made a decision about what I was going to do.

We rode side by side as we talked, and after I'd told Deray I hadn't made a decision, he looked over at my wedding finger and said, "Well, I don't see your engagement ring anymore. What does that mean?" he asked curiously.

"I gave it back to Adonis, but I also told him it didn't mean never. It just meant not now."

"Don't you think you're giving him false hope, Dezzi?"

"I might be, but since my mind has so many things going through it right now, I just can't give up on him like that. I don't want to make any rash decisions right now."

"Understood," Deray said, as he loosened his horses reins to speed up, which let me know he didn't want to hear anything else about it, so I wouldn't bring it up anymore.

I released my reins on Eva and she still wouldn't speed up.

"Hey! Deray! I need a little help here!" I shouted.

Deray turned back around, and came back to help me, as he laughed at me and my horseback riding techniques the entire way back to help me.

When he and Ninja finally made it back to save me and Eva, I said, "Oh, that's how y'all do us? Just leave us lost in this cruel ole world, huh?" I said, laughing.

"Now you know I wouldn't leave you like that!" Deray said.

"Well, you just did!"

"And you see all you had to do was call, and I came running. That's how it would always be. You would never have to worry. We have to work on this horseback-riding thing, though. You got Eva looking a little confused!"

I enjoyed my time with Deray, but I also enjoyed my time alone sometimes just to be able to clear my mind. My stay with him was supposed to be only a few days, but a few days turned in a week, a week into two weeks, and then I looked up and I had been there over a month. In the beginning, Adonis would text me every couple of days to let me know he was thinking about me, which would sometimes get in my head. I didn't let Deray know he was contacting me, though, and I would never respond because I didn't want Adonis to confuse me more than I already was. Ess would also text me quite often just to make sure I was ok. As long as I texted her back, she was cool. Those texts from both Adonis and Ess became less and less, to the point they were now non-existent. It bothered me a little at first, but now I felt like I would really begin my new life, fresh without stress and drama.

I felt safe with Deray, and he made me feel at home. I didn't have to worry about a thing. I knew for a fact I was taken care of. I didn't have to get on any stage and get naked for complete strangers, and I didn't have to worry on a daily basis whether or not my house was going to be taken from right up underneath me. All I had to do was go to school, and I had plenty of studying time.

Deray always made sure he had plenty of time for me, and made sure we had an activity planned at least twice a week, just so we could get out of the house and do something fun. We communicated constantly, and Deray always considered my feelings. I didn't have to ever really worry about our schedules conflicting because Deray would go check on the club, but he had things in order, and everyone who worked there was fearful of him, so he didn't have to worry too much about things going awry. He was a real businessman in my eyes. He would stop by the club unexpectedly a few times a week to make sure everything was in line, but he would only stay for a couple of hours and no one ever knew what happened to Desire. Deray told me that Monét apologized to him for bringing me in, and then I performed a disappearing act. What was funny was Monét tried to call me one time, and never again. She didn't even leave a message. He just told her that they'd find another "Desire" and not to worry about it.

Deray continued to run his other business, but he always made sure that I was out of the picture when he was taking care of business, and kept me clear of anything that would put me in danger. I didn't know where he and Adonis were doing their business, but one thing for sure was that Deray made sure that I didn't see Adonis at all.

Tonight was one of the nights Deray would pop up at the club. He asked me if I needed anything before he left, but I had everything I needed and wanted, including this alone time that I was about to get. It was nice to be able to see Deray so much, but my "me time" was nice, too. Before I left Adonis, we had gotten to the point where we almost never got to see each other because our schedules conflicted so much, and that was probably where our issues began, but I was over that. I just took every moment that I got alone, and did whatever it was that I wanted to do. While Deray was gone tonight, I was going to light some candles, turn on some music, and take a nice hot bubble bath.

As I began running my bath water, Deray came in the bathroom, looking and smelling good. He gave me a kiss on the lips and told me he'd be back soon, and to enjoy my bath. He walked out, but it was like he was still there because I could still smell his wonderful smelling cologne lingering in the air. I waited a few minutes before getting in the tub. I liked to know for sure that I was alone, so five minutes after I heard the front door shut, I ran downstairs just to be sure, and ran back up and turned on the intercom to play my music throughout the entire house. Music, no matter what kind, always gave me an extra sense of peace.

I removed my robe, and as I was about to put one foot into the tub, I thought that I'd grab my mom's journal since it seemed I was at a peaceful place in my mind and should be able to handle anything. I hadn't read anymore of it since I'd read about my own daddy fondling me. I couldn't take anymore after that.

After I got into the water, I took a deep breath, and found where I had last left off in the journal. The last date I had read was October 3, 2002, and I kept flipping through trying to make sure no pages were stuck together or torn out because the next entry wasn't until July 4th, 2005. Before reading, I flipped beyond that entry, and nothing else was there. All of the other pages were blank, which saddened me, because I wanted to be able to read more into my mom's thoughts. There was nothing I could do about it, so I began to read.

July 4, 2005

Today would have been one of the best days of my life if I hadn't found out something that completely broke my heart. The Fourth of July is another one of my favorite holidays, and this one was ruined. I was beginning to believe that all of my favorite holidays were jinxed. Brandon had bought every type of firework that you could possibly think of just so he could make the day perfect for me and Dezzi. We had the perfect weather outside, and the three of us had our cute Fourth of July outfits on. Lots of family came over, as always, since no one else could afford all the fireworks that they knew we'd have. Brandon was on the grill, grilling hot dogs, burgers, and ribs most of the day, while the kids ran around playing hide and seek, and tag.

I closed my eyes for a second as that memory came back to me. I could smell the burgers like they were right in front of me. I remembered not having my two front teeth, and I had two long ponytails hanging down both sides of my head. I couldn't remember anything bad happening that day, so I wasn't sure what my mom was talking about at the beginning of the entry, but maybe I was just too young to understand. I was six at the time, so I should've at least remembered if something happened that was as devastating as my mom made it seem. I opened my eyes and continued to read.

Everyone was so happy, and I took a million pictures. At the end of the night, after all the fireworks had been lit, and the kids had played so hard that they were deliriously tired, I walked everyone out, and decided to do a little cleaning before turning in. I called Dezzi to tell her to go get in the shower and put her pajamas on, but she didn't answer. The last time I'd seen her, she was sitting at the kitchen table with a milkshake Brandon had made for her. I looked over at the glass, and it was completely empty, so I grabbed it and put it in the dishwasher with the rest of the dishes.

I went upstairs to find her. I figured she was probably knocked out somewhere after all the fun she'd had. I found her, and she was knocked out in her bed with Brandon standing over her with his pants down. I ran and jumped on top of him, screaming, telling him to leave her alone. Throughout this entire ordeal, Dezzi didn't budge. I pushed Brandon out the way and put my ear close to her mouth to make sure she was breathing.

Dezzi was breathing, but she was out of it, but not out of it due to being tired. She had to have been drugged! I asked Brandon what he had given her. At first he told me he hadn't given her anything, and then when she wasn't moving, I think he started to freak out and told me he put a little something in her milkshake just to relax her after the long day. I grabbed him by his shoulders, asking him was he crazy. I knew then that Brandon definitely had a problem. I picked Dezzi up and felt how warm she was. I went and ran a cold shower while still holding her, and stepped into the cold water with my baby girl.

She slowly began coming out of what seemed like a coma. Brandon stood in the doorway of the bathroom crying. He kept saying that he didn't want to, or mean to hurt Dezzi. The first time I caught him fondling her, we went to counseling. Brandon had admitted during that time that he had been molested by his father, which was what messed him up so badly. I wasn't willing to leave him for a problem that wasn't his fault. He promised me it would never happen again, and I trusted him. The psychiatrist he was seeing had put him on some medication, and as far as I knew, everything had been fine for all this time, but now I wasn't so sure. It wasn't like Dezzi could tell me if Brandon had been doing things to her if he had resorted to drugging her!

After I got her to wake all the way up, she looked around wondering why we were in the shower with our clothes on, and I had to lie to her and tell her that she had a fever and I was trying to get her well. I dried her off and put on her pajamas. Brandon was nowhere in sight. After I gave Dezzi plenty of water and laid with her for a while until she fell asleep, I went into my bedroom, and there Brandon was, sitting on the edge of the bed with bloodshot red eyes.

I shut the door, walked over to Brandon and slapped the shit out of him. He didn't move. I shouted his name and he looked at me. I told him this could not happen, and Dezzi was my baby girl, not his! He hated when I said that, but at that moment I didn't care. Brandon was a good man, and Dezzi loved him, but I wasn't always around. I told Brandon that her real father, Deray, would have never done anything like that to her! Yes, he left us both for the streets, but I just knew he was not that kind of man, and even though Deray had never even laid eyes on Dezzi, if he knew what another man had done to her he would've murdered them! I began blaming Deray for leaving and putting our daughter in this position, but then I blamed myself for allowing Brandon to adopt and molest her. If Deray had just fit me and his daughter into his life, I know we could have been happy. We would've been Carlisa and Desireé Goodland . . . Not Carlisa and Desireé Kimbrough.

Life happens in a certain way for a reason, and Brandon was put in my life for a reason. I felt like I was truly his helpmate, and I would help him through this problem. We would do all the counseling in the world to make things right. I am extremely hurt right now for me and my daughter, but I couldn't give up on Brandon. I have to accept the fact that Deray was no longer in my life and never would be. Brandon took over his responsibilities as a father, and if it kills me, I will make this right!

~Carlisa

Chapter Thirty-Four

I began hyperventilating in the tub. I threw the journal across the room before I dropped it into the water, then somehow slid my body out of the water onto the floor. I felt like someone was suffocating me. I couldn't believe a word of what I had read, and all I could think about was why I hadn't read it sooner. I had been living with, and fucking my own father . . . My flesh and blood who abandoned me and left me with a man who molested me probably for years! As I laid on the floor, I tried to calm down. My breathing began stabilizing, but I still didn't know what to do! My body was numb, and I must've passed out, because when I came to, Deray was standing over me asking me if I was ok.

I felt my eyes get big as saucers and I jumped up off the bathroom floor and quickly began getting dressed. I needed proof.

Deray, panicking, said, "Baby! Tell me what's wrong!"

"Me and you! That's what's wrong!"

"Did something happen while I was gone?" Deray asked, as he was walking around the room just as quickly as I was, following closely behind me.

After I got completely dressed, I said, "Deray, let me ask you something."

He looked at me with fear in his eyes, waiting on me to ask my question, not knowing what was about to leave my mouth.

I folded my arms and said, "Do you have any kids?"

Deray had never mentioned any children to me, but I had never asked either.

Deray looked at me with honest eyes, yet, knew he was lying, and said, "No, Dezzi. I don't have any kids. I can't even have kids. I got that taken care of a long time ago when I realized I didn't want to have children."

I couldn't believe after all the times he told me I could trust him, he stood in front of me and told that bold-faced lie. All I could do was exhale and shake my head at him.

"I gotta go," I said as I walked out of the room, down the stairs and out the door.

I jumped in my car and sped down the road to get home as quickly as I could. This was the wrong time to have a long drive ahead of me. I wished I could just snap my fingers and be there. I knew I would have to go back to Deray's house because I realized after I had already pulled off that I forgot to grab the journal. I was just hoping he didn't read it and try to destroy it.

When I finally got to the house that belonged to me, surprisingly, I noticed Adonis' car outside. He would normally be out working this time of night. I put my key in the door, and the knob wouldn't turn. He had changed the locks on me. I still had my garage opener, so I went back to my car to press the button on that, but he must've changed the code on that, too, so I had no option, but to ring the doorbell.

Adonis came to the door without a shirt on and a pair of sweats. I looked him up and down before asking why he had changed the locks to my house.

"You didn't wanna be here, and I'm paying the mortgage every month. That's why I changed the locks," he replied.

I pushed Adonis out of the way, and just as I did, I saw Ess coming down the stairs wearing only a robe and house shoes.

"Everything good?" she said as she was coming down the stairs, before seeing me standing there.

"Naw! Everything ain't good! So this is what it is now? My ex-fiancé and best friend laying up in my house together?"

"Oh, Dezzi," Ess said in shock.

"Yeah, it's me bitch. Is this why you started taking Adonis' side when I tried confiding in you? Was this your plan the entire time?"

I looked at Adonis since Ess wasn't answering what I was asking.

"Was this the plan, Adonis? Were you always attracted to her, or is she just the rebound chick?"

"You know what? I ain't got time for this. Let me get my shit," Ess said, as she began walking back up the stairs that she never completely came down off of.

"Dezzi, trust me. This was not the plan. It just happened. I missed you so much."

"Shut the fuck up! This is some bullshit that I didn't come here for. Let me go get what I came to for."

I ran up the stairs to find Ess, not in my room, but in my mom's room. She and Adonis were both dirty as hell. They had been fucking in my mom's bed, which was the only place in the house where I could still find her scent!

"Bitch, if you don't get out my momma's room right now!"

As Ess was putting her clothes on, she sarcastically said, "Why? She's not coming back. Yeah, Donnie told me your little secret."

Trying to act as if I didn't know what she was talking about, I said, "What secret?"

"Bitch, you killed your own mother! So try something with me! I will spill the beans and won't think twice about it."

I looked back at Adonis, who had entered the room. He had stressed, and stressed, and stressed to me to keep my mouth closed about the situation, and he had told himself!

"So that just happened, too, I assume," I said.

Adonis shrugged his shoulders.

While arguing with those idiots, I pulled my mom's box of important documents out of her closet. I found the folder that read, "Birth Certificates", and opened it up. The first one I saw was mine. I pulled it out and there it was, right in front of my face. The proof was in the pudding. At birth, my mom had listed Deray Goodland as my father, and my name was Desireé Goodland. It then made a lot more sense. She named me after him . . . Deray and Desireé. That molestation was what my mom was finally going to come clean about before her accident. It had to have eaten her up for years, but she tried her best to keep me safe and keep her family together at the same time. I was too young to know that Brandon wasn't my real dad because Deray left before I was even born, and Brandon came into the picture before I could remember.

"Oh my fuckin' God!"

Adonis and Ess stood there, looking puzzled, as I went through the rest of the folder and found the adoption papers of when my "dad", Brandon, adopted me. My life had been all fucked up from the beginning and I didn't know it. I suddenly heard someone downstairs calling my name.

"Dezzi!" Deray yelled.

"Who is that?" Ess asked.

"None of this is your business, Ess, so why are you still here?"

I could hear footsteps coming up the stairs, and then down the hall.

"Dezzi, are you up here?"

Deray walked into my mom's room where we were all standing.

"Deray? What are you doing here?"

"I'm here to check on my girl."

Adonis frowned up and said, "This the nigga' you messing around with?"

I looked at both of them and said, "No, this is my father!" I said as I threw my birth certificate at Deray. It hit him in the chest before he caught it and looked at it.

"Damn girl! You murdered your mom and now fucking your daddy?" Ess said, annoyingly.

"Get out!" I yelled.

I looked a Deray as he stared at the birth certificate. He looked up at me and said, "Dezzi, I'm so sorry."

Adonis, still in disbelief, said, "So this is really the dude you dumped me for?" He looked over at Deray and said, "So is this why you decided to help me out? Because of her?"

I looked over at Essence who had her cell phone in her hand.

"Who are you calling?" I asked, as I lunged towards her, trying to grab her phone.

She ran out of the room onto the catwalk.

"I'm doing what should've been done a long time ago. Your mom didn't deserve this. I'm gonna tell the police where they can find the body," she said as she breathed heavily, trying to run from me.

"Ess!" Adonis yelled from my mom's doorway. She stopped and looked back, waiting on Adonis to say something.

"Don't do it. It's not worth it. What about us?"

"What about us? I know you still love her!"

While Adonis had Ess distracted, I ran and grabbed her arm, trying to take her phone out of her hand.

We tussled on the catwalk, and Ess continued to talk shit as we fought as if we had never been friends. We both kept hanging close to the rails that were never repaired after my mom's accident. I was getting tired and didn't have much strength left. Half of my body hung over the edge of the catwalk. I struggled trying to hold myself up and fight Ess off at the same time. This bitch was trying to kill me! I could see Adonis coming up behind Ess as I continued to use the last bit of my strength to hold on. He put her in a headlock, while I attempted to pull myself up.

"You dirty bitch. How do you murder your mom, and then bury her on top of your dad? She deserved at least a proper burial. I see why she treated you the way she did!"

"With my dad?" I yelled.

That was the only thing I'd heard out of everything she'd said. Finding out where Adonis buried my mom pissed me the fuck off. It probably wouldn't have bothered me as much if I hadn't found out that bitch ass muthafucka had molested me! That was probably the last place she would've wanted to be buried. I immediately regained my strength, pulled myself up, and kicked her in the stomach as Adonis held her. Ess fell to the ground still trying to push me over the edge. I jumped on top of Ess and grabbed her hair with both of my hands, banging her head against the hardwood floor. Adonis jumped on top of me, and pulled me up off of her. After I stood up, I looked down at what I had done . . . again. Ess was looking up at me, but she wasn't breathing. Blood started gushing from her head, into her wild hair. I instantly began crying, uncontrollably.

Adonis turned my body towards him, and hugged me. I stood there, crying on his shoulder, when part of this was his fault.

Deray stood in the doorway and softly said, "I'll take care of it. Donnie, take her in the room and close the door. Be there for her, and console her right now."

Adonis did as Deray told him, and Deray did as he said he would. He took care of Ess. After about an hour, when we came back out of the room, it looked like nothing had happened, and Deray was gone. I went into my mom's room, and he had left my birth certificate lying on the bed. Deray walked in the room after me, and picked the document up off the bed to look at it with his own eyes. As he read it, he shook his head.

"There's just so much more that you don't even know," I said, as I took my birth certificate out of Adonis' hands to put back in its place. I knew that all of this would have to be addressed sooner or later, but I'd let things cool down. I never imagined that my best friend would try to kill me. I was still in shock knowing that Ess and I had been so close, and it came down to this. I didn't have anyone else left, but Adonis was still there for me. I was upset with him for burying my mom in the grave with the man I now called Brandon, but I knew his intentions were good at the time. We didn't have all the information we had now at that time. Either way, I know my mom did love Brandon even though he had some issues. She made that quite evident in her journal. That did give me some acceptance for what was already done.

Neither, Adonis or I had talked to Deray after he'd left my house that night. Adonis didn't ask me any questions about the time I was with him, and I tried my best not even to think about it since I had officially committed incest. I wished so badly that my mom had not waited to try to tell me the truth about my life. All of this could've been avoided.

Adonis and I tried to start over, and get our life back in order. I didn't think either of us would ever look at each other the same after knowing so many secrets about each other. I had come clean about stripping so I could help with the expenses, and that was how I got connected with Deray, but that was the only thing I ever said about him. At least we did have the opportunity to try again with things out in the open.

With some of the money Adonis had made, we got an attorney and were able to get some of our money back from the bad deal that Adonis had entered into with the other people who invested in the Record Label, and gained primary ownership. It was now truly called "Dezzigner Records" with a big beautiful sign in front! I was now in charge of the contracts and accounting portion of the business, and it was running a whole lot smoother, without us having to sacrifice our time with each other. Our relationship began to get stronger and stronger every day. One thing I learned from all this was when the love is real, there's no coming between it. If it's meant to be, it will be. Another thing I learned is that karma will come back for you, but if you make things right, everything will begin to fall back into place.

I continued to go to school, because I still had my own dreams. I supported Adonis, and he supported me. One day, coming home from school, I walked into the house to get ready to do some studying. I dropped my books and purse off in the house and went back outside, across the street, to the mailbox. As I sorted through the mail, I saw an envelope that was addressed to me, but did not have a return address. The rest of it seemed to be junk mail.

I walked into the house and sat at the dining room table as I began to open the envelope.

"Hey Dezzi. I didn't even know you had made it home," Adonis said as he came down the stairs. He came straight over to me and began asking me about my day.

I was silent, and my mouth almost hit the floor.

"What's wrong? What is that you're looking at?"

I handed the envelope, and the check that was inside the envelope, to Adonis.

"Oh shit," he said, as he handed it back to me.

The envelope was from Deray. In addition to the check, the envelope also contained a letter. Adonis stood behind me and massaged my shoulders as we read the letter together:

Hey Dezzi.

I know it's only been a little while, but I couldn't let things just end the way that they did. I don't like the way things were left at all, and it has haunted me every day since. I don't know how credible I am to you right now, but I want you to know I loved the hell out of your mother, and if I ever got to meet you, I would've loved you just as much, or more. Shit, the time I did get to know you as an adult, I loved you. Just in the wrong way. I was young when your mom and I were together, and I became greedy and allowed those streets to suck me in, causing me to neglect my family. I am so sorry! I can't express how sorry I am! I read Carlisa's journal, and I can't believe everything the two of you endured once I was out of the picture. I never wanted anything bad to happen to either one of you. I promise I didn't. I just made some bad choices, and I'm regretting them now. I hope I don't sound too violent, but Brandon better be glad that he's already dead, because if he wasn't, after finding out what he did to you, I would've killed him myself!

I know it's a hard subject to talk about, but we also have to address what happened between us. It wasn't right, but honestly, we didn't know it wasn't right. Those things would have never happened between us if I knew you were my daughter, and I know you already know that. I'm not that kind of man. I don't know if we can ever have a father/daughter relationship any time in the future, but I hope we can after the smoke clears. I knew it was something about you that was special. I just wish I had recognized what it was before we crossed that line. Now things are uncomfortable between us. I would've also never done this to Adonis. Yeah, he stole money from me, but he was still like a son to me. Please send my apologies to him as well. All I really have is you and him, so I truly hope we can somehow get past this. I would like to begin the process by giving you what's owed to you. I know I didn't take any money from you, but I wasn't there to provide like a dad should have, either. Please accept this token of love, and I'm hoping to hear from both you and Adonis one day in the future. I have placed your mom's journal in a safe place. It's all I have left of her. If you would like it back, just let me know, and I'll be sure to get that back to you.

Take care, and please, please, forgive me for everything because I am where it all began.

Love,
Your Dad

As Adonis read the letter with me as he stood behind me, he kissed me on the forehead and said, "So, what now?"

After all these years, my blood father sent me a check for five million dollars and wanted to be a part of my life. I felt he was very sincere in his letter, but I just wished he had never left me and my mom. I believed we could've been one big happy family, but, like I always said, everything happens for a reason. Will I ever be able to allow Deray back into my life to play the role as Daddy Dearest? I don't know. Only time would tell.

I looked back at Adonis and said, "Your name will definitely not be going on the account this time! You have to earn that, and you are a long ways from earning your way back to the bank account!"

"How about I start working on it now!" Adonis said as he lifted me up out of the dining room chair, carried me up to my bedroom, and made love to me the way a man makes love to his woman right before he says, "Dezzi, that's the only blood you have left. Let's at least try to let him into our lives. If you're good with it, you know I'm here, and I got you. If it just doesn't feel right, we'll leave it alone, and it'll just be me and you."

"I knew there was a reason why I love you," I said.

"I love you too, Baby."

I kissed the man of my dreams who was nowhere near perfect, but he was perfect for me. We shared a lot together. Some was good, some was bad, and some was horrible, but we would be able to enjoy the good memories, and help each other through the horrible ones. We had purpose in each other's lives, and a lot of our purpose had been served, but we were nowhere near done.

The End

www.ingramcontent.com/pod-product-compliance
Lightning Source LLC
Chambersburg PA
CBHW071130170626
46809CB00002B/562